T0367927

A CREATURE
UNLIKE
ANY OTHER

A CREATURE UNLIKE ANY OTHER

CAROLYN BESSETTE KENNEDY

ALLISON LANG COOK

ARCHWAY
PUBLISHING

Archway Publishing books may be ordered through booksellers or by contacting:

Archway Publishing
1663 Liberty Drive
Bloomington, IN 47403
www.archwaypublishing.com
844-669-3957

Because of the dynamic nature of the Internet, any web addresses or links contained in this book may have changed since publication and may no longer be valid. The views expressed in this work are solely those of the author and do not necessarily reflect the views of the publisher, and the publisher hereby disclaims any responsibility for them.

Any people depicted in stock imagery provided by Getty Images are models, and such images are being used for illustrative purposes only. Certain stock imagery © Getty Images.

Cover art illustration by Brandyn Aikins

ISBN: 978-1-6657-6188-8 (sc)
ISBN: 978-1-6657-6190-1 (hc)
ISBN: 978-1-6657-6189-5 (e)

Library of Congress Control Number: 2024912467

Print information available on the last page.

Archway Publishing rev. date: 8/22/2024

To Emma Margaret, for showing me rainbows

CONTENTS

INTRODUCTION

The Kennedy family fascinates people worldwide, and many biographies and other works have been published about their personal and political dynasties. According to *Marie Claire Australia*, when Carolyn Bessette was first seen with John Kennedy Jr. in 1994, she "became the most famous woman in America overnight, but she loathed being written about and struggled with being constantly tailed by the press."[1]

Twenty-five years after her tragic death, Carolyn still makes headlines. Fashion media regularly refer to Carolyn as *the* style icon of the 1990s.

A Creature Unlike Any Other is the biography of Carolyn Bessette Kennedy set in a fictional context loosely based on *The Wizard of Oz*. Her story is told through biographical text, as presented by the protagonist, Guy, a literary editor living in Vancouver, Canada. Nearly thirty, Guy yearns to shed his bland life and procures a job interview in New York. He buys a van and schedules a road trip. On Friday, just before departure, Guy receives a manuscript about Carolyn Bessette Kennedy's life, which he must review while traveling.

---

[1] Davies, "Remembering Carolyn Bessette-Kennedy 20 Years After Her Tragic Death."

Guy tangles with his neighbors, twin sisters whom he secretly calls the twitches, members of a motorcycle gang known as the Broomsticks. The twitches mysterious dog, Ruby, sneaks into his van during a storm and is Guy's first companion on the adventure. However, the Broomsticks demand Ruby's return and a cross-country chase ensues.

As the journey progresses, Guy meets three characters: Stacey, a spacey waitress with a knowledge base of many random facts; Tina, the cynical and sometimes cruel daughter of an aging Hollywood movie star; and Leanna, a former supermodel assistant with a troubled past. And who is Doc Aus, the Australian animal communicator?

I hope you enjoy your journey with *A Creature Unlike Any Other.*

CHAPTER 1

THE CRASH

Friday, July 16, 1999, Off the
Coast of Martha's Vineyard

"Martha's Vineyard. Martha's Vineyard. Over."

"Martha's Vineyard. Martha's Vineyard. Over." John Kennedy Junior, the son of the late President John Kennedy and Jacqueline Kennedy Onassis, spoke into his headset's microphone. He piloted N253N, a Piper Saratoga, under visual conditions, maintaining the plane's speed and direction from the cockpit. His wife, Carolyn, and her sister, Lauren Bessette, sat behind him and belted into the rear-facing seats.

Carolyn Bessette Kennedy drew a long pale strand of her golden hair and tucked it behind her ear. She sensed John admiring her out of the corner of his eye, and in a gesture of playful flirting, she twirled the mass of ponytail toward him. It was never hard to get his attention.

Seizing the moment, Carolyn tapped John's arm and motioned for him to pass the bottle of water purchased back at the airport. He had already finished a banana, and its peel lay slumped on the front-facing passenger seat. John handed back the bottle with a smirk and a playful wink.

The flight's departure was later than planned.[2] By 8:38 p.m., when finally cleared for takeoff from New Jersey's Essex Airport, the day's light had been entirely replaced by an expanse of humid, inky darkness. The only light was a faint sliver of the crescent moon, and because it was so hot, a haze lifted upward, blurring the sea and sky. These were not ideal conditions for a novice pilot flying at night.[3]

They were almost forty-five minutes into their journey, flying at 3,600 feet, some 150 nautical miles northeast of New York City, heading toward Martha's Vineyard to drop off Lauren. Their plan

---

[2] "According to communication transcripts, the pilot contacted ground control at Caldwell about 2034, and stated, ' ... saratoga niner two five three november ready to taxi with mike ... right turnout northeast bound.' The ground controller instructed the pilot to taxi to runway 22, which he acknowledged. At 2038:32, the pilot contacted the tower and advised he was ready for takeoff. At 2038:39, the tower controller issued a takeoff clearance, and the pilot acknowledged the clearance at 2038:43. A few seconds later, the tower controller asked the pilot if he was heading toward Teterboro, to which he replied, 'No sir I'm uh actually I'm heading a little uh north of it, uh eastbound.' The tower controller then instructed the pilot to make a right downwind departure. This was acknowledged by the pilot, at 2038:56. There was no record of any further communications between the pilot and air traffic control'" Muzio, "Group Chairman Factual Report," 3.

[3] "Maintenance records from the pilot's Cessna 182, logbook entries from known flight instructors, witness statements, and training records were used to reconstruct the pilot's flight time from December 1998, to the date of the accident. The combination of the first logbook and the reconstructed flight time indicated that the pilot had a total flight experience, including simulator time, of 326.5 hours, of which 55 hours were at night. In addition, the pilot had 35.6 hours in the accident airplane, of which 9.4 hours were at night. He also had 3.1 hours of solo time in the accident airplane, with 0.8 hours of that being at night. His last known flight without a flight instructor onboard was on May 28, 1999, in the accident airplane" Muzio, "Group Chairman Factual Report," 4.

ALLISON LANG COOK

was for John and Carolyn to continue to the Kennedy family's Hyannis Port compound, where they would attend the wedding of John's cousin Rory.[4]

"Martha's Vineyard. Martha's Vineyard. Over." John repeated.

The scream of the wind against the plane as it sliced through the sky made it hard for the trio to hear one another. Lauren looked up and mimed something to her sister. The girls exchanged a few knowing raised eyebrows and smiles before returning to the pages of fashion magazines they had been flipping through in the dimly lit cabin. Now and then, they pointed out pictures of handbags and outfits they liked to each other to kill the time.

Carolyn unscrewed the water bottle and held it to her lips. The decision to accompany John to his cousin's wedding was important. The past few weeks, months even, had proven to be stressful for their marriage. They spent the week apart for various reasons, with John taking a suite at the Stanhope, close to his political magazine, *George's*, headquarters. He had just checked out earlier that day, making tonight their reunion.

She smiled while recalling his playful banter when she arrived in her town car at the airport. Still using his crutches from the hang gliding accident in early June, John hobbled almost expertly over to greet her and help load her bags onto the plane.[5]

---

[4] "Witnesses stated that the purpose of the flight was to fly to Martha's Vineyard, drop off one passenger, and then continue on to Hyannis, Massachusetts" Muzio, "Group Chairman Factual Report," 2.

[5] "Witnesses at Caldwell airport observed the pilot and a female near the airplane. One witness observed the pilot on crutches. The same witness also observed the pilot loading luggage into the airplane." Muzio, "Group Chairman Factual Report," 2

"My lady." He offered her his hand gentlemanly, tucking both crutches under his left arm to escort her from the car.

Carolyn spun her wedding ring, using her right hand's thumb and index finger to stroke the thin gold band while cradling the open water bottle between her thighs. She recognized that the excitement of their marriage soon gave way to the reality of their union. John Kennedy was an American prince, and as his wife, she was enslaved to his family legacy—the *Kennedy curse*, some dared to say.

Carolyn used that week apart from John to consider their path forward. While she loved her husband, the fame he attracted challenged her. They could not even walk their dog on the streets of New York without being harassed. And then there were always nasty, unfounded rumors in the tabloids. John swore that, eventually, the photographers would grow bored of chasing her. However, to date, if anything they were worse.

She thought about moving away from the city and the constantly scrutinizing media. Even though John tried to get them to back off and leave her alone, his plea only intensified their curiosity and increased their persistence. They chased her mercilessly, and she felt trapped. It was all so painfully public.

One of her solutions was to relocate upstate, where they could have property, fences, and gates. She reasoned that they needed seclusion to start a family. Growing up in the fishbowl was unnatural, and any kids born into their union required protection from the constant paparazzi cameras. Perhaps as soon as next year, they would move away from the two-one-two area code, the honking horns, the chaos, and the smog.

Carolyn was all too aware that John disagreed. He wanted to stay in the city where he grew up. It was part of his identity, like family. His mother raised him and his sister there, and they turned out OK, John would joke. But after almost three years of endless harassment, even he had to admit that things were becoming different. The public's thirst for details of their private moments made it challenging to live quietly.

Carolyn screwed back on the water bottle cap and attempted to pass it back to John, letting him know she was ready for him to take it by tapping his arm once again. He seemed preoccupied, irritated even by the request, and ignored her. He was attempting another radio call, and Carolyn strained to hear what her husband said.

"Martha's Vineyard. Martha's Vineyard. Over."

"Skippel. Over."[6]

Something did not feel quite right.

— — —

As the plane passed by westerly Rhode Island, radar detected that it had dropped to 2,500 feet, half its intended cruising altitude. Suddenly, it fell 300 additional feet in only four seconds, 300 more in the next five, and 500 more in the five seconds after that. It would

---

[6] "Mr. Perez is employed at Republic Airport, Farmingdale, New York. He preferred not to release his employer's name. On the night of the accident, between 21 00 and 2230 Eastern Daylight Time, he was monitoring the Unicorn frequency, 122.95 Mhz. During that time, Mr. Perez heard several transmissions from a pilot that used a call sign similar to N9253N. During a period of several minutes, the pilot attempted to contact 'Skipple'. Mr. Perez believes this may be a fixed based operator at Martha's Vineyard, Massachusetts. The pilot received one response that was unintelligible to Mr. Perez. Then, the pilot responded 'I'm not trying to speak with you, I'm trying to contact the facility.' One last transmission was heard. The pilot stated 'We're not going to make it if we don't get a hold of the facility.'" Muzio, "Group Chairman Factual Report," 99.

be impossible to know when or if the passengers realized the acute problem or their impending doom.

Shortly past 9:40 p.m. on the evening of July 16, 1999, the plane began to spin wildly out of control. John could not recover from the g-force of the graveyard spiral, and the three were likely already unconscious as the aircraft slammed, nose first, into the sea.[7]

---

[7] "On July 16, 1999, about 2141 eastern daylight time, a Piper PA-32R-301, Saratoga II, N9253N, was destroyed when it collided with water approximately 7 1/2 miles southwest of Gay Head, Martha's Vineyard, Massachusetts. The certificated private pilot and two passengers were fatally injured."
Muzio, "Group Chairman Factual Report," 2.

ALLISON LANG COOK

CHAPTER 2

RUBY

63 Days Later, Upstate New York

Donna, a wife and mother of five, sat on the sofa in the sunroom of the family home, watching television while folding the three hampers of clean laundry made by a family of that size. Windows encircled three sides of the room as it was an addition that jutted out from the living room and into the side garden. With the television's placement on the living room's exterior wall, Donna was oblivious to the lovely light of the afternoon sun and the first hints of autumn developing in the lush tree canopy.

"Mama!" Donna's youngest daughter, three-year-old Tangie, called out in alarm. "Mama, there's something wrong wif Sweetie." She sniffled.

"What's that, baby?" Donna replied absently, her attention riveted to the screen. She took little notice of her daughter as the drama of Genoa City on *The Young & the Restless* played out. *The tension with Jill and Mac, the Jabot deadline, and Jack's deal with Victor! Maybe his arms are tied, but really, Jack and Victor? And Nikki and Brad are kissing!* She felt like squealing.

Things were heating up on her favorite soap, and Donna was equally oblivious to the clothing she folded. Guided by instinct, her hands picked up garment after garment, matching the sleeves of shirts and the legs of pants and halving the fabric neatly into squares. The final basket sat beside her feet, sorted and nearly filled by her half-hour-long effort.

"Mama!" The stubborn child persisted, tugging at her mother's sleeve while insisting, "Come on, Mama!"

A commercial for an artificial sweetener separated her from the world of Genoa City and the lives of the Abbots and Newmans. She turned her attention to her daughter. "Yes, baby," she replied.

Tangie stood in front of her mother, clearly agitated. Her auburn pigtails were riddled with flyaway hairs as if from a static shock, and she fidgeted with her fingers on the hem of her T-shirt as she tried to gather words to address the problem. A developing cold labored her breathing, and Donna could see a stream of liquid beginning to drip from the rim of her daughter's nostrils.

"There's something wrong wif Sweetie," the child repeated.

Donna got up to fetch a Kleenex. She pulled the tissue from the box and wiped Tangie's runny nose.

"Where is she?" Donna asked as she instructed Tangie to blow into the Kleenex.

"In there." She gestured toward the front-hall closet, visible through the adjoining living room.

Donna rose, crossed the living room, and opened the closet door. Her eyes widened. The family dog, Sweetie, a petite lab mix, lay comforting two tiny, whimpering puppies. She called for her daughter to bring a towel from the pile of fresh laundry. Tangie scurried off quickly, returning with her favorite purple one. She proudly handed it to her mother.

"Is Sweetie going to be OK?" she asked with concern.

"Yes, baby. Sweetie had puppies. See—there they are. Can you count them for me?" Donna asked.

She coiled her daughter's pigtail between her thumb and index finger to smooth it out while Tangie counted: *One. Two.* Suddenly, she squealed excitedly, "Mama, Mama! I see another. I see another. It's coming out of Sweetie. Look! Mama!"

Sure enough, a third tiny puppy was born. Donna took the towel and tucked it underneath the tired dog's head. Sweetie looked up with weary eyes. "That's a girl," she said, stroking the dog's crown and floppy ears.

She looked down at the three tiny puppies beside their mother, clinging to her warmth. It was a miracle. She had not even suspected that Sweetie was expecting. And now there were puppies. She couldn't believe it. In the background, she could hear the closing anthem of *The Young & the Restless*, but suddenly it seemed not to matter.

"Come on," she instructed her daughter. "Let's leave Sweetie alone with the puppies."

Donna closed the closet door partially, giving Sweetie privacy to nurture. She guided her daughter by placing her hand on Tangie's upper back. Together, they strode past the dining room off the front hall and toward the kitchen at the back of the house. Donna opened the freezer and withdrew the last blue, white, and red rocket Popsicle. Her daughter jumped up and down, tore away the white, sticky wrapper, and greedily stuck the tip into her mouth. She hopped happily from the kitchen, around the back of the stairs toward the sunroom, and switched the channel to her cartoons.

Sensing that Tangie had settled, Donna picked up the phone and called her best friend, who answered after two rings.

"Lydia, it's me. You'll never guess what just happened." She was breathless. "Sweetie just had puppies."

"What?" her friend exclaimed, surprised.

"You heard me right. Three puppies." Donna was awed.

"No way!" Lydia responded in disbelief.

"You want to come see them?" she asked.

"Sure, I'll be right over." Lydia hung up.

Donna replaced the phone in its cradle and moved toward the kettle on the kitchen counter. She unplugged it, brought it to her sink, filled it with water from the tap, returned the kettle to the counter, and plugged it in. She removed two white ceramic mugs from the cupboard above, turned away from the counter, and folded her arms across her chest to wait for a boil. Soon enough, the water stirred. She stood, listening to the robust bubbles while smiling at the afternoon's surprise. *Puppies!*

Tangie ran back into the kitchen. She carried with her the Popsicle stick sucked clean and cried excitedly from a stained mouth, "Mama, can I play with the puppies?"

"No, baby. They are too little to play. You must let Sweetie be alone with them until they get bigger," Donna explained.

"Oh." Tangie's face contorted into a sulky pout.

"Would you like another Popsicle?" The child's face instantly brightened. Donna opened the freezer door and removed a grape one.

"No," shrieked the daughter. "I want pink!"

"But Tangie," Donna reminded her, "you ate the last pink one yesterday."

"Oh." Tangie assumed her cross face, pouting deliberately with her bottom lip.

"How about you have an orange one?" Donna offered.

"OK." Tangie agreed with a slight shrug.

Tangie snatched the treat from her mother's hand and dashed back to sit in front of the television. From the kitchen, her mama could hear the child slurping happily away on the frozen stick, Sweetie's puppies forgotten.

"Be careful. You have dance pictures later. Don't make a mess!" Donna warned her daughter.

The kettle began its shrill whistle, indicative of task completion. At the same time, Lydia appeared at the back door.

"Hi!" She hugged her friend. "I brought you this." She extended a copy of their shared passion, *People* magazine. Donna recognized the late couple on the cover. "I've already read it. It's a commemorative issue. I want it back after, though. It could be worth a lot one day." Lydia winked.

"Thanks. It's so sad what happened to them. I can't believe they died." Donna traced a finger across the man's jaw on the cover, John Kennedy Junior. "He looks so much like Jackie."

"I know," Lydia commiserated, "and that poor mother of Carolyn and her sister. I can't believe it. To lose two daughters."

"I know. It's so sad. Nothing could be worse than losing a child. So shocking." Donna echoed her friend's sympathetic tone before changing the conversation by asking, "Do you want some tea? The kettle's boiled."

"Please, but shouldn't we have champagne under the circumstances?" Lydia teased, fully knowing it was only just after one.

"I can't. Tangie has her dance pictures today, and I must pick up the other kids from school." Donna drove the family minivan.

Donna poured the kettle over the tea bags in two mugs. She let them steep for a few moments before removing them with the tip of a small spoon. She got the milk carton from the fridge, poured it into the dark liquid, and returned the milk to the refrigerator door while reaching for the sugar in a nearby cabinet. Using the same spoon, she twice measured a heaping spoonful and dumped it into both mugs, pausing to stir the clouded, steaming beverage, creating a whirlpool effect. She passed the first mug to her friend and kept the second for herself.

"So," Lydia began with a smile, "how does it feel to be a mama again?"

"Very funny." Donna rolled her eyes and leaned in to take a small sip of her tea. The liquid felt too hot on the tip of her lip, so she blew on the surface to cool it.

Lydia quickly changed the subject. "So, what are you going to do with the pups?"

"I don't know. Find new homes for them and give them away. They will be ready around the new year, I think." Donna calculated correctly.

"That is if we all make it!" Lydia laughed, referencing the upcoming Y2K, end-of-the-world hysteria. "But seriously," she continued, "I'll take one." Donna gave her a puzzled look. Lydia's husband was allergic to Sweetie; he couldn't even enter their house without breaking into hives.

"Not for us, silly, but for my sister. She's been talking about getting a dog." Lydia reassured her.

"Your fancy sister, who likes expensive things and always goes on vacation, wants to get a dog?" Donna rolled her eyes.

"What?" Lydia laughed in mock protest. "She's trying to become more grounded. Plus, she's got a new job near San Francisco, and having a dog is a great way to meet people. I know she will be a good owner. She'll spoil her!"

"Well, OK." Donna agreed. "You will get the first pick."

"Can I see them now?" Lydia eagerly insisted.

"Of course." Donna nodded. They stood and went to the closet, where Sweetie and her puppies slept peacefully.

"*Ooh*," Lydia cooed. "Aren't they just the cutest things ever! I'll take all three," she said, sounding like she was buying a purse, belt, and shoes. "That one, I'll take that one." Lydia pointed at the one born last. "Look at that one's coat. It's different from the others. It's blonde. White, golden blonde."

They leaned in for a closer look. Sure enough, one of the dogs was much lighter than the others. While the first two seemed brownish with scattered black spots, the blonde one was unique, almost luminescent. *So pretty*, Donna thought.

Tangie entered the room hysterically, screaming something about having dropped her Popsicle. She looked down at her chest as fat tears swelled in her eyes. She was covered in orange sweetness that stuck like thick sap to the corners of her mouth. A sizeable wet stain soaked the youngster's T-shirt as a colored blob.

"I made a mess, Mama," she whispered in a small voice full of regret.

"Don't worry, baby," Donna soothed, extending her arms to comfort the girl. "We'll clean you up for picture day."

CHAPTER 3

FOUR SHADOWS

*Friday, April 27, 2001, BlackJack Publishing
Head Office. Downtown Vancouver, Canada*

Centered like a bull's-eye amid a boxy arrangement of cubicles, Guy Myles sat alone at his desk facing his computer. The overhead fluorescent lights were dimmed in an Earth Week effort to conserve energy, amplifying the dullness of the gray walls, carpet, and furniture. Guy could not help but feel the drought of vibrancy that came with color and light. Even the digital ring of the office telephones were monotone hymns of gloom and lost inspiration.

His workspace wasn't much more than an eight-by-eight section of heavy industrial-grade flooring with tall, chrome-rimmed, fabric-covered dividers on three sides. It was so positively lifeless that Guy felt six feet under, waxy and cold. When he closed his eyes and drew a deep breath, the space held the sterile scent of bleached-white paper, a faint iodine sweetness of black toner, and background notes of acrid old coffee left too long on the break room burner.

Guy looked at his muted reflection in the backlit computer screen. It was the same face he had stared at for twenty-nine years: the same clean-shaven mouth and chin, the same brown hair trimmed neatly above the ears, the same long, pointed nose, and the same hazel eyes. If he attempted to mess up his bangs by parting them differently, they always bounced back into place as though they had been denied permission to change.

Guy, the only child of a reverend father and a librarian mother, was used to a life void of dramatic excitement. Perhaps it started as early as preschool when the teachers and students mispronounced his christened name, Guy, which his mother had intended to sound French as in *ghee*, with the flat, bland Guy, like "that *guy* over there."

Even his attire mimicked the tone of the office. He unintentionally sported a white buttoned polo topped with a charcoal crewneck and navy necktie to complement the industrial decor. Only recently did Guy wear blue jeans to work, not just on dress-down Fridays, and that was because his three favorite colleagues, Alisen, Alyson, and Alison, whom he collectively anointed the Three Amigos, teased him about being too bland.

The Three Amigos liked Guy and would pass by his desk on their way out of the building most nights. "Hi, Guy!" they always chimed together. He wasn't sure how or when the ritual started, but it had become an expectation and often his day's highlight.

Is it time to go yet? Guy wondered, poking his head above the walls of his cubicle, hoping the Amigos would pass by. When they were nowhere to be seen, he used the pointed index finger of his right hand to raise the cuffs of his shirt and sweater to check the time on his watch. The dials were spinning, but each minute seemed to stretch longer than the last. Departure felt past due, though this quick clock reference told him otherwise. It was only four twenty.

ALLISON LANG COOK

Make that four twenty-one. He sighed, sat back down, and hung his head in his hands.

A mound of papers lingered like a nuisance at the edge of his desk. The package had arrived hand-delivered earlier that day, and he even removed it from the envelope before becoming discouraged by imagining the chore ahead. Several coffee breaks, corresponding visits to the men's room, thumb twiddling, and other variations of time-wasting prevailed. All added together, these avoidances had erased nearly six hours of the workday.

Time to get focused.

He extended his arm and drew the pile toward the desk's center. While securing the top page of the lower right corner with the tips of his fingers, he flipped through the document from bottom to top. *Riff.* His initial observation was that the manuscript was substantial. It would take days to get through it all. That was time he wanted to spend away from his work as an associate book editor, not engrossed in this new project.

The workspace was sterile and quiet, save for the sounds of his invisible coworkers, proofreaders, and editors clicking away at their keyboards behind tall, cubed walls. They were like animals in pens, passing the time. Occasionally, one would jump up and go out for a break. Some had meetings to attend and announced this importance, causing as much disruption as possible as they assembled for departure. The colleague to his left always muttered to herself as she collected her files, which annoyed Guy incessantly.

Nothing bothered him more than an unnecessary distraction while he worked. It seemed the office was stacked with those types. They made meetings to waste time and fussed over tiny details in overblown debates. Often, this nonprogress delayed the completion of the project, and by the time it went to print, it was considered history, not contemporary. That was the thing about Guy. He preferred to work alone, and he was efficient.

At least, usually, he was.

Maybe it's the weather, he considered. An unprecedented forty-eight days of continuous rain were beginning to weigh on Guy, like everyone else. Everything he owned, including his bedding, was damp. They were used to the precipitation, living in the Pacific Northwest, but it felt cruel when it lasted for over a month.

Whatever the excuse for his lackluster mood, life at BlackJack Publishing wasn't measuring up. He was tired of working hard for nothing but the promise of something that never materialized. Like a pun on its name, BlackJack was where the dealer always won, and he could barely put anything resembling twenty-one together.

Guy annulled any feelings of guilt associated with pondering a career change, grabbed his computer mouse, and drew it across a BlackJack desk pad with a swishing motion. This action caused the backlit box to leap alive, revealing his bright-blue screen. He dragged the icon arrow to the top of an orderly list of files and landed on the explorer *e*. With one rapid double click, he was off into cyberspace.

Guy quickly entered his seven-letter password on the Hotmail home page and examined his new emails. He did so cautiously, often looking over his shoulder, as Hotmail was illegal, a corporate no-no because of viruses and such. Guy no longer cared if he got caught. Or, truthfully, he knew the threat of being discovered was minimal unless they monitored his activity, which he considered unlikely.

He scrolled down the stack of messages to find the one received earlier that month. It confirmed a job interview at a publishing house in New York. Not even the bleakness of the office could ease the thrill he felt reading the email title: *Guy Myles/Ideal Publishing Wednesday, May 2, 2001, 1:00 p.m.* Those words precipitated his booking off a week's vacation from work, which snowballed into the decision to make the journey a road trip, necessitating a vehicle purchase.

He logged off and looked around his desk, which, save the manuscript, was practically empty. Usually it stood covered by papers, stacks, and stacks in piles as high as half the way up the cubicle wall. He even dreamed of paper at night, the words stressfully blurred and unfamiliar. He diagnosed this as a consequence of the job, reading so much content day after day.

Needing a stretch, Guy rose and paced the twenty steps beyond his cubicle, past the outer bands of the bull's-eye formation, to the water cooler. Natural light from a section of floor-to-ceiling glass backlit the transparent cylinder, and he noted the cooler's level was half empty. *Or is it half full?* he pondered while pouring a paper cone of cool refreshment. He stood momentarily sipping while looking out the window toward the ground-level courtyard.

With all the rain, the city was a mélange of gray and black and mirrored glass reflecting more gray and black dullness. The clouds hung low in the sky. It was hard to feel motivated under such bleak conditions. *But this will soon end,* he reminded himself as he tugged at his tie to loosen its tight grip.

Suddenly, the courtyard burst into activity as dozens of workers popped open their umbrellas and strode outside, determined. Guy glanced back at his watch. *Finally, it's five. How many others are rushing home?* He watched enviously from above as the buildings hurriedly emptied, spilling crazed people starving for fresh air into the streets. They scattered through the asphalt maze of roads that patterned the downtown's core into what seemed like an endless grid.

Guy was raised to believe that hard work and perseverance would be rewarded. Up until recently, he believed in that mantra. He was serious about his job, never took sick days, and self-volunteered to clean out the communal fridge on the last workday of each month. As an editor, Guy read umpteen awful works, sprinkled in with some that made it. He rewrote pages of misguided prose, edited countless run-on sentences, and suggested better word choices for those that seemed ill-fitting to the text.

After all the extra hours, hard work, and dedication, Guy wondered why he cared: *No one would probably notice if I left, so why am I making this easy for them and hard for me? I want to get going. Why don't I go?*

Unable to ignore the churning rot of displeasure that manifested within, everything became crystal clear as Guy stood, sipping water and looking out the window. *I must color outside the lines.*

Using his right hand's fingers, he slowly pulled the knot of his tie and removed it from the clasp of his shirt collar in a long, smooth, snakelike motion, absently rolled it around his four fingers, and stuck it in the back pocket of his jeans. He unbuttoned the top of his polo, crossed his arms across his chest, and leaned in to watch the progression of the mass exodus.

Guy wasn't surprised when a new, darker storm quickly gathered above the city core, and heavy, leaden clouds threatened the few remaining fleeing workers. As the sky inevitably erupted, he pressed his cheek against the building's glass to feel the sharp beads of the downpour reverberate, driven with enthusiasm by a ferocious, howling wind. He thought about the promise of the week ahead while crumpling the empty water cone in the palm of his hand.

It's almost time, he reassured himself, returning to his cubicle to toss the garbage into the trash. He sat down as he switched on his desk lamp, illuminating the manuscript.

Guy sighed, reclined, and swept his hands across the crown of his head to the back of his neck before freeing his hair with a spring. The first time felt so good that he repeated the gesture, rocking back farther while scraping the nails of each finger against his scalp. The release left his body tingling. He rolled his neck from side to side, listening to how it cracked as he motioned slowly from left to right. He leaned forward and pressed his shoulder blades together until they burned from the effort of the exercise, paused for an excruciating hold of ten seconds, and then released them back to their natural position.

He had diligently reworked manuscripts from that chair at that same desk for over three years. Forty-plus hours a week spread over five, sometimes six, days, he spent them all, minute by minute, draining pens of their ink. He followed the careful regulations structured by BlackJack to ensure reputation and respect in an industry where so many mistruths made it into scandalous black-and-white permanency.

BlackJack's brand was a serious, no-nonsense operation. Guy questioned whether he wanted to be in alignment with such a rigid policy anymore. After all, what was the fun of a Woody Harrelson biography without detailing his rumored marijuana smoking? Or Pamela Anderson's *Secret to Hollywood Success*, which overlooked her noticeable cosmetic enhancements and focused instead on her childhood in Ladysmith, British Columbia?

It was apparent to Guy that permitting such tidbits would help BlackJack sell more books. But the higher-ups didn't agree, so his job was to cut all the fun stuff out. He often felt like a scientist dissecting a butterfly's wings, condemning flight. It was becoming frustrating and demoralizing.

Guy's attention returned to his latest editing victim. He scanned the front page, looking past the cursive writing on an obtrusive yellow Post-it stuck to its cover.

CBK: Eternity. The Carolyn Bessette Kennedy Story

The author's name and contact information stood inscribed below the title, and Guy took little notice of either line. This manuscript was the burden of his vacation, his killjoy.

He imagined a fantasy where he could send the work to the rejection pile. He closed his eyes and crafted a letter that went something along the lines of:

> Dear author,
> I regret that we cannot proceed with your submission.
> On behalf of BlackJack Publishing International Inc.,
> I wish you all the best in your publishing career.
> Yours truly, Guy Myles

But he knew it was impossible. He could not dismiss the text. It all had to do with that Post-it stuck to the cover page. Its message bore the distinctive scrawl of his boss, the founding literary editor at BlackJack, known only by the initial *M*.

He reread the note:

Dear Guy, thoughts? Needs more oomph. Due one week from Monday, SVP, M.

Thanks, M. Guy sighed as he flopped back into his chair and closed his eyes. *Thanks a lot.*

Guy recalled his first meeting with M. Guy's impressive credentials—a BA with honors and a master of English literature—combined with his experience as a postsecondary teaching assistant helped him secure a coveted interview at the newly created BlackJack.

M greeted him warmly in the reception, her graying hair piled atop her head in a messy yet styled bun. They met for an hour, exchanging witticisms and quips quickly, as though they had known each other for years. Guy knew the job was his when M nodded, stood, and extended her hand, which he shook as a done deal. He started the week later as a proofreader and was assigned his currently not-so-beloved cubicle.

Their instant rapport grew as they worked together. True to his upbringing, Guy was always willing to stay late and come in on weekends. This dedication impressed M considerably. She took him under her wing and became a mentoring figure. M usually assigned Guy solid projects, mostly from their biography division. He was thankful for this, as detailing textbooks was like pulling out fingernails individually.

On more than one occasion, M invited Guy to grab a bite in the bar at the bottom of their building. Guy appreciated the inside scoop on the industry. He noticed a bit of wine allowed her to relax, and she would often speak about gossipy details that BlackJack usually rejected. Guy always listened attentively as she recalled her early days at American publishing powerhouses such as Viking and Doubleday.

"Guy, I started my career at Viking, much like what you are doing here at BlackJack," M would usually begin.

By now, Guy had it memorized. In the late seventies, M went to Doubleday as a book editor, rising through the ranks first as an associate and then as a senior editor. At some point, she decided to move away from New York. She never explained why she left the city, and Guy knew enough not to ask such personal questions.

One night, after a healthy dose of red wine, M revealed that while at Viking, she was delighted to learn that her idol, Jacqueline Kennedy Onassis, was also on staff. She described how the office was always abuzz with rumors about their celebrated colleague but that Jackie played no part in cementing them. The former first lady preferred to earn advancement. She came to work to do her job, avoided the spotlight, and refused special treatment.

M glowed when she spoke of those days when she interfaced daily with the soft-spoken and stylish Jacqueline. She spoke of how it inspired her to be close to such an icon. Once, she boasted about how they both were embarrassed about their size-eleven feet. Whenever Jackie heard about a shoe shipment in their size, she would leave a little monogrammed notecard on M's desk, letting her know, "They're here!"

Jackie left Viking for Doubleday in 1977, resigning—M would whisper the following tidbit as it was speculative and unconfirmed— because of a controversy surrounding a book that portrayed Ted Kennedy as the focus of an assassination plot. Hearing that Jackie was gone, M decided to do everything possible to get a position at Doubleday. It took her nine months to land the job as a book editor, but she felt it was worth it to be closer to her mentor. Soon, M became a senior editor alongside Jackie. She reminisced that, ironically, the move was the best thing she ever did to advance her career.

Doubleday was sold to Bertelsmann, AG, a German-based worldwide communications company, in 1986. In 1988, it became part of the Bantam Doubleday Dell Publishing Group, which Guy knew would eventually become a division of Random House. Ideal was formed in 1996 as an offshoot of Doubleday to contrast their Christian offering, WaterBrook Press.

By then, M had abandoned New York with a handful of colleagues to found BlackJack in Canada. They grew the company into a viable contender, publishing professional books, biographies, and nonfiction that appealed to international audiences without compromising the integrity of the works by relying on what M referred to as "smut" publishing.

After Carolyn Bessette Kennedy received unsavory publicity posthumously, M wanted to publish a flattering piece. She believed strongly that the public wanted to know more about her mentor's daughter-in-law, and she wanted to be the one who brought the work to life. She made it a mission, sending out feelers across the industry.

One day, M arrived at the office in a fluster, her hair wind-tousled and her signature polka dot cape tossed about her neck. She urgently paged Guy and outlined the project. "An agent friend of mine has told me of a super new work," she announced breathlessly, wriggling her fingers in excitement, "It should be here within the week, so I'll lighten your review schedule for the next while, Guy. I want this project to be special."

She reminded him about her SOS policy for a biography, which stood for "search out soul." Broken down roughly, this meant submerging into the subject. While doing this research, one should oscillate between favorable and unfavorable opinions of the individual in question for a well-rounded view. Eventually, one would become inspired by the person because of their humanity. The biography would transcend clichés and be a representation of truth. Or so it went.

Realizing it could be the most significant career break granted by BlackJack, Guy enthusiastically tackled the project. He online searched Carolyn Bessette Kennedy, visited fan blogs, and read her eulogy and obituary in more than one microfilmed newspaper. Guy took his familial mantra seriously, submerging himself in Carolyn's e-shrines.

But, as the days of rain accumulated, M brought nothing to his desk. Guy began to doubt that there would ever be a manuscript to review. The Carolyn e-groupies irritated him with their endless exchanges over where a particular white wrap shirt came from or what Egyptian musk perfume she wore. Guy felt that if he were to continue with the SOS, his opinion would almost certainly sway into the unfavorable sector, negating the value of the exercise.

So he decided to pivot and research the city of New York itself, which opened Pandora's Box. Guy read blog after blog about the city scene, restaurants, art galleries, parks, and even one solely dedicated to its bridges. Then there were the movies set in New York, which he would watch in earnest succession on weekends. The sheer mass of concrete, architecture, height, density, and grit proved enchanting, and Guy quickly found his daily chats with his three favorite colleagues more personal because they, too, loved New York.

"It's the best!" The Amigos repeated while interrupting each other with restaurant suggestions and walking tour itineraries. "Seriously, Guy, It's the best!"

Guy had never thought to dream about leaving Canada, but the pull of the majestic Big Apple was magnetic. With no promised extensive manuscript to edit and few other ones that usually sat stacked and unread around him, Guy reasoned he could spend time on the company clock searching job boards for the perfect New York opportunity.

His efforts resulted in an impossible nibble. It was a position with Ideal, a company that operated under just about the opposite philosophy as BlackJack. It was practically the smuttiest, worse than the worst, Jerry Springer–inspired publisher of books. In early April, they emailed the meeting confirmation to his Hotmail.

Guy immediately booked himself off for a week to travel for his interview. Shortly after that, the Three Amigos passed by his desk.

"Hi, Guy," they chanted in unison.

A lengthy conversation ensued, and Guy revealed his intention to travel to New York, although he was careful not to let them know about the interview. Somehow, the suggestion of a road trip was tossed into the conversation.

"Come on, live a little, Guy! Be young. Be restless," Alisen coaxed before pointing out, "I mean, you don't even do dress-down Fridays, Mr. Insipid." She laughed, pointing at his crisply ironed trousers.

Tired of being thought of as *"that* Guy," the Guy in the center of the cubicle arrangement who lived by the mantra of hard work and dedication but had yet to be treated to the taste of its exotic fruit, Guy took action. His path was set. He sourced a vehicle: a van. That following workday, a Monday, he wore blue jeans, even though it wasn't officially a dress-down day.

And then, as if by design, M delivered the manuscript on his last day before his scheduled road trip to New York. Guy sighed, resigned to the idea that he could not escape the burden. It was coming with him whether he liked it or not. *A working vacation*, he groaned quietly inside.

The raging weather outside threw great torrents of rain against the tower. The gale-force winds rattled the windows so effectively that it seemed the glass was swaying in and out of its framework. Guy took notice of the storm from his position in the room and renewed his eagerness to depart. He gathered the manuscript and slid it into a Mountain Blue attaché case beside some other materials he had collected for the project.

"Another rejection, Guy?" Alyson asked, peering over the edge of his space.

Guy looked up to find the Three Amigos. *Finally!*

"What are you ladies still doing here?" Guy tried to pretend they had not startled him.

"Why, we were waiting for you!" Alisen, a midthirties marketing executive, spoke a little louder than Guy preferred. "Do you want to join us for a drink? Maybe watch the new episode of *Survivor*?"

She was the boldest of the three, the one his BlackJack colleagues greeted with trepidation. She had the reputation of a demanding diva. Her fearless attitude, however, granted her many successes. It seemed that without much more than muscle, she ascended into her own office, a real coup in a space that seemed an open sea of squares. To make matters worse, he had no idea what she did or what made her important enough to deserve her own office. She certainly had courage; Guy gave her that.

"No, ladies, I'll have to pass. I have some tidying up to do here," Guy said. In truth, he didn't have anything more to do. Even his suitcase was packed for the trip and waiting for him in the van.

"Why are you working late?" The nerdy Alison asked as she pushed her glasses up against the bridge of her freckled nose. Guy classified her as being the sharpest. She always seemed to get the story behind the story before anyone else could figure out what the story even was. Alison also had her own office, but it was undoubtedly, in his opinion, deserved. She was part of the accounting team, and every time he walked by her office, the screech of her adding machine would echo as an earworm for hours.

He opened his case and held up the CBK manuscript.

"What is this one about?" Alisen asked.

"Biography of John Kennedy Junior's wife, Carolyn Bessette," Guy announced as he lightly shook the papers.

"Ooh, I loved her," Alyson said, touching her heart while Alison added, "I'd love the inside scoop!"

"Ladies, I would love to say more, but sadly, I just got it this morning and haven't had the chance to start. Plus, remember I'm on vacation to New York next week, so I won't be able to report until the start of next month." Guy returned the manuscript to his case and snapped the buckles closed.

His announcement sent Alyson's mouth into an exaggerated pout. "Not a whole week!" she complained.

"I'm afraid so," Guy confirmed, adding, "but when I get back, hopefully, I'll have some work to pass on to you." He tapped his case gently to remind them of the manuscript inside.

"Great!" Alyson perked up, releasing her curled lip. "I'm going to love this project. I'm sure of it." She worked as a book jacket art director. Her work was stunning, evidently carefully designed with passion to be unique in an industry where so much was patterned the same. It didn't hurt that she also touted movie-star looks, Guy noted as her pout transformed into a dazzling smile.

"Well," Alyson sweetly continued, "we'll miss you around here. Have a great adventure, Guy!" She and Alison linked arms and started to walk away from Guy's desk.

"Don't let anyone give you trouble out there," Alisen whispered as she slipped in to link with the other two. The Three Amigos began to walk together toward the exit.

"Bye, Guy," they chanted in unison, turning to wave at him. At that exact moment, the overhead office lights flickered off, as they did every night precisely at six. A sudden flash of electric-blue lightning startled them still. It seemed they froze eternally, their blackened images and his head and shoulders together as a row of shadow puppets against the pale-gray backdrop of the neighboring cubicle.

CHAPTER 4

THE STORM

Friday after 6:00 p.m., Vancouver, Canada

Guy stood and waited until he was sure the girls were gone. Despite their growing friendship, ceremonious goodbyes were not his thing. They made him uneasy. He hated the back-pat hug and was uncertain of the protocol for exercising the single-, double-, or triple-cheek kiss. Each Amigo did it differently, and Guy could never remember which gesture was for whom. Instead, he avoided the entire experience and stayed at his desk until they left.

When he could no longer hear their commotion, he jumped up, slung his attaché over his shoulder, and snapped off his desk lamp. One last survey ensured that nothing was forgotten. It would be ten days before he would see the place again. He crossed his fingers for luck, thinking maybe then only to resign and pack away his favorite coffee mug.

He dashed through the dark cubicle maze toward the elevator. He turned one corner and another before arriving at the hallway with the four Otis doors. He inserted his plastic ID card into the wall control panel. A green light replaced a red one, indicating the elevator was ready for instructions. Guy pressed the down button twice with an impatient thumb. The doors automatically swung open as though waiting for him. He took a long stride into its cavity, turned around, and illuminated the P3 button.

The doors closed, and he descended to the parking garage. When the lift rested at the base of the shaft, he budged the doors open with his shoulders, annoyed by the relaxed ease with which they parted. He pushed through the glass door from the elevator chamber and then the next into the dank parking garage. Across the nearly emptied space, he saw the round headlights of his newly acquired van waiting for him.

Tossing his bag onto the passenger seat, Guy slid in and inserted the keys into the ignition. The engine started with a rev and pop. He wouldn't call it an official backfire, but he knew the sound wasn't healthy. With all the recent rain, Guy figured that the system was waterlogged.

Guy quickly discovered that the 1985 Volkswagen Vanagon was susceptible to many vehicular issues. For instance, there was no heat or AC; the radio was stuck on 88.9—The Voice of Eighties Rock—and on one occasion, the oil leaked. Even with its noisy and messy flaws, Guy liked the van as it was. He had bought it a few weeks prior. It seemed like a sensible choice to purchase a vehicle created for road trips. The man he bought it from repainted it charcoal gray, aesthetically because the original reddish-bronze color was dated and preventatively because the van was beginning to rust ever so slightly around the rims.

Not everyone was as enthusiastic about Toto. He christened the van as such when, on the drive back from its purchase, a retrospective on the band *Toto* filled his ears with an endless rotation of their greatest hits. Afterward, it seemed that either "Africa" or "Rosanna" played at some point on his trip to or from work. The name stuck, and as the past few weeks together unfolded, Toto became an extension of Guy, like a metal companion.

But some people weren't van people, as Guy shortly discovered. For no apparent reason, Toto drew the ire of his angry neighbors, twin sisters who lived next door in his apartment complex.

The twitches, he secretly called them, were superintendents for the small four-story building Guy and a handful of others called home. They were profoundly unpleasant. Even on sunny days they wore sour expressions accentuated by their sharp, pointy features and pinched, tight lips. He suspected they were sisters because they resembled each other so identically. But Guy rarely addressed them by name because he could never decipher who was who. So he created the moniker twitches, the union of twins and witches. The name seemed utterly appropriate.

Guy, being uncomfortable with confrontation, avoided the twitches. He kept to himself, never played loud music, and cooked with inoffensive seasonings. Since the twitches were equally disinterested in casual communication, the adopted "don't bother us, and we won't bother you" understanding seemingly worked well for everyone.

It all changed when Toto came on the scene.

Before he picked up the van, Guy went to the twitches and paid for April's parking up front. One took his money from the threshold of their slightly ajar apartment door while snarling. From behind the doorway, the other shouted that he was finally becoming a grown-up by getting himself wheels. Guy said little, hoping silence would end the conversation sooner. Once they assigned him a spot, he darted back to the sanctuary of his apartment.

It was clear that the twitches were not expecting a vehicle quite as large as Toto. When he drove the van in from the street, he encountered them in the parking lot. As he tried to position it in the farthest slot, his assigned space, the twitches protested angrily.

"What do you think you're doing?" one shouted, her shrill voice reverberating off the adjacent garbage box.

"Um, parking," he answered after rolling down his window.

"Don't give me that smart aleck tone, mister. You can't park there. That's for the babies." She practically cooed.

The twitches were members of a predominately female motorcycle gang called the Broomsticks. Their "babies" were their two shiny, silver motorcycles. When riding, the twitches sported uniforms of black leather pants and matching jackets trimmed with yellow tassels. The back of the jackets came embroidered with the group's logo, a broomstick circled by the slogan, "We'll sweep you *away*." A smaller version of the emblem, less the slogan, was painted on their helmets.

The group was a North American phenomenon, with chapters in practically every major city. Formed in a town whose name Guy could never remember, the organization was initially known as Your Tornadoes. The year after being established, a massive Category 5 Tornado passed through the town and demolished the gang's clubhouse and a neighboring animal shelter.

It was a tragic loss, and the media grabbed the story. CNN arrived only hours after the sun rose, revealing the flattened remnants of the buildings. Empty pet cages lay strewn across the rubble alongside a mess of mangled motorcycles. The reporters stayed all day and

ALLISON LANG COOK

through the next night, partially due to the story's multistate public interest and partly because it was a slow international news day.

Due to this publicity, Your Tornadoes enjoyed community assistance, who pitched in to rebuild the clubhouse and animal shelter. They renamed themselves the Broomsticks to rebrand after the tragedy and honor the neighbors with brooms who cleaned up the debris.

Over the next twenty years, the Broomsticks enlisted a staggering one hundred thousand members. Guy knew this because he had done an SOS on them and discovered the website www.broomsticks. usa. He created a false login identity, guy123, and an easy password to remember: *12345. From there, he maneuvered through the well-run site's chat rooms and message boards. Much material was accessible for viewing, covering a mélange of topics, including, perhaps not so curiously, dogs.

Apparently after the tornado, the Broomsticks decided to take on the cause of lost and abandoned dogs. Working with the local community, they took over daily management of the adjacent shelter. Through their established network, they found homes nationwide for pets and even delivered them to their proud new owners. Some dogs would ride in sidecars that resembled crates on wheels. In the colder areas, the sidecars were enclosed and heated.

Almost overnight, the service grew in popularity. Animal rights activists and dog lovers across North America applauded the initiative. Guy knew that one-tenth of all canine adoptions in the United States ran through the Broomstick organization. The group wasn't as well known in Canada and Mexico but had a growing presence in both countries.

On the website, he found the dogs divided into sizes: toy, small, medium, and large. The most popular size seemed small, categorized as twenty pounds. Size large was listed at over one hundred pounds and required a special license since the sidecar needed to be proportionally as big, making the motorcycles more challenging to ride.

The twitches were involved in this program. When they brought them home, the adoptee would stay for a few days at the apartment and then they would move along to deliver the canine to its new owner. Their dog transportation crate was anchored to the sidecar of one of the twitches' babies, and Guy thought it could hold a small dog.

Due to the duration of their absences, Guy assumed that the twitches delivered mainly across the border. On closer inspection of their bikes, he found stickers on the sidecar representing cities like Seattle, Portland, and even San Francisco. They were usually gone overnight and sometimes for several days.

Simultaneously with the appearance of small dogs, Guy also noticed that the twitches appeared to be gaining rank in their organization. The arms of their jackets boasted increasing tassels, which Guy knew from his research represented accomplishment and a translating hierarchical upward movement. They were doing well in the Broomstick organization.

But their charity did nothing to warm Guy to them. They had been too disagreeable and worse since the day he brought Toto home. He reasoned that maybe bike people didn't like VW vans, although it seemed impossibly stupid that anyone would care enough to cause such a fuss.

Once, they reluctantly assigned him a new parking spot, changed it for another, and then changed it back to the first. He found this out when he found Toto missing. A neighbor suggested that the vehicle had been towed, pointing to a freshly installed No Parking sign. When he knocked on the twitches door for the name of the towing company, they scolded him for parking in the spot, insisting that they had never assigned him the stall in the first place.

The headaches ensued from there. It seemed the twitches had daily issues with Toto. Sometimes, it was the sound of the engine starting in the morning. Then it was a stain from dripping oil on the pavement. Whatever it was, they loved to complain, and Guy heard an earful. He had taken to leaving early in the morning and returning home late at night, hiding in his apartment on weekends to watch the New York movies. That way, he would avoid them and their constant complaints.

Guy refused to engage in their combat. Denied the occasion of a face-to-face battle, they left notes taped to Toto's window. He ignored the messages, tucking them into the glove compartment. When that began to fill, he took an old shoebox and kept the array of unpleasantries under the passenger seat.

Somehow, they discovered his Hotmail address and began a second-wave assault of harassing e-messages. They sent cyber one-liners like, "Hey hippie! The hunk of junk belongs in the dump!" Or "Pay attention—Guy driving the Van." His favorite, "You're smelting," referred to their desire to eliminate Toto entirely.

One day, it came up in conversation when the Three Amigos passed by Guy's desk as usual on their way out of the office. Guy had just finished an "illegal" search of his Hotmail account, where he found the first of the twitches' messages.

"What's wrong?" Alyson asked with heartfelt concern, noticing Guy seemed slightly perturbed and out of character.

"Oh nothing," Guy replied.

"Come on, Guy. We can tell something is wrong," Alison said astutely.

"Well," Guy began, "ever since I bought the van for my road trip, my neighbors have pestered me about it."

"You should just tell them off!" Alisen exclaimed.

"Wait," Alison asked, laying a hand on Alisen's shoulder to calm the situation. "How are they pestering you?"

"Well, first they left me paper notes, but now they have taken to sending messages to my Hotmail. I received one today. It said, "Hey Hippie! The hunk of junk belongs in the dump.""

"Well, that's funny on multiple levels." Alisen roared with laughter. "First off, you are hardly a hippie. I mean, what did I call you the other week? Mr. Insipid!"

"Guy, do you think they could be joking," Alison interrupted. "It would make sense if they were teasing you, right?"

Guy shook his head no.

"I'm sorry, Guy," Alyson said caringly.

Thankfully, as the rain poured from the skies the week prior, the twitches departed on their latest canine mission and did not return for several days, permitting Guy respite from the ugly situation. They had only recently reappeared—and with them a new dog.

Guy usually paid little to no attention to the rescued pets. The newest one was different. The dog found its way into his apartment just the day before. He was home after work reading a magazine from his treasured *Vanity Fair* collection. Guy, a *Vanity Fair* enthusiast, was passionate about the Dominick Dunne diary and the magazine's various politically-relevant articles.

That evening, he was rereading the September 1999 issue commemorating Carolyn Bessette Kennedy. The cover featured a black-and-white photograph of her side profile. Inside were more pictures, some with her dog and a brief article. He found it in his collection a week earlier after as part of his SOS on Carolyn, an e-groupie on www.carolynsanicon.com had referred to the issue in one of their comments.

As he was expecting the manuscript from M, he did not return the issue to its regular slot on his organized bookshelf after finishing the article. Instead, he kept it decoratively on his living room coffee table. This placement fostered a habit, and Guy eventually explored the issue's other stories.

His favorite was the one about George Mallory, the mountaineer who may have been the first to summit Mount Everest. Mallory and his companion Sandy Irvine died on the mountain in 1924, and no one could confirm whether the men had reached the summit before their unfortunate demise. The *Vanity Fair* story even included gruesome pictures of Mallory's heel frozen in the top of the world's permafrost.

Although his third-story bedroom window was open, Guy could not figure out how the dog could have made it high enough to sneak in. Nevertheless, he looked up from the magazine to find the twitches' new foster dog staring at him from his bedroom doorway. There was something about her and how she stared that was disquieting. When he put down the magazine and stood to approach her, the petite dog darted from the doorway out the window and disappeared into the night's damp fog.

The strangeness of the event baffled him, and he wondered if the dog's appearance and hasty departure had any sinister purpose. He worried that the twitches were up to something. He pushed it from his mind while at work, but now that he was heading home, the perplexity occupied his thoughts as he twisted through three parking levels up to the street-level exit.

Parking so deep in the belly of the building was typical for someone at his pay scale. The first level was reserved for upper management and other VIPs. The bootlickers and suburban commuters took the second level. Both groups seemed to be at their desks before 7:30 a.m. Guy's usual arrival time was a respectable 8:30, but he could have easily come later, as M had never arrived before the first coffee break.

As he left the protection of the building, a wall of water slammed across Toto's windshield as though dumped from an enormous overhead bucket. Flicking on the wipers, he carefully turned right and drove slowly through the streets. The rainfall refused to ease, and he was amazed at the storm's chaotic strength. The wind churned and gusted, causing swirling clouds of heavy moisture to descend deeper into the city. Loud sessions of thunder boomed and echoed, and lightning lit up the darkened sky.

While wet weather was typical for the Pacific Northwest, the brutal example of an electrical storm was uncommon. The downtown seemed eerily abandoned, almost a ghost town, and Guy was glad when he turned onto the familiar bridge that took him toward home. Amid the chaos, his only solace was the swish of water against the tires as he drove through random midstreet ponds.

Toto chugged at an alarmingly slow pace as they approached the base of a hill, so Guy pushed forcefully on the accelerator to propel upward. Slowly, the van crept to meet the hill's crest. Once on flattened terrain, Toto lurched and released a mighty sigh, which Guy thankfully echoed. He turned the radio on as the announcer finished the six o'clock news.

"They are calling it the storm of the century, ladies and gents. If you are on the roads, be careful out there tonight. And now, Tears for Fears," the announcer said huskily.

88.9 began to play Tears for Fear's hit "Broken."

When Guy arrived at the turn onto his street, it seemed darker than usual, and it took him a moment to realize that the street lamps were unlit. He prayed it didn't mean a loss of power for the entire block. So often, when that happened, it took them several hours before reconnection, which was always a huge hassle for the residents.

Suddenly, as he spun Toto's wheel, a great gust of wind ferociously ripped branches off trees and scattered leaves around the street in a swirling mess. Guy swerved around multiple fallen branches and wove toward the driveway, third in on the left. Lightning streaked a bluish-yellow crackle across the clouded sky. He counted one, two, barely reaching three before an ear-splitting boom of thunder rumbled, rattling Toto's windows and shaking his seat so fiercely that, for a moment, he felt he might bottom out.

The lightning announced intense rain, forcing Guy to hunch his upper body over the wheel to see out the front windshield. Toto's wipers flipped from side to side in a powerful frenzy, clearing the water, yet visibility was impaired. He turned into the driveway and made the short journey past the apartment building into the back parking lot.

Someone—Guy thought he made out the image of a twitch in a dark rain slicker and a matching hat—was holding a flashlight as though hunting for something. As he approached her, he became blinded by an intense flash of light that beamed directly and purposefully as a warning of her presence.

He saw only brightness and heard only the wind howling as it viciously bent the trees. In stunned reaction, he slammed on his brakes. The entire van lifted from the ground, weightlessly suspended in the air, before landing on a patch of uneven pavement with a thud.

The upheaval confused Guy, impairing his instincts. In that instant, he pressed the gas before correcting his error by slamming his foot abruptly on the brake pedal. Toto lurched forward just enough to bump the twitch's motorcycle, causing it to tip over and fall onto the attached sidecar. In reaction to the impact, Guy's brow met the abrupt swat of Toto's loose sun visor as his chest landed against the steering wheel.

After moments of darkness followed by static light, a faint recognition overcame Guy. A drizzle of water from the crack between the door and jam rolled slowly down his arm like a tickle that he had no energy to itch. He rested there for a pause, unable to move, think, or even do anything. His eyes felt heavy, weighted by the uncooperative muscle mass of his brow. He saw dots of color. They swirled and twirled inside the lids of his eyes.

ALLISON LANG COOK

"What have you done to my baby!" The twitch screamed.

The sudden shriek of her cry was worse than any bolt of thunder the storm could have produced and snapped him out of the momentary swoon. In that instant, Guy regained control of his movements, although they were thoughtless and lumbering. He reversed the gear shift, and Toto rolled away from the twitch's motorcycle. Guy jerked the van into park and exited the driver's side, leaving the door ajar despite the rain.

Guy took a few steps toward the motorcycle to inspect it for damage. At first glance, he detected nothing more than a cracked side mirror. The twitch without the flashlight turned and snarled at him, making such an ugly face that Guy was genuinely afraid.

"I'm so sorry," Guy felt inclined to say.

"You, Mister Guy Myles, I'll ensure you never drive that junk again! I'll get it taken off the road! Do you hear me?" The twitch seethed threateningly as she took a step toward Guy.

"We will make you pay for this. You and that van!" The sister twitch agreed with a wicked laugh as she shone the flashlight's beam onto Toto.

Eyes wide, Guy backed slowly toward the open van door and returned to Toto's driver seat. The chorus of Bronski Beat's "Smalltown Boy" was playing on the radio, and Guy took the serendipitous suggestion. *"Run away, turn away, run away."* He performed a swift three-point turn, fled past the building onto the storm-ravaged street and set his course toward the highway leading to Seattle.

CHAPTER 5

GLINDA

Saturday Morning, Interstate 90,
King County, Washington

The first rays of daylight shot up from the horizon like the points of a crown. The announcement of the sun's arrival aroused a chorus of birds from their nocturnal slumber. Their collective song trumpeted through the hills and valleys to greet the new day. It was a fresh morning, with a calm breeze and a brilliant azure sky.

Guy woke in a motel room's bed to the sensation of moisture spreading across his hand, painted in delicate lines with a brush that felt like sandy leather. It stirred him from the depths of sleep. *What time is it,* he wondered? It didn't take long to remember that he was on the first day of his road trip. He was heading to New York for his interview with Ideal. After several weeks of anticipation, all was finally happening.

A small yip commanded Guy's attention. Ignoring the shooting pains caused by such immediate action, he sat up and bent across the bedside to find the source of the strange noise. Two big blue eyes stared back at him. He blinked, startled. They were familiar eyes, and he recognized their owner instantly. He reached out to gently stroke his canine companion's brow.

"That was quite the storm last night," he offered aloud. "I didn't realize you were with me."

She released a soft sigh while Guy took notice of the space. The room was a vibrant, eclectic mash of hues so disjointed that he knew he wasn't at a Ramada. The curtains were shiny gold, and the bedspread was multicolored floral. The carpet was bright red, and the wallpaper had a vibrant pale blue hue. It was like he could count almost every color in a Crayola box. They came together in a disorganized prism. Final touches included a set of chartreuse lamps, a turquoise-rimmed mirror, and a magenta chair in the corner.

Guy turned the television on and found the sound no more than a low muffle. He turned up the volume. A succession of cereal and fruity beverage commercials came across the screen and then a sunny female anchor was back, grinning from ear to ear.

"Good morning, and welcome back. You are watching the *Saturday Show*, and I'm your host, Katie Carson," she said.

The camera pivoted and zoomed in as she spun to the left and continued.

"Have you ever owned a pet you felt was close to being human? For many of us, our pets are our children, best friends, and special family members. As absurd as it sounds, a recent survey showed that more than 50 percent of us feel a connection to our pets that extends beyond the traditional role of alpha/beta. But what if there was more? What if your beloved Fido was, in fact, a reincarnated person? Joining us today to discuss this theory is world-renowned animal and spiritual communicator and Australian veterinarian Doctor Greg Osmond. Welcome, Doc Aus," Katie said.

The camera changed angles to reveal a man wearing a finely tailored, three-piece suit. When he smiled, his eyes sparkled. "G'day, Katie," he said.

"Your book *Living Ghosts: The Study of Human-Animal Reincarnation* is rapidly becoming a bestseller. Please tell us a little bit about your theory," Katie said.

"Well, in my early days as a veterinarian, I encountered a few suspect patients. These animals just seemed a little more human than ordinary. I began to study their behavior and soon discovered a common thread that helped me understand them: they all had unfinished business in this world. My role was to help convey their messages to the appropriate individuals," Doc Aus replied.

"Amazing, Doc. Bear's story from our last segment gave me the chills," Katie said.

"Crikey, Bear was a terrific example. Once Bear made his discovery about his past life, he was able to release and function as a pet. The soul of his human counterpart was allowed to rest, and he went on to live a life of pure animal joy," Doc Aus replied proudly.

"Can you share another story with our viewers?" Katie asked.

"Indeed. Recently, I met a lovely parakeet. The owner contacted me after he became curious about why the bird repeatedly sang the melody of 'Somewhere, over the Rainbow.' The bird sang nothing else, and it was beginning to annoy his owner, especially at three in the morning. So he brought the bird into my New York studio, and we performed a spiritual search for what I like to call Esprit, the spirit the animal has channeled or bound. Well, the bird arrived, and we were able to make contact. I determined that the bird did indeed have a slight possession of the spirit of the late Judy Garland," Doc Aus said.

"Of course, she starred in *The Wizard of Oz*. How did you make that connection?" Katie asked.

"I assure you it wasn't easy. It was around the time that Judy's daughter, Liza Minelli, married David Guest. The story was on *Entertainment Tonight*, *Extra*, and all the networks. Under hypnosis, the parakeet's owner could recall that the singing began during these moments. This confirmation and information I received from the spirit world, which must remain confidential, led me to an obvious conclusion. Esprit emerged while the bird discovered Liza was married. Judy was singing her delight," Doc Aus said.

"Does the bird still sing?" Katie asked.

"Not so much anymore. The novelty of the news has worn off," Doc Aus replied.

"Interesting. Tell me, Doc, how do you respond to your critics who suggest that your tactics are nothing more than smoke and mirrors?" Katie asked.

"Come again?" Doc Aus replied, surprised.

"Well, for instance, a woman, Esther Harris, from Florida, suggests that you falsely led her to believe that her hamster, Sammy IV, was the reincarnation of her late fifth husband," Katie said.

"Well, Katie, I was getting a message from the hamster, and I communicated it to Ms. Harris plainly and simply. I call ignorance that she did not believe me," Doc Aus said defensively.

"Let's see—you told Ms. Harris that the husband died because he wanted to, and I quote, 'be rid of her' and that he was only back as the hamster as a way of reminding himself why he wanted to leave the human world in the first place. Don't you think that's a little harsh, Doctor?" Katie asked inquisitively.

"Well, that was the information conveyed to me through Esprit. But I see why she may have had an issue with the truth," Doc Aus said.

"Ms. Harris also indicated that some of your methods were unorthodox, even dangerous. She notes that a confidentiality clause in your contract with her prevents her from elaborating further," Katie said.

"Unorthodox? Nonsense! Katie, my work is ultimately based on the secret teachings of Ursa, an eighteenth-century veterinarian who founded the underground society Animalia. Ursa believed that reincarnation was a natural progression of the soul toward its eventual maturation and infinite release. Ursa adapted the theory as a hierarchy, with humans passing into the animal world, progressing into reptiles, and then aquatics, eventually descending the order until one is a mere amoeba; Zen ultimately achieved. The information I received during the séance came via methods taught in the *Book of Animalia*, the most sacred of the society's texts," Doc Aus replied.

"But the hamster died under your care, didn't it?" Katie asked while raising her eyebrow.

"We were performing a rather tricky exercise, and sadly, the hammy passed during the affair. We took many precautions, but these things sometimes happen," Doc Aus replied.

"Ms. Harris claims that your fingers were on the hamster's throat, causing asphyxiation," Katie stated.

"It was unfortunate, but I assure you that we made all efforts to save Sammy IV," Doc Aus replied.

"But, Doctor, wouldn't it be that the animals are your responsibility during these spiritual communications?" Katie asked.

"Why, yes, Katie, but why don't we concentrate on the hundreds of examples of my success? I've connected with many deceased individuals living successful lives as reincarnated pets. I have heaps of satisfied customers," Doc Aus boasted.

"Well, your work is certainly interesting. We will surely hear much more from you in the future, Doc. Thank you for your time this morning," Katie said with a smile.

"Thank you, Katie. Glad to be here," Doc Aus said with a final wink to the audience.

The segment was over, and Guy flipped off the television. Deep concepts were too heavy for his tender brain so early in the morning. He slowly rose from the bed and stood beside it, pausing to offer the dog a light ear tussling.

"Do they know you're with me?" he wondered aloud.

The dog cocked her head as he spoke, as though she understood what he was saying. Guy was mesmerized by her eyes. They were so blue, unnatural even.

"You know they weren't my biggest fans before this. I'm willing to bet I'm a persona non grata around the apartment block today. That is if they know where you are." Guy paused. "And if I can figure out how far along our journey we are."

Curious, he went to the window to part the curtains, pushing the fabric back until it met the wall. Sunlight poured into the room, forcing Guy to squeeze his eyes tightly shut until they adjusted to the sensation. The dog started to pace at his feet. Guy wondered if it meant that she needed to go out to pee. He looked down at his boxer-short clad physique. "Just a moment, girl. First, I need to get dressed."

There was a bathroom behind the door next to the closet. Guy opened and entered. It was, in contrast to the decor of the bedroom, white and clean. He went to the sink and drew a blast of cool fresh water into the depths of the basin. Cupping his hands, he splashed the water across his face, ran his fingers through his hair, and then wiped them dry using a starched towel hanging in short reach by the sink. He rinsed his mouth with another handful of water and then rubbed his teeth clean with the cloth. Feeling a bit revived, he was ready to greet the day.

Guy found his clothes in a hurried heap on the floor. He pulled on yesterday's jeans, removing the tie from his back pocket to act as a dog leash for his new companion. He partially buttoned his white polo and rolled the sleeves. He slid into his loafers and crossed the room toward the motel door, took the knob, and pulled, stepping into the bright sunshine.

"Come on, girl." Guy gestured for the dog to join him.

The parking lot outside was nearly empty except for a couple of parked vehicles, so Guy felt little need to leash the dog with his tie. The highway was at the far side of the lot, and Guy could see a giant sign announcing the motel. He turned and ventured toward the business office at the far end of the one-level structure while the dog trotted happily beside him. Guy was pleased to find a bowl full of water at the office entrance and smiled as the dog found it and began to drink.

A chime rang as he opened the door and passed through the entrance. The room was small, with a high counter against the side opposite the door. Two floral-print armchairs and a couch stood arranged to the left, with a small wooden table in the middle. Guy stepped up to the counter and found no one on duty. A shiny silver bell rested on top of the desk counter. He slapped it with the palm of his hand and waited for a response.

In no time, a short man shuffled up to the desk and climbed up onto a stool tall enough that his height soon paralleled Guy's.

"Checking out, sir?" he asked in a strange, chirpy voice.

"Um, yes, I am." He paused and then placed the motel room key on the counter. "I was hoping that you could help me. Where am I?" He knew he was several hours into the journey but needed clarity.

"Why you're in King County." He gestured toward a sign on the wall.

THE COUNTY, WHERE EVERYONE'S KIN.

Guy noted that the *G* from *King* was missing and replaced with a crown that dangled from the upper right edge of the letter *N*.

"You'll need the key to your Vanagon." He pointed to his van parked beside a large blue sedan. The man spun around on his stool and took a ring of keys from a hook marked 9. Turning back, he extended the set to Guy, who took them. Next, the man picked up the room key from the counter and hung it on the same hook.

"You were in quite a state last night, driving in through the storm. Lucky that you found us," the man said.

"Yes, indeed," Guy recalled the stress of driving in the terrible weather. He had been so tired on arrival that he hadn't even brought his luggage in from the van.

"Where are you from originally, Guy?" the man asked.

"Originally, um, I'm from Canada," Guy replied.

"Ah, the funny money place." He paused. "Hold on a minute." He hopped off the stool and hurried off into the back room. He returned a moment later with a map. "I reckon it is a few days' drive to the Big Apple. Last night, you asked for a road map to get to New York City. I had one in the back. It's an older edition, but the routes are the same. I took the liberty of tracing the route with a yellow highlighter. You must only remember to follow the yellow-lined road, and you'll get there."

"Thank you," Guy said, taking the map. He moved toward the office door, pausing to ask, "Do you know where I can get a bite to eat?"

"Across the road and down a way is as good as any," the motel man concluded.

Guy thanked the man again, exiting the office with a repeat of the door chime, and went to Toto's side door. The dog was waiting for him beside the van, so he opened the door for her. She hopped onto the front seat. He closed the door behind her, walked to the other side of the vehicle, and entered to sit on the driver's side. Guy took a moment to collect himself. He took a sip of water from a bottle in the cup holder, opened the sun visor, and slid open the mirror.

He surveyed his appearance, noting that something seemed different. True, the unbuttoned polo and lack of a tie showed more of his neck than he was used to, but that wasn't it. It took Guy a few seconds to realize that his hair had taken a new part, perhaps when he had splashed his face with water. Regardless of how it came to be, Guy admired himself for a few moments longer.

"What about you?" he asked the dog as he closed the visor's mirror. "How did you get here?"

Guy remembered the bright flashlight and the twitches looking for something outside by the garbage boxes. He wondered if they had been looking for the dog. It made sense that she was frightened by the storm, and he knew she was agile as she had previously escaped from his apartment window.

But how did you get into the van?

He studied the pet who sat quietly on the seat, staring back at him. Guy felt strangely compelled to continue holding her gaze for an extended period. At that point, he noticed a tiny charm attached to the collar. It was red and glittered in the light. He pinched it between two fingers and read the name etched into the enamel: RUBY.

"So, your name is Ruby," he said aloud, fully aware that she would not speak back to him. "Welcome aboard."

Ruby cocked her head slightly to the right each time he said her name. She was lovely looking, beautiful even, despite being a dog.

Her coat was a shimmering pale white gold, almost platinum in hue and angelically luminescent. Something about her blue eyes seemed familiar.

Ruby broke their gaze by standing and shaking her coat from nose to tail, which alerted Guy to a second, more petite charm hidden behind the red name tag. It was silver and gleamed in the way that expensive things do. This charm was from the renowned New York jeweler and read, "Please return to Tiffany & Co, New York 925."

A New York connection, of course. Guy guessed the dog knew he was heading to New York and took the opportunity to sneak a ride during the storm. She must have hopped in when he inspected the damage to the twitch's bike and hid from the sisters in Toto's back seat.

"Ruby." He felt pleased to know her name. "We'll get you home. But first, we should eat."

Guy attempted to orient himself to the surroundings by peering over the steering wheel. The road to his right, the west, was long and straight, marked only by a thick line that split the pavement into two equal lanes. That was the direction he had come from. To the left were a few buildings and houses, the route seemingly leading toward the central part of town. Eastward was the way to go.

The decision was made, and Guy slipped the key into Toto's ignition. He flipped it forward, springing faithful Toto to life with a familiar rumble. He pressed the clutch, released the parking brake, and popped onto the road, hoping no one was around to witness the clumsy bunny jump.

They quickly arrived in town, finding the main strip quite deserted. Guy saw none of the locals, yet cars sat parked in the driveways, and toys from last evening's play lay scattered across the crisp green lawns. It was apparent that life lay somewhere behind the cheerfully painted doors despite the absence of people.

Just as the man promised, there was a diner down the road. Guy pulled into the parking lot and found a space in the shade. Ruby seemed disinterested in coming with him, so he left the side door open so she could hop in and out as she pleased. She was a dog used to riding in a motorcycle sidecar, savvy enough to dart in and out of his apartment window, and, after her behavior at the motel, Guy was not worried about her running off. As he left the van, he thought to grab the map. It would be good to study the route while he ate.

Guy crossed the parking lot toward a door marked Diner North. At first, he thought the place was locked, as the way inside would not budge. After several docile attempts to rattle and pull the handle, he used the strength of both arms and pushed open the heavy glass to enter the establishment.

The diner was bustling in sharp contrast to the stillness of the town's main street. Nearly every table and a generous row of barstools was occupied. Old and young, they chatted noisily between sips of coffee and toast bites. The air smelled heavily of grease and bacon. Guy's mouth watered with anticipation. He found the last booth empty, save for a local paper, and slid onto the bench facing the restaurant so he could observe.

From his position at the back, he detected one waitress working. Despite the hustle and bustle, the dirty plates, and the cluttered countertop, she seemed oddly pristine. She swung from table to table as though contained in an effervescent bubble, smiling as coffee swooshed around inside a glass carafe with an orange plastic top. There was an upside-down mug on the table, and Guy turned it over to signal his interest in a fill of the brew.

Despite Guy estimating her age at fifty, the woman seemed to glow with an unmistakable aura of youth. Her hair was a golden mass of curls, and her cheeks seemed brushed with a kiss of rosy color. Her makeup perfectly complemented the pink uniform that hugged her body through the waist and hips before fanning into an A-line that swirled as she floated around the diner.

Within moments, she passed him a laminated, single-page menu. She filled his cup, handed him two sugars and two creamers, spun on her toes, and set off without saying a word. She returned in an appropriate amount of time with a tiny pad and silver pencil whose tip was the shape of a star. She indicated her readiness for his order by cocking her head slightly as she looked directly at him.

"What will you be having today, Guy?" Her white teeth sparkled when she smiled.

"I will have number five, please," he replied.

"Are you sure about that?" she asked. "Our special is divine. And you'll need extra energy with the day you have ahead."

He nodded in agreement, not because he wanted the special but because he was speechless, stunned, and inclined to obey. The waitress winked with one long flutter of an eyelash and was gone. He watched her as she passed inside the counter and through the swinging doors into the kitchen.

ALLISON LANG COOK

She returned a while later with a plate of hot eggs fried over easy, pancakes and syrup, two links of sausage, a slice of watermelon, a segment of orange, and seasoned home fries. She delicately slid the plate underneath Guy's nose so no item rolled out of its appointed place. Guy ate every last morsel of the delicious food. He had not realized how hungry he was.

She returned at the perfect moment to refresh his coffee, sliding an extra creamer and sugar alongside the mug.

"Looks like you were right about the special being the thing for me," he offered bashfully.

"A good waitress always knows," she said as she placed a small Styrofoam container beside his plate. "This is for that sweet little girl you have outside. She is lovely."

"You mean Ruby?" Guy asked.

"Of course, silly." She giggled. "A young pup needs her strength, too."

"I'm taking her on a trip," he indicated, unfolding his map on the table. He wasn't sure why he had told her. Guy watched as she traced her long, manicured finger across the route marked by the motel man in yellow highlighter.

"To New York City," she noted, "is quite the adventure. Just follow the signs, and you'll get there." She must have sensed his puzzlement. "You may feel lost and misplaced for now, but there is no need to worry. Your journey will be quite enlightening, I'm sure." She placed a black plastic tray marked VISA on the table. It contained his upside-down check.

"A word of wisdom," she began, closing her eyes to recite the words: "For long you live, and high you fly. / The smiles you'll give and tears you'll cry. All you touch and all you see / Is all your life will ever be."[8] She paused with her eyes closed in pensive reflection before her great lashes sprung open. "Pretty, isn't it?" She sighed. "Pink Floyd from the song 'Breathe.'"

Guy nodded as though he already knew the source.

"Here." She pointed to an exurb in the bottom right corner of the local newspaper leftover from the booth's last occupant. There, Guy discovered her quote printed in prominent, bolded ink. She gently coaxed the words away from the remaining paper with a careful tear and handed the clipping to him.

"It's the saying of the week. Take it with you to remember when things become unclear," the waitress advised.

He picked up the square of paper to study the saying more closely. As he did so, the waitress bid him farewell. "Goodbye, Guy. Travel safely."

"Wait." He stopped her. "How do you know my name?"

She said nothing, her bee-stung lips pressing together softly. She offered a subtle wink before seeming to float behind the swinging kitchen doors. Guy waited a moment or two for her to reemerge. When she did not, he gave up, shrugging his shoulders as he flipped over the bill and paid what he owed. In typical diner fashion, she wrote a little note in bubble cursive at the top right corner of the bill.

Until we met again, Glinda from Diner North ☺

---

[8] (David Jon Gilmour 1973) Carolyn Bessette Kennedy's high school yearbook quote taken from Pink Floyd's "Breathe (in the Air)"

He folded the map and stood to leave, almost forgetting the carefully torn quotation. He grabbed it so hastily that the paper slipped out from underneath his fingers, swaying like a feather in the breeze, until it met the sticky floor. As it fell, it became inverted, revealing the details of the flip side. Guy bent down and retrieved it, pleased that it was not soiled. He scanned the advertisement, which was also written in bold.

Does your pet seem to have something to say?

Do you want to know their most profound thoughts?

Get answers from world-renowned spiritual and animal communicator Dr. Greg Osmond. E-MAIL ME WITH YOUR QUESTIONS.

Or visit me in my Marvel Studio in New York, New York.

Doc Aus, the Australian veterinarian.

Guy folded the torn piece of paper in half and tucked it into the back pocket of his jeans. He gathered the Styrofoam container and left the diner with the yellow-routed map securely in his hand. In contrast to Guy's difficulty entering the diner, his exit was effortless. As he passed the doorway, bells chimed a friendly jingle as he stepped away from the establishment and returned to Toto and Ruby.

CHAPTER 6

CBK: ETERNITY BEGINS

Post-Diner, King County, Washington

Guy found Ruby happily lying underneath the shade of a nearby hemlock. He went over, opened, and placed the Styrofoam takeaway container, which contained bacon, nearby. He did so close enough that she could smell the gift but far enough that she would have to make some movement to eat. She looked at him, stood, and moved away from the food. Guy thought she seemed almost offended that he would offer her something so basic.

Guy closed the container and placed it in the back of the van. He figured that perhaps Ruby wasn't hungry but would want it later. Leaving the rear door ajar, he circled Toto's nose to sit behind the wheel. Guy pulled the attaché case from behind the gearbox and laid it onto the passenger seat. He opened the case and withdrew the vacation-interrupting manuscript and his Carolyn Bessette *Vanity Fair* issue. The Carolyn article was marked by a fold in the top right corner of the page, and Guy quickly opened it to the correct section.

He laid the manuscript in his lap against Toto's wheel and swapped the unfurled *Vanity Fair* with the attaché case on the passenger seat. He opened the case's front zipper pocket and fumbled through it for his favorite editing pens, one red, and three black, as was customary for him to use while working. Guy put the tip of the red Bic into his mouth, bit the plastic cap off, and stuck it on the opposing side. He moved the empty attaché into the back seat and used Toto's cup holder to store the extra pens he didn't need.

"Let's get started," Guy said aloud.

Guy cracked his knuckles over Toto's wheel and picked up the manuscript, leaving the *Vanity Fair* open on the Carolyn article in the passenger seat. Without wasting another minute, Guy flipped over the title page and began to read.

– – –

CBK: 1

The expression "cool," not that of the weather or one's temperament but the one meaning intensely good, gathered popularity in the 1930s. It was a way of describing someone or something that broke from the mundaneness of mainstream culture. A "cool" person was self-confident and gifted with a bewitching quality that evoked amazement and admiration from others.

Carolyn Bessette was cool.

An actor is famous for their roles, a model for her portfolio, a politician for winning an election, but rarely is someone christened cool without a platform. Carolyn was cool just by being herself. It is apparent in every recollection, photograph, and shared memory from all stages of her life. She was the "it" girl of her time, even though she gave minimally to the evolution of her hype.

Who was Carolyn Bessette?

After exchanging vows on tiny Cumberland Island, just off the Georgia shore, it was apparent that she had captured John Kennedy's heart. Yet millions of American women wondered who this Barbie doll was and how she had bewitched the coveted John-John.

The details surrounding the sumptuous woman remain scarce. First sightings labeled her as a "mystery blonde." Why would Kennedy be with another woman if he was supposedly dating Darryl Hannah?

The typical five Ws (who, what, where, when, and why) had no immediate answers. Indeed, Carolyn was as beautiful as any actress or model but was neither. As a trained publicist, she was a master of image. Employing silence was her secret weapon. By saying nothing, she became all the more alluring. Everyone wanted to know more about her.

What was her name? Carolyn Bessette.

Where did she work? For Calvin Klein.

As what? A publicist. A stylist.

Was she American? Yes, from Connecticut.

Who did she date before John? There were rumors of heirs, models, and athletes.

One New York magazine described her using an array of adjectives like *bright, ambitious, wickedly funny,* and a *master of men.* Had she studied the 1990s how-to for single ladies looking for Mr. Right's bible, *The Rules*? No one will ever know. Not one editor, *Vogue, Glamour,* or even *Cosmo,* landed that coveted interview and photo shoot of the newest Kennedy bride for their cover.

To some, she was mere tabloid fodder. There was that prized shot of her bikini-thong bottom aboard a Hyannis Port speedboat, the other of her embracing John on a gold-plated chair at some Hilton Hotel function, those of her walking the dog on the New York streets, and the infamous shots of her clashing with her Romeo in a public New York City park.

To others, she embodied a significant shift in her generation's style. Carolyn's careful study of streetwear and love of avant-garde designers, paired with a beautiful physique, made her the most famous fashion-forward influencer of the decade. Her name immortalized the minimalist chic movement of 1990s New York.

Yet to a select few, she was a daughter, a sister, and a treasured friend.

Carolyn Jeanne Bessette was born on January 7, 1966, in White Plains, New York. She was raised in Greenwich, Connecticut, by her mother Ann (née Messina), a school administrator, and her orthopedic surgeon stepfather, Richard Freeman, alongside two older sisters, twins Lisa Ann and Lauren. Her father, William Bessette, remained in White Plains, where he worked as an architectural engineer.

By all accounts, their childhood was typical. Carolyn attended the local public school, Greenwich High, for two years until her parents decided to switch her to the Catholic high school, St. Mary's. She told friends the change occurred because she was having "too much fun,"[9] and her social life was moving in on her studies.

---

[9] Bumiller, "Enter Smiling, the Stylish Carolyn Bessette," 31.

At St. Mary's, Carolyn wore a uniform, dated athletes, and was voted the "Ultimate Beautiful Person."[10] As former classmate Claudia Slocum told *People* magazine in 1997, "She was the only one who could pull off wearing the ill-fitting school uniform pants."[11]

After graduation, she attended Boston University, where she studied early childhood education. In her senior year, she was featured on the cover of the 1988 *Girls of BU* campus calendar.

In an interview with *W* magazine in 1995, when they profiled her as an up-and-coming New Yorker, Carolyn revealed her reason for not pursuing teaching as her chosen career. "At the time, I felt a little underdeveloped myself to be completely responsible for twenty-five other people's children. And to a large extent, I felt it wouldn't be provocative enough for me."[12]

After graduating in 1988, she remained in Boston and worked for the Lyons Group, a nightclub consortium. There, she booked the club's entertainment and cared for VIPs. Through connections at the club, she took the job that led her to Camelot II; she began working for Calvin Klein in his Boston-based boutique on Newberry Street.

Carolyn was a natural. She was an astute study, knew which pieces would look best on each shape, and had a natural rapport with the women who frequented the Newberry shop. In no time, clients would ask for her by name. Her career as a stylist began.

A short while later, Susan Sokol, then the president of Calvin Klein's women's collection, needed talent to work with celebrity clients in their New York boutique.[13] Carolyn expressed her interest, won the

---

[10] Johnson, "Carolyn Bessette Kennedy Echoes of Camelot."
[11] Staff, "A Man in Full," 66–71
[12] Ganem, "An American Princess Lost."
[13] Bumiller, "Enter Smiling, the Stylish Carolyn Bessette," 31.

job, and relocated to Manhattan. Within no time, she was drawn into Calvin's inner circle and moved quickly from retail into public relations for the designer's shows. There, she gained attention for her incredible style and self-confidence.

It was a natural fit. Many felt that Carolyn represented the healthy, beautiful American woman who inspired and was the target buyer of Klein's attire. Paul Wilmot, a former Calvin Klein publicity manager, adds, "She looked every bit the model herself, knew the clothes, and possessed wonderful people skills."[14]

The first public sighting of John Kennedy with mystery girl Carolyn happened on a street curb during the running of the 1993 New York Marathon. The newspapers published their combined image with a great song because it was no secret that John was involved with on-again / off-again flame, *Splash* actress Daryl Hannah. Indeed, it was Hannah, not Bessette, whom he brought to visit his dying mother shortly before Jacqueline Kennedy Onassis's May 1994 passing.

John and Daryl Hannah first met in the early eighties on respective family vacations. Hannah was the stepdaughter of billionaire Jarrold Wexler, who significantly contributed to John's uncle Ted Kennedy's 1980 presidential campaign. They began to see each other in 1988 after attending the wedding of John's aunt Lee Radziwill to director Herb Ross. At the time, they were both dating other people. Hannah was a decade into a love affair with LA-based singer-songwriter Jackson Browne, while John was in a three-year relationship with actress Christina Haag.

John and Daryl began as nonexclusive but became serious about one another in the summer of 1992 when she lived in New York to study film at NYU. In late September 1992, Hannah announced

---

[14] Johnson, "Carolyn Bessette Kennedy Echoes of Camelot."

her intention to end her relationship with Browne for good and flew to LA to collect some items from her and Jackson Browne's home. The encounter led to reports of an alleged domestic incident in which Hannah received injuries requiring medical attention. John Kennedy Jr. had never been a fan of Browne and, on hearing this news, flew to LA to aide Hannah and return with her to New York.[15]

From that point, John and Daryl Hannah were a couple, so the first sighting of John with Carolyn, a mysterious blonde, curbside on Sunday, November 14, 1993, became all the more curious.

Crafty, as some say was her skill, Carolyn managed to entice Kennedy away from Hannah and into a love affair that would lead to their eventual wedding three years later. John bid farewell to Daryl Hannah in August of 1994, three months after the death of his mother, and began to date Carolyn exclusively. In no time, Carolyn moved out from the East Village apartment shared with designer Gordon Henderson and into Kennedy's Tribeca loft on North Moore.

"Carolyn was a girl who got what she wanted," a Kennedy insider shared. "She was very sharp, played her cards close to her chest, knew how to handle men, and was not afraid to be aggressive. When Carolyn felt John's attention drifting, she would play on his insecurity to make him jealous, using ex-boyfriends or other obliging men she encountered. Of course, Carolyn loved John, but a little hint of competition never hurt."

Many who knew Carolyn said that Jackie would have approved her for John. Something about her insistence on a private life rather

---

[15] Staff, "Say Goodbye to the Pretender."

than using her newfound fame for self-promotion would have made Jackie particularly warm toward her daughter-in-law.

"She was hypnotically attractive. There was something about her eyes; she just had that quality, the one that top models possess. She was über," one fashion insider confided. "Carolyn was placed on the best-dressed list several times, not only for her excellent taste and inert sense of style but also for encouraging an entire substratum of society to shuck the jewels and gaudy accessories and align with the pared-down Prada look of a fashion editor."[16]

The sparkle of her gaze out from under the cock of an expertly arched eyebrow, Carolyn's signature move was tossing her gorgeous hair while focusing on her partner in conversation. "She made people feel special like they were the only ones in the room," recounts a New York socialite who wishes to remain anonymous. "I attended many charity functions with the Kennedy couple and was forever impressed with Carolyn's ability to work the room. She was private but a welcome addition to any group. When they arrived, the party always seemed to start."

– – –

Guy picked up one of his black pens to make a few notes on the side margin of the manuscript. He reordered a few paragraphs and corrected a few spelling errors. He also scribbled notes requesting citations in the places they were missing.

– – –

"Her many business colleagues also respected Carolyn," notes Paul Wilmot, Carolyn's friend and coworker at Calvin Klein

---

[16] (B. N. Services 1997) Bee News Services, "Brits and Bessette-Kennedy make best dressed list"

"She was very sophisticated, and everyone in the business loved her. And she had the most spontaneous, crackerjack sense of humor. We'd go to these dinners, and she'd be the life of the party. It's got to be one of the things that attracted him to her—she had such a repartee and such wit. She had just enough sense of sarcasm. All the things that seemed so serious in the fashion world—she would cut right through them."[17]

But not all portraits were flattering. A jilted ex-boyfriend complained, "Carolyn was cunning and manipulative. I never even saw the end of our relationship coming and then suddenly, I went from the top of the totem to the bottom with no explanation. I guess she had no time for anyone else when John Kennedy came on the scene."

New York gynecologist Dr. Ruth Ann Moore, who didn't know Carolyn personally, said in an interview on *Good Morning America*, "In a city with almost one hundred thousand reported STDs per year,[18] I was disgusted by how the media portrayed Ms. Bessette as a man-hopper. Surely, a woman like that would have had more sense than to become another New York statistic."

A Manhattan waitress who was not authorized to speak on behalf of her employer said, "Most women would have flaunted the Kennedy engagement. I saw her at the bar when she met with Narciso Rodriguez, maybe plotting the wedding dress. No one would have ever known what they were doing. They just looked like a couple of longtime friends, sipping a round of cosmopolitans and sharing a laugh. She was that discreet."

---

[17] Ganem, "An American Princess Lost."
[18] Office of Sexual Health and Epidemiology, *Sexually Transmitted Infections New York State.*

And then there was the hair. Everyone seemed to agree that it must be highlighted and bleached, but what was the toner that gave it the illusion of spun gold? What, indeed, was the secret to her hair?

Carolyn's hair was darker with honey highlights in the early years after the first sighting on that New York curb. She wore it messy as she had just gotten out of bed, a holdout look from the early '90s grunge trend. As their relationship took hold and she became John Kennedy Jr.'s number-one armpiece, Carolyn's hair lightened and became a statement; some would say her trademark.

Manhattan colorist Brad Johns was responsible for this transformation. When Carolyn became a client, she was already dating John and was looking to refine her image. He brought her into the realm of Grace Kelly, a platinum blonde with a silky texture. Was it true that blondes had more fun? Looking at pictures of Carolyn out at galas, dressed in fabulous designer clothing, one must say, "Yes!"

When asked what a woman should do if she experiences a bad hair day, Johns said, "Stay home! This is not a dress. This is not a bag. You can't leave it behind. You can't take your head off. The only thing to do if your hair is awful is to stay home."[19]

At Carolyn's request, appointments at Johns's salon were under tight secrecy. There was such an intense public interest in her life that even something as benign as a haircut became a mission to avoid the attention of the paparazzi. Carolyn learned which of her friends, colleagues, and associates she could trust with the more private details of her life. It was rumored that when Brad Johns broke her trust by publicly speaking about his relationship with her, she became infuriated and switched stylists.

---

[19] Staff, "JFK's Lawyers Called in to Gag his Wife's Ex-hairdresser.

In the spring of 1996, Carolyn resigned after seven years at Calvin Klein. Some said she had tired of the role and wanted to free herself to work more closely with her future husband; others had her unhappy with changes in management at the fashion house. One insider suggested Klein himself wanted her gone when the attention she received from the media overshadowed his collections.

As a newly anointed fashion icon, Carolyn was expected to dress the part. She was the first call from the stylist at Saks and Bergdorf when they received new shipments from her favorite designers. Speculation about the clothes worn made the chatter around various New York social events. Did she enjoy Yamamoto because of the fit or because he did not advertise? Once John Kennedy launched *George*, some felt she could not wear designers who bought space in the magazine for fear of bias.

Carolyn was the envy of American women who had the looks, height, fantastic figure, affluence, and perfect husband. But there was a darker side that trapped her in a gilded cage. This impression would outlast most others after her untimely death.

– – –

Guy's attention was drawn away from the text when Ruby suddenly hopped through the van's rear door. As though her legs were springs, she jumped up on the small fold-down table nestled between the seating ensemble in the back and then leaped again into the front passenger seat, landing on the open issue of *Vanity Fair*. The sequence startled Guy, and he put down the manuscript to discover what Ruby wanted.

Ruby sat on one side of the open magazine, gazing downward. On closer examination, Guy found that Ruby sat on a Brooks Brothers ad adjacent to page 130. He looked curiously at the image underneath the dog's left paw because the way she held it indicated he should. There, he found a picture of John and Carolyn together, and it seemed to Guy that Ruby was intentionally showing him the photograph.

Guy gently pulled the magazine out from beneath her paw to look closer. He read the caption underneath, which stated the date as October 5, 1998, and the event, a gala to celebrate the renovation of New York's Grand Central Station. Guy looked back and forth between Ruby, who was staring at him, and the photograph in the magazine. The way Ruby looked up at him eerily mirrored the fashion by which Carolyn gazed up at her husband.[20]

This is too weird, Guy thought.

Guy found the torn quotation passed along by Glinda in his back jeans pocket and used it to bookmark page 130. He closed the magazine, stacked it on the manuscript, and tucked both inside his attaché case. He checked his watch, noting that it was almost eleven and time to get moving if they wanted to get some distance on the journey.

---

[20] Michaelis, "Great Expectations," 130.

CHAPTER 7

STACEY

*Four hours later, Interstate 90,
outside Spokane, Washington*

Time and distance passed without incident through noon and the early afternoon hours and Guy noted how driving Toto was an almost soothing experience. Despite the van's age and issues, its connection with the road resulted in a fluid sensation. Nobody would have believed him if he had told them how smooth the ride was or how easy it was to manage the gas pedal. He did not have to press too hard to maintain speed, and the wheel required little movement to keep a straight course. Toto was built for road trips.

Guy glanced at Ruby, who was staring out the window from the passenger seat. He was never granted the childhood privilege of pet ownership, so he was unused to dogs' behavior. From his limited experience, he always assumed they were stupid, mangy, yappy, and smelly. Ruby defied these stereotypes. She never barked; her scent was clean, perhaps even slightly fragrant. She sat patiently and demanded little.

Guy reached out to lightly tousle the crown of Ruby's head between both ears.

"You're a good girl," he praised. "And those twitches should be thankful I'm taking you to New York."

They were at a place where a fork in the road forced him to consult the motel man's highlighted route. Guy slowed Toto, pulled off onto the shoulder, and withdrew the map. Except for the mark of the yellow-lined road, everything suddenly seemed blurry, and he squinted for clarity. Between the stress of driving and the time spent reading the CBK text, it was time to rest. He looked up to see a sign confirming where to go and started toward the next town.

Guy quickly discovered the main street. He located an Internet café between the local post office and a barbershop where he could get a jolt of caffeine and check his emails simultaneously. In addition, the restaurant's door boasted the national canine acceptance symbol for eateries. The logo meant Ruby could join him inside. While Guy had previously avoided such establishments, it seemed fortuitous under his current circumstances that he would find a place that accepted dogs so easily.

The sun lowered from its prominent place in the sky, casting a lovely, warm, late-afternoon glow over the town. He parked Toto and dropped a handful of thin silver dimes into the parking meter. He helped Ruby out of the van, affixed the leash he fashioned from his necktie, slung his attaché case over his shoulder, and crossed the street to enter the café.

Once past the threshold, Guy found a darkened room with various armchairs scattered around the space, their seats boasting inviting depressions. The window coverings were thick navy velvet sheaths knotted with heavy braided rope. Scattered around the room were several giant candelabras of wrought iron covered by drips of wax that spilled like fountains from their diminishing source.

"Welcome," a woman with raven hair, dark lips and nails, and kohl-lined eyes greeted him by the door. Her skin was pale, making the effect of the black clothing she wore all the more drastic. "Are you looking for Internet in the back, or do you want to sit out here?" she asked with a yawn.

"Out here is fine for now. Do you have a menu?" Guy asked.

"Sit yourself," she replied flatly. "Our menu is bologna."

"OK, then," Guy nodded. "Bologna it will be. And a coffee, please."

The waitress went behind a curtain, leaving Guy and Ruby alone. Guy chose a table for two beside the window. Ruby jumped up on the seat that faced him, pawing at the cushion to plump it a few times until she settled into its cozy seat. After considerable rustling, rattling, and banging, the girl returned with a small silver tray. She set it down beside him on a round table that stood in between the two chairs.

Guy surveyed the tray's contents. It held a white ceramic mug filled with steaming coffee, two sugar cubes, a tiny pitcher of cold milk, and a glass of drinking water tied with a white napkin. He felt the presentation only lacked chocolate or a biscotti to be perfect. He offered the water to Ruby, who lapped it directly from the glass before sighing and closing her eyes to nap.

Guy went about his ritual of reading his manuscript by organizing a series of three fine-tipped black ink pens and one red Bic pen at the side of his coffee. He stirred one sugar cube into the mug and opened his attaché case to find the manuscript under *Vanity Fair*. Guy withdrew it, smoothed the top, and flipped over the cover containing the title, author's information, and M's Post-it note, landing on the first page of the second chapter.

– – –

CBK: 2

Long before she added the desirable Kennedy hyphen to her name, Carolyn was much in demand. The combustion of her icy blonde looks with the warmth of her personality made the nearly six-foot beauty a natural man magnet. She dated several famous personalities over the years before her move to New York. At Boston University, future NHL player John Cullen and clothing heir Allesandro Benetton were Carolyn's rumored suitors. Cullen, touted as the most handsome man at school, fell hard for Bessette.[21]

What was it about Carolyn that made everyone so positively intoxicated? Thousands of beauties light up the New York scene, some with the benefit of being well-bred and exceptionally wealthy, some not quite as fortunately bequeathed. The common thread between them is the understanding and practice of meeting rich, good-looking, powerful men and marrying well. Carolyn Bessette was no stranger to this doctrine.

As effortless as she made it seem, Carolyn and John's mating dance had ups and downs. Rumor was that the pair met while jogging in Central Park in 1993. Smitten by her beauty, he stopped her on the path to ask for her phone number. Carolyn obliged, scratching out her digits on the palm of his hand. She smiled and ran off, unsure if the *People* magazine–anointed Sexiest Man Alive would call. But, of course, he did.

---

[21] Jeffreys, "Blonde Ambition," 158–159.

Other versions of the story had the pair meeting through friends, most likely Kelly Klein, Calvin's wife. Or perhaps she was assigned to him as a personal shopper when working with private clients in New York. Whatever or whoever could claim credit for the introduction, John was in love.

John Kennedy's friend, former Grateful Dead lyricist John Perry Barlow recalled:

> The first time he told me about Carolyn was a night at Tramps in early '94. John was still going with Daryl. And he said that there was a woman that he'd met who was having a heavy effect on him. He wasn't going to pursue it, because he was loyal to Daryl. But it was hard for him, because he couldn't get his mind off her. And I said, "Well, who is she?" And he said, "Well, she's not really anybody. She's some functionary of Calvin Klein's. She's an ordinary person." Which of course was not so, she was anything but an ordinary person, but as far as the rest of the world knew, she was. And he maintained a platonic relationship with her until after he and Daryl had broken up.[22]

It was not only John who had other dating interests on the go. Before John, Carolyn's most recognizable conquest was the handsome and sculpted CK underwear model and *Baywatch* actor Michael Bergin. At the time, Bergin was the star of a larger-than-life billboard advertisement in Times Square, selected as an unknown successor to Klein's wildly-popular advertising campaign that featured rap star Marky Mark. Carolyn was reportedly heavily involved with the twenty-five year old when she first met John.

---

[22] Roshen, "Prince of the City."

ALLISON LANG COOK

Many speculated that Carolyn teased Michael along, retaining him in her back pocket only to bring him out whenever she felt it appropriate to make John jealous. If she thought John's attention was waning, she would remind him that Michael was always a willing partner, waiting in the wings.[23]

Michael Bergin was not the first man Carolyn may have played. At St. Mary's, she dated an athlete named Eugene Carlin, who would later describe their relationship as "hot and heavy."[24] When interviewed, Carlin described Carolyn as someone who would make a man jealous if she felt it was beneficial. When Carlin retorted with an attempt to do the same back at her, Carolyn ignored him and moved along to her next conquest.

"Was she an opportunistic man hopper? I can't say that for certain," a friend from college confides. "But I always admired her and wasn't surprised when she wound up on John Kennedy Jr.'s arm. Carolyn always came across as better than the rest of us. Or maybe that was just our opinion. But the proof is in the pudding."

– – –

Guy picked up his red pen and scribbled the word source followed by three question marks. He liked to use the red pen for urgent items and felt backup was needed for sensitive statements. He didn't want the author to face libel accusations if they were preventable.

– – –

When Carolyn met John Kennedy in New York, employing the same tactics that worked for her in the past was most certainly on her agenda. In 1994, after formally breaking it off with longtime

---

[23] Jeffreys, "Blonde Ambition," 158–159.
[24] Staff, "Crazy for Carolyn."

lady love Daryl Hannah, John was free to pursue Carolyn. Judging by comments made to his friends and colleagues, after a short time, John was infatuated.

It was easy to see why. According to friend Paul Wilmot, Carolyn was

> A touch-and-feel person. When you talked with her one-on-one, she'd touch your arm and grab your hand in a sort of affectionate way. She was much better in a small group of people. So you take the looks, the charm, the style, and that wonderful voice and sense of humor and incredible warmth and love of conversation—she was the best company you could ever have.[25]

If the theory was true, Carolyn chose to toy with John, giving of herself and taking only as much from him as necessary until she could ensure he was hers. Some would say she played him perfectly; she was available and unavailable as it suited her and was not against faking engagements when John called for a last-minute interlude. Sometimes, she hinted that she saw other men, perhaps Michael Bergin, which drove John to the edge.

John was relentless in his quest, and Carolyn willingly succumbed. She moved in with him in April 1995, and they became engaged that September.[26] To fully appreciate the talent necessary to cement such a swift courtship, one must look deep into Carolyn's essence to uncover her depth, sensual play on life, and luminous beauty.

Friend and fashion designer Tom Ford confided:

---

[25] Peretz, "The Private Princess," 274–281.
[26] Johnson, "Carolyn Bessette Kennedy Echoes of Camelot."

In photographs, she always appeared quite cool and aloof, but in person she was exactly the opposite. She was warm and engaging and had an almost magnetic sex appeal. She was polished and slick, yet she had a great charm and, of course, great style. She was an individual. She was a true beauty.[27]

In addition to her obvious physical attributes, cool Carolyn Bessette will forever be known as highly intelligent, profoundly engaging, and wickedly funny, a consummate "Ultimate Beautiful Person."

— — —

Sensing that someone was watching him, Guy drew his attention away from the text and looked up to find the waitress a few feet away.

"I'm going now." She motioned toward the door. "Stacey's here, though. She'll hook you up in the back online when you're ready. But just to let you know, we close at five."

Guy nodded to acknowledge he heard her and returned to the paragraph she had interrupted.

— — —

Early media photographs show Carolyn as a bushy, honey-blonde woman with considerably more eyebrows than in her sleeker New York days. In fact, between her *Girls of BU* cover and her triumphant Cumberland Island chapel shot as Mrs. John Kennedy Jr., much about Carolyn was reimagined.

---

[27] Peretz, "The Private Princess," 274–281.

Her style flaunted minimalism, inherited from working as a Calvin Klein publicist. Her hair was longer and glossier, and her roots were bleached from root to tip by one of New York's finest colorists, Brad Johns of the Clive Summers Salon on 57th Street. Her eyebrows were plucked into a sleek arch, allowing the features of her face, eyes, and cheekbones to stand out. She wore little makeup, face powder, and a dab of vivid red lipstick: her signature.

John Perry Barlow continues,

> I didn't meet Carolyn until the fall of '94, by which time he and Daryl had broken up. Carolyn was as charismatic as John was. Charisma, you know, was once a theological term meaning "grace." And she had that. I was also impressed with the fact that she was a bit eccentric. She was not conventional in any sense. Carolyn seemed a lot like John's mother in her quirkiness and also in her unbelievable capacity to engage one's attention. Jackie could be talking to six people at one time and make everyone feel like the only one in the room. Carolyn had the same ability. It was based on genuine interest. Having a beautiful woman want to know all about you is not such a bad thing, you know (laughs).[28]

Declared a trendsetter by the national press, Carolyn was often compared to her late mother-in-law, Jacqueline Kennedy Onassis. They were decades apart but united by their fashionista status. Where Kennedy Onassis had encapsulated the structured look of the 1960s, Carolyn was the embodiment of the emerging sleekness of the 1990s.

---

[28] Roshen, "Prince of the City."

"So very much like Jackie O!" The paper headlines accompanied shots of Carolyn striding around Manhattan with a Jackie-esque scarf fold and strappy sandals.[29]

Designer Carolina Herrera insisted:

> Millions of women copied Jackie when she was in the White House. Jackie never met Carolyn; I don't think. But her love of privacy would have made her a favorite of Jackie's. She would have loved Carolyn's simplicity.[30]

– – –

"Hi," a small voice shyly interrupted. "Are you the bologna?"

Guy looked up, expecting to discover a clone of the first waitress, whose persona seemed inspired by the gothic decor of the cafe. Instead, he found Stacey. She was pert and messy-haired and sported a T-shirt layering over a long-sleeved top and a sprinkle of freckles across the bridge of her nose. Around her hips hung a denim wrap skirt whose front pocket revealed the bulge of a shoved-in paperback book.

She placed a plate on the table beside the coffee. In contrast to the elaborate ceremony the coffee seemed to offer, the dish on the table was as simple as advertised: a bologna sandwich on white. It wasn't even cut into two. Guy picked it up and bit the edge while Stacey watched as he chewed, looking for approval. He felt obliged to nod, smile, and place the sandwich with the missing bite back on the plate.

---

[29] Gerhart, "Bessette Tried to Avoid Kennedy Spotlight," A20.
[30] Peretz, "The Private Princess," 274–281.

"It's good. Thanks," Guy said as he picked up the manuscript, resting on his knees to signal his intention to return to work.

"What are you reading?" Stacey asked with such buoyancy that Guy could not help but push aside his budding irritation. While he hated being interrupted, the waitress seemed so genuine. Stacey continued, "You look so into it, and I thought I'd ask."

"This," he began by raising and lightly shaking the document, "is a manuscript from an author. I'm an editor."

"An editor, wow!" she exclaimed. "I've never met a real-life editor before! Tell me," Stacey moved to sit on the arm of Ruby's chair, "have you met anyone famous?" She begged to know.

"Well, my job is more of a behind-the-scenes gig, if you know what I mean," he said.

"Oh wow!" She paused and blinked, cocking her head to the side before uttering, "That's so rad."

Stacey led the conversation for several minutes, asking Guy every question he felt could be asked about his work. The waitress was thorough. When Guy felt the topic had been exhausted, he changed the conversation and asked what Stacey was reading.

"What? Oh this?" Stacey withdrew the book from the waistband of her skirt and held it up for him to see.

"*THE RULES: Time Tested Secrets for Capturing the Heart of Mr. Right* by Ellen Fein and Sherrie Schneider." Guy read the cover aloud. "Do you mind?" He raised his hand, asking for the book.

Stacey happily handed Guy the paperback. Well loved by its owner, the spine was loose from consistent bending. Guy noticed that the corners of several pages were folded into tiny triangles, marking their importance. He flipped the cover. The first page read:

A Rules Sampler

- DON'T MEET HIM HALFWAY OR GO DUTCH ON A DATE.
- DON'T OPEN UP TOO FAST.
- DON'T CALL HIM AND RARELY RETURN HIS CALLS.
- DON'T EXPECT A MAN TO CHANGE OR TRY TO CHANGE HIM.

He flipped over the page and read on. "Rule #1: Be a 'Creature Unlike Any Other.'"[31]

"Be a creature unlike any other?" he questioned.

"I also have the second book, *The Rules II, More Rules to Live and Love By*," Stacey announced, "I've read both like a thousand times. I want to be prepared for when I meet him," she explained. "My Mr. Right, that is."

Guy knotted his brow, puzzled, forcing Stacey to continue.

"Well, you see, it's a bunch of rules, apparently from someone's grandma in the early nineteen hundreds and passed down from generation to generation of women. They teach you what to do and what not to do when dating men. Like, um, they say not to see a guy more than once or twice a week. That's so that they want to see more of you. You always play them into calling you up and never

---

[31] Fein, *The Rules.*

calling them back. I mean, these rules don't work around here as much. You have to be in a cosmopolitan environment, like a big city. That's where the kind of men you want to attract live. The guys around here are, well, pretty bad."

To solidify his understanding, Guy asked Stacey to confirm: "If you were interested in some person," he paused, "would you, for the most part, act as though you weren't?"

"Yeah, you play hard to get. I know—it sounds so odd. But yeah, that's how these gals tell it. Plus, kissing is not recommended until after at least a few dates. Play hard to get and make them chase you." Stacey sang sweetly, adding, "I'm reading up to try it out when I visit my eldest brother, Herb. He lives in Manhattan, you know, New York City."

"Oh really? What does he do there?" Guy asked.

"He's a student at Columbia. He's all smart and stuff, unlike my *other* brothers." She rolled her eyes and explained, "Yes, I have four older, smelly brothers. And they are incomprehensible, like from a different planet." She raised a palm to her brow and shook her head in mock disbelief. "A bunch of clowns, I say, but they're all mine!" She laughed.

"I wouldn't know. I'm an only child," Guy shared.

"An only child!" Stacey squealed. "I'm pretty sure I've only met one other person who was an only child, and that was because they were adopted."

"So your brother wants you to visit Columbia in New York?" Guy asked.

ALLISON LANG COOK

"Herb? Well, he's trying to get me to enroll there too. But I don't know." She shrugged.

"You don't know what?" Guy asked.

"Well, what I'd study for one. I've read a lot," she considered, "and I know a lot, but I don't think I'm college material."

"Why not?" Guy asked.

"Well, I was never a good student. The teachers always said I had my head in the clouds and didn't apply myself enough. But I couldn't help it! I'm just not interested in quadratic equations or the theory of evolutionary development." Stacey sighed.

"Yeah, me neither," Guy commiserated with a laugh.

"Did you go to college?" Stacey asked.

"Yes, I did. I studied English literature," Guy said.

"Like Shakespeare?" Stacey asked, adding proudly, "I've watched the Romeo and Juliet movie starring Leonardo DiCaprio and Claire Danes about ten times."

"Shakespeare was my major," Guy revealed.

"Wow, how did you become an editor?" Stacey was impressed.

"The English degree helped, and working at a publishing house seemed a good idea," Guy answered.

"It must be super-duper interesting, reading all day," Stacey speculated keenly.

"Sometimes." Guy laughed aloud. "Other times, it's just a huge burden."

Stacey seemed confused by the comment, so Guy clarified, "You see, I'm supposed to be on vacation right now, but my boss gave me this," he said, holding up the manuscript.

"You have to read it on your vacation?" Stacey said, "That doesn't sound so bad."

"Read, edit, polish, and prepare it for her review," Guy said.

"Well, at least you have company." She pointed at Ruby. "I love dogs! They have such a passion for life. Come here, girl!"

Stacey held her hand out to Ruby and began scratching the top of her head, tickling down her back before returning up the opposite side. Ruby sat with her eyes closed and paws crossed in quite a ladylike fashion. Guy noticed that Ruby seemed annoyed rather than pleased by the attention. Regardless, she tolerated it.

"I read a book once on dog massage, and they are supposed to love this technique," Stacey approached Ruby for a second round of affection.

"Apparently," Guy observed as Ruby abruptly jumped off the chair, shook, and stared at him as if to say, "Let's go."

"Where are you going for your vacation?" Stacey asked, taking Ruby's abandoned seat to face Guy at eye level.

"We are going to New York. It's a road trip," Guy told her.

ALLISON LANG COOK

"You are driving *all the way* to New York." Stacey was amazed. "From here?"

"I have a VW van," Guy answered, wondering if the waitress would disapprove of him taking the dog across the country in a small car.

"Really?" She stopped and laughed aloud. "My parents were Deadheads, and they had all my brothers while traveling around in their VW back in the day."

"Suddenly, the name Herb makes sense," Guy teased astutely.

"What? Herb?" Stacey laughed again. "No, my parents named my brothers after the presidents who sat in office after Calvin Coolidge. Herbert, Frank, Harry, and Dwight. I was supposed to be John. But then, oops, I was a girl!"

"Like, as in John Kennedy?" Guy asked before realizing how uninformed the question seemed.

Not missing a beat, Stacey replied, "Of course, silly. He counts, even though he was assassinated."

"Yes, of course," Guy agreed.

"So, you are going all the way to New York?" Stacey repeated.

Guy cleared his throat and took the final sip of his now cold coffee. "Yup. It should be about three days, I figure. I have to get there by Wednesday. I have a job interview."

Guy didn't know why he revealed that small, secret detail. Perhaps it was because the waitress was so easy to talk to and seemed to take a genuine interest in what he had to say, or maybe it was because she was a stranger in a café in the middle of nowhere. But there was something about Stacey that made Guy feel at ease in her company. It was as though he had known her for ages.

"You don't think that maybe … gosh, I'm just being silly. Well, it's just that I barely know you, but you seem trustworthy, like a fifth brother," she offered the compliment before the actual request. "Can I ride with you to New York?"

Guy started to answer, but she interrupted before he could say anything.

"Please, please," she begged, pushing her hands together and pouting slightly. "You see, today's my last day working here, and I was already planning to go. I could help with the driving and pay my share of the gas. It's so much easier than taking the bus. Please, take me with you."

Guy looked to Ruby, seated on the floor beside the chair. Her blue eyes shone vividly in the dark light of the café, and she wagged her tail with moderate enthusiasm. "Please," Stacey repeated, addressing the plea directly to the dog.

Ruby's tail began to swing back and forth with increased velocity. She stood and walked toward Stacey, sat at her feet, and looked up. Stacey pet the top of Ruby's head, using a variance of the dog massage technique. "Pretty please," she repeated as Ruby closed her eyes and began to pant.

"Sure, I guess you can come along," Guy decided.

Stacey stood and began to hop up and down on hearing the news, clapping in delight. She pressed her hands together and spun around so that her hair and skirt flared outward in perfect synchronization.

"You won't regret it! I promise. I have to email Herb and tell him I'm coming. He'll be so excited." She seemed already preoccupied with the composition of her email as she returned the book to the waistband of her skirt.

"While you're at it, I have some web work before we head out." He held out a twenty-dollar bill. "Can you set me up?"

"Sure thing." She pointed to the back of the café. "Come this way."

Once Guy packed away the manuscript and his pens, Stacey led him to four empty computer terminals. Each was separated by long velvet curtains behind and on the sides, creating strange cloak-wrapped, closet-sized spaces. Stacey hurriedly signed him onto the first terminal before darting to a neighboring one to log on herself.

Guy clicked through the familiar MSN homepage and typed a search for Hotmail. The computer chugged at an annoyingly slow pace. The connection was most definitely not urban, he noted. The hourglass icon tilted over and over while he waited. Finally, after almost three full minutes, the page loaded, and he entered the password for his account.

Guy spent the first few minutes cleaning out all the spam messages that seemed to amass like flies to nectar in his inbox. He knew that, ultimately, he would have to shut the account down and enroll in another, better version—maybe Yahoo!. It was a hassle he didn't yet feel up to, so cleaning out the unwanted messages was just part of the penalty of apathy.

Once he finished deleting, he went into his trash bin to find their email address and quickly composed a note to the twitches.

I am on a cross-country road trip and discovered your Ruby somehow got into the van. She has a "Return to New York" charm on her collar, and since I'm already en route, I thought I'd do you a favor and deliver her. Sorry about the bike. I'll pay for any damage. Guy

He reread the composition and pressed send. Since he was in his Hotmail, he took a moment to reread the job interview confirmation in his saved file. As usual, it evoked a smile. He was caught up in that moment of euphoria when his inbox icon suddenly lit up, announcing a new message. Guy froze momentarily before his index finger won the battle and clicked on the envelope icon, opening the email.

GUY, GIVE US BACK OUR PRECIOUS RUBY. CHOOSE TO DISOBEY, AND WE WILL SWEEP YOU AWAY! IT WILL NOT BE PRETTY. BROOMSTICKS UNITE!

The all-caps message included two attachments. The first was a poor-quality digital picture of Guy beside Toto in the apartment stall parking. They must have taken it when he was going to work one morning because his hair looked as though it was still wet from the shower and had yet to dry into its usual style.

The second was a photo of Ruby, head down, perched on one twitch's motorcycle seat. The email signature bore the unmistakable logo of the Broomsticks, and Guy knew that it meant trouble. The population of the CC address bar confirmed that the email was copied to every motorcycle gang member from one side of the country to the other.

Guy looked at Ruby, who had quietly joined him. In the dark space, her big eyes shone like full moons.

"Well, Ruby," Guy addressed the dog. The twitches have declined my offer to drive you to New York. Now they are sending their riders to find you. Ruby, you must be exceptional to warrant all this attention."

"Who are you talking to?" Stacey asked from the booth next door. "You sound just like my brother Harry. He's always talking to someone." She laughed.

Guy switched off the computer and said to Stacey. "OK, let's hit the road."

"OK, mister-in-a-hurry, I'm coming!" She giggled, adding, "Wait, I don't even know your name." She stopped and faced him.

"It's Guy." He extended his hand. "Guy Myles."

"Well, Guy Myles," she said, shaking his hand up and down three times. "I'm Stacey. Stacey Crowe. No relation to Sheryl or Russell."

She began to laugh hysterically at her joke, and for a moment, Guy regretted his offer to take her to New York. Temporary cold feet, he soon realized when he thought about how much easier the trip would be with two drivers. Also, the Broomsticks were looking for him alone and would not be looking for a couple in a van. So bringing her along was also a semidisguise.

Stacey approached the hostess stand to gather her possessions. After rooting through the tip jar for her portion of the month's gratuity, she tossed a small cloth backpack over her shoulder, went to the door, and flipped the sign of the café to closed.

"Bye, old life," she said without a hint of nostalgia that Guy could detect.

Together with Ruby, they exited the café. Stacey turned back to lock the establishment's front door, slipping her key into the mail slot while Guy surveyed both ways up and down the main street. There were only a few cars on the road—and no motorcycles, much to his relief. As a precautionary measure, Guy led Ruby to the van while shielding her like a celebrity with his attaché case.

"Sweet Westie," Stacey commented on spotting Toto for the first time, "is it an eighty-six?"

"Thanks." Guy smiled. "An eighty-five."

"Oh my god!" she exclaimed gleefully as she rounded the front to circumvent Toto. "Of course it is. It has round headlights. The eighty-six went to the rectangle."

Guy opened the rear door, and Ruby jumped onto the seat.

"I love these vans!" Stacey gushed. "You know, my parents were Deadheads, and they used to travel in one of these vans until I was a baby. Then they settled here. I've always wanted one. But yours has no kitchen," Stacey said astutely.

"Yeah, the person I bought it from customized the interior. It's not an actual Westfalia camper; it's a Vanagon passenger van. But he made the interior like a camper, so these back seats fold down." Guy pointed to the rear.

"Super cool!" Stacey exclaimed.

"Well, Stacey Crowe, how do you feel about driving?" Guy asked as he tossed the keys toward her. He handed her the map as he got into the van. "That's for you to follow."

"Oh I get it." Stacey slid into the driver's seat and picked it up. "I follow the yellow-lined road. Perfect, Guy, that makes sense. Why don't you get back to whatever you need to do? I'm going to get us where we need to go."

"Sounds like a plan," Guy agreed.

"Well, now you sound just like my brother Dwight. He's always got a plan!" Stacey laughed as she started Toto.

Guy flopped into the back with Ruby. Having been interrupted from his work inside, Guy opened the attaché case and withdrew the manuscript. With no distractions and a Stacey as the driver, he could finish in no time. He found where he left off and continued reading as Stacey adjusted the mirrors, put the van in gear, and guided Toto toward New York City.

CHAPTER 8

QUEEN OF CAMELOT II

Through Montana, Interstate 90

The front passenger seat was empty except for Stacey's small cloth backpack. She held the wheel with her left hand while rummaging through it with her right. Guy noticed that when she finally found a pop can, she withdrew and abandoned it in Toto's cupholder. Returning both hands to the wheel, Stacey hummed quietly to herself.

Guy removed his loafers and put his socked feet on the seat occupied by Ruby, who sniffed his toes. She grew bored, curled up, closed her eyes, and lay still. With the brilliance of the day fading behind them, Guy bit the pen cap of the red Bic and continued to read the manuscript.

– – –

CBK: 3

Blessed with perfect bone structure and natural beauty, Carolyn Bessette was destined for the attention often besotted on attractive people. Her height, hair, and physique gave her that sought-after, all-American look made famous by models like Elaine Irwin.

Carolyn personified the classic look of a refined New Yorker, the way she wore her clothes, pairing everyday essentials with bolder pieces, punctuating color against basic black, or wearing a skirt to meet the lip of a knee-high boot.

Carolyn dabbled in modeling while working in Calvin Klein's Boston boutique. Photographer friend Bobby DiMarco helped Carolyn assemble a modeling portfolio. When interviewed in 1996, DiMarco revealed:

> I knew her when she was wild as she's ever gonna get, when young guys were hitting on her all the time. She liked to party but she doesn't drink and she doesn't do drugs. She was a well-mannered, well-brought-up little rich girl. She decided she didn't want to teach but wanted to be a model, so I helped put her portfolio together. It wasn't difficult: she's just the right size and has just the right look.[32]

An alternate perspective would be that Carolyn's mother and stepfather disapproved of a modeling career, especially when sisters Lauren and Lisa Ann were highly accomplished academics. In all likelihood, Carolyn's inherent desire for advancement, her knack for interpersonal connections, and her skill for making long-lasting impressions propelled her into her life as a New York "it" girl.

– – –

"What are you reading?" Stacey interrupted his concentration.

"The same thing as I was before." Guy did not want to engage in a discussion and replied almost curtly.

---

[32] Jeffreys, "Blonde Ambition," 158–159.

"I know that, silly. I meant, what is it saying?" Stacey prodded.

"Um, things about Carolyn," Guy answered.

"What kind of things?" Stacey asked.

Guy tried not to be annoyed. She was behaving just like his worst work colleagues. He wouldn't finish any of the reading if she kept interrupting him. But he didn't want to be rude, so he offered Stacey the perfect carrot.

"I tell you what, Stacey," Guy bartered. "I'll let you take a peek later."

"Really! That's not, like, illegal or something?" Stacey smiled broadly in delight.

In truth, it wasn't something that was usually done. But Guy was interviewing with Ideal, the edgiest, most unscrupulous publishing house around. He wouldn't be suitable for the job if he followed the rules.

"Oh, now, you sound like my brother Frank," Stacey said while sucking in her breath.

"Just drive," Guy said in a light joking tone and returned to the text.

– – –

Photographs from her college days show a full-faced woman with a teased mass of wheat-colored hair and pouted lips. Carolyn, though untrained as a model, portrayed sensuality like an expert. She knew how to stare into a camera lens to gain the maximum hypnotic effect, and so many found this allure memorable.

A few years later, when Carolyn emerged as one of the most photographed women in America, her look was radically different. She was several pounds lighter,[33] cheekbones prominent, and eyebrows plucked into a delicate arch. Once a mass of highlighted hues, her hair was eventually bleached and toned from root to tip into a sublime champagne blonde. It was longer and straighter, silky, and often worn tied back into a neat ponytail or chignon at the base of her neck.

Slick as the city itself, Carolyn knew how to make an impression. Her daily wardrobe was mostly black, with the occasional white or beige variation. Her accessories were simple, and her makeup minimal. As designer Oscar de la Renta told *Women's Wear Daily*, Carolyn was "the incarnation of modern style."[34]

Canadian freelance fashion consultant magazine editor Ian Hylton recalls meeting Carolyn in her early years, noting that she wore her long blonde hair spaghetti straight alongside a yellow sweater, a daring combination for a blonde. "Carolyn's style was really one of her own making. It wasn't about what was going on in the runways. She stayed true to herself in all that she did. That's what true style is all about."[35]

At the time, fashion was evolving from a world of fussy detail to cleaner, sleeker lines and muted palates. No designer embodied this trend more than Calvin Klein. Carolyn worked as a publicist for Klein, and it was rumored that she inspired the designer. Her natural way of wearing the look certainly made her a fit, but there was more to her image than simply the fabric and cut of her garments. Her whole package of height, clothes, hair, eyebrows, and

---

[33] Goldsmith, "Kennedy's," 45.

[34] Staff, "A Man in Full," 66–71

[35] Fulsang, "Carolyn Bessette Kennedy 1966–1999."

makeup—paired with a look of indifference—cemented Carolyn as the embodiment of a shifting generation.

Education in the world of fashion came quickly. Carolyn's experience working for Klein, first in sales at his Boston store and later in New York, meant she was privy to expert craftsmanship and refined tailoring. She attended fashion shows displaying the latest trendy outfits and was likely permitted, as many fashion houses allow, to obtain designer goods at little to no personal expense.

One client of Calvin Klein recalled meeting Carolyn, who wore jeans with loafers, a white T-shirt, and an oversized blue blazer[36]. The client noted, "I would have looked ridiculous in her getup, but she pulled it off effortlessly. It was like she hadn't even tried, although I suspect that every piece was purposefully selected. It was the perfect assembly of expensive, cheap, tailored, bulky, street, and chic. Carolyn had the best eye."

Many admired her incredible personal style, and much like her mother-in-law, the former first lady Jacqueline Kennedy Onassis, Carolyn helped cement the reputations of several designers as serious contenders in the fashion world.

Like Jackie's fondness for Oleg Cassini, Carolyn had her favorite designers. She once commented that she wore Yohji Yamamoto like a uniform. His designs were based on men's garments, and he used uncluttered shapes and dark, washed fabrics. They permitted the wearer comfort and the illusion of anonymity. Often, Carolyn allowed the clothing to make the impression, leaving her attributes bare, except for a dab of powder and a smack of red lipstick.

---

[36] Johnson, "Carolyn Bessette Kennedy Echoes of Camelot."

Carolyn Bessette was instrumental in making Narciso Rodriguez a household name. She selected him to design the gown for her top-secret nuptials. The hush-hush event took place on Saturday, September 21, 1996, and completely overshadowed the other celebrity wedding of the day: model Christie Brinkley to her fourth husband, architect Peter Cook.

News of the abrupt end to John Kennedy Junior's bachelorhood hit the newswires the following day, breaking women's hearts and dreams worldwide. About the bride, everyone wanted to know that one thing: What did she *wear*?

Along with the preparation for the wedding itself, Carolyn Bessette's wedding dress was the best-kept secret in America. In it, she embodied sleek elegance. Further, the gown was instrumental in changing how brides looked and felt. Copycats scurried to imitate the one-of-a-kind creation, and brides at boutiques begged, "Not meringue, think Carolyn Bessette!"

Her spectacular "no frills" dress created by Narciso Rodriguez, her former Calvin Klein colleague, was an overnight worldwide sensation. A departure from the usual taffeta bodice, Carolyn's dress symbolized the minimalist movement, and Rodriguez became well-known for being its celebrated designer.

At the time, Rodriguez worked to establish himself as a leading designer at Nino Cerruti. Based in Paris, he took on the project as a personal favor for Carolyn. She placed the order for the gown on June 9, 1996. It was thought to be worth an impressive $40,000.[37]

> "It's a very sensuous dress," said her friend and designer, Narciso Rodriguez of the Design House

---

[37] Johnson, "Carolyn Bessette Kennedy Echoes of Camelot."

of Nino Cerruti, who made his pearl-colored silk crepe creation a gift to the bride. "That's what we both wanted from the beginning."[38]

For weeks before the wedding, John and Carolyn were thought to have purposefully tried to throw the press off the scent of their plan. While Carolyn was in Paris, John was seen around New York. One publication gave an account of Carolyn's night out with a handsome Frenchman at a fashionable restaurant. The man turned out to be Narciso Rodriguez, who later joked, "I am her supposed French lover."[39]

Born in New Jersey in 1961 to Cuban parents, Rodriguez studied at the Parsons School of Design in New York. Initially planning to be an architect, Rodriguez diverted into fashion illustration. While in high school, he took commercial art classes on the side, learning about shape and form, which would become fundamental to his design practice.

His first collection debuted in the spring of 1998 and was featured in virtually every major fashion magazine. He won Best New Designer at the 1997 VH1 Fashion Awards and a CFDA Perry Ellis Award 1998. He was also awarded the Hispanic Designer of the Year in 1997, an honor bestowed on such designers as Oscar de la Renta and Carolina Herrera.

In an *Elle* magazine interview, Rodriguez said, "I create a frame for a woman's personality, one that celebrates her beauty."[40]

He carried this design philosophy into his creations. His clothes were understated and comfortable. They appeared neither modern

[38] Bumiller, "Enter Smiling, the Stylish Carolyn Bessette," 31.
[39] Collins, "By George, He Got Married!" 44–47.
[40] Davis, *Narciso Rodriguez: Celebrating Beauty.*

nor classic, tailored to the woman's body while allowing her persona to shine instead of the garment. Rodriguez was known for giving the ease of wear a lot of thought without compromising elegance. The dress flattered the woman wearing it, adding to her beauty.

At no time was that more apparent than in the wedding photograph of the newlywed Kennedy couple. Carolyn was a glowing vision in white.

Her gown was a slinky display of silk. Floor-length and cut on the bias, it was a form-fitting creation that hugged the twenty-nine-year-old bride's statuesque figure, accentuating her stunning physique. Rodriguez constructed the gown in pearl-colored silk crepe. The veil was silk tulle with a hand-rolled edge. As a finishing touch, this sheer fabric became gloves that extended up the arm to the elbow. Open-toed shoes and a small bouquet of lily of the valley rounded out the bridal accessories, her bare collarbone a stark reminder that for this woman, less was more.[41]

Carolyn's look exuded such elegance and grace. With the backdrop of a white, late-1800s Baptist chapel illuminated by candlelight, the scene seemed something out of a fairy tale. The wedding was intimate, a family affair for a couple who craved privacy while exchanging their vows and commitment to one another.

The headlines of newspapers and magazines alike screamed the news of the sudden and secretive wedding. Readers scooped up copies quickly, scouring page after page for exclusive details.

"Well Done!"
"By George: He Got Married!"
"JFK Jr., Hitched to Tradition."

---

[41] Johnson, "Carolyn Bessette Kennedy Echoes of Camelot."

"Caroline, Meet Carolyn!"

The setting was secluded Cumberland Island, located eight miles off the coast of Georgia. Boasting one of the ten best beaches in America, the island is a wildlife haven, home to wild horses, deer, armadillos, and hundreds of species of birds. The couple wed in a simple ceremony inside the First African Baptist Church built by formerly enslaved people after the Civil War. The couple is said to have received special permission from the Catholic Bishop in New York to conduct the ceremony in a non-Catholic location.[42]

John's sister, Caroline Kennedy Schlossberg, dressed in a navy Rodriguez creation and acted as matron of honor for her new sister-in-law. Caroline's two young daughters, Rose and Tatiana, were the flower girls, and her son, Jack, was the ring bearer. A humorous moment occurred when the three-year-old Jack asked, "Why is Carolyn all dressed up like that?"[43]

John's cousin and best friend, Anthony Radziwill—the son of Jackie's sister Caroline Lee, known as Lee, and ex-Polish nobleman and London businessman Prince Stanislaw Stas" Radziwill—was the best man.[44] The Reverend Charles J. O'Byrne of Manhattan's Church of St. Ignatius Loyola presided over the ceremony.

Additional security was present on the tiny island, accessible only by air or sea. "It was important for us to be able to conduct this in a private, prayerful, and meaningful way with the people we love,"[45] Kennedy said through a spokesperson.

---

42 Collins, "By George, He Got Married!" 44–47.
43 Gerhart, "The Bridegroom Wore Blue."
44 Collins, "By George, He Got Married!" 44–47.
45 Gerhart, "The Bridegroom Wore Blue."

Kennedy wore a dark suit and his father's watch during the ceremony[46]. His uncle Senator Edward Kennedy reflected on the absence of John's parents as he made the statement about Carolyn and John. "I know Jack and Jackie would be very proud of them and full of love for them as they begin their future together."[47]

The couple released only one picture to the media. In it, they exited the church, arm in arm, grinning happily. The worn clapboard steps of the church were visible beneath the hem of Carolyn's stunning silk dress. The contrast of the world's newest, most-fêted couple elegantly positioned against a plain, unadorned venue was iconic. The image ran on the covers of magazines and newspapers around the world.

After the ceremony, the wedding guests returned to Greyfield Inn, a grand and graceful turn-of-the-century mansion built in 1900 for the Carnegie family. Dinner was held on the porch and lasted well into the night. Guests feasted on caviar, roasted lamb with minted potatoes, and a three-tiered buttercream cake. The couple's first dance was to Prince's "Forever in My Life."[48]

A beaming John was said to have toasted his bride, stating, "I am the happiest man alive,"[49] a pun on his *People* magazine Sexiest Man Alive title of 1988.

– – –

"OK, I'm prying, but I'm just too excited. I have to know what the book is saying. Is it gossipy?" Stacey asked in a tone laced with urgency.

---

[46] Collins, "By George, He Got Married!" 44–47.
[47] Gerhart, "The Bridegroom Wore Blue."
[48] Collins, "By George, He Got Married!" 44–47.
[49] Johnson, "Carolyn Bessette Kennedy Echoes of Camelot."

"No, not exactly," Guy said as he lifted his gaze to meet her eye in the rearview mirror. "The publisher I work for doesn't like that approach. It's more like information. This chapter's about her style."

"Yeah, right, I remember. Carolyn Bessette was totally a rad dresser! She was always in the style beat section of *US* magazine. I would read them during my lunch break in the school library. My brother Dwight always said reading is better than getting into a food fight in the cafeteria," Stacey said while laughing.

"I guess so," Guy remarked, returning his attention to the manuscript.

– – –

The world's most eligible bachelor was off the market. Carolyn began her role as the spouse of the scion of the nation's most prominent political dynasty. Soon, she would learn the true meaning of her commitment and how it would force her to adjust her life in ways that often proved difficult.

There were the shots of the newlyweds honeymooning in Istanbul, Turkey, where Carolyn sported a large pair of Jackie-inspired sunglasses and a blue scarf folded into a triangle and secured around her long blonde ponytail. The couple was spotted sightseeing, hand in hand, looking relaxed. While John wore shorts, Carolyn chose ankle-length pants, sandals, and a navy blazer buttoned atop a white T-shirt.

On October 6, 1996, she was introduced to the swarm of New York media as Mrs. John Fitzgerald Kennedy Junior on the front steps of their home at 20 North Moore in trendy Tribeca. Carrying what would instantly become a sought-after Prada handbag, Carolyn exited the building hand in hand with John. She wore a black, long-sleeved, crew neck top, a midlength camel skirt, brown boots, a sleek ponytail, and a facial expression of such fright that many reckoned she seemed like a deer caught in the headlights.[50]

She could not hide the extreme discomfort of being in the limelight, and her new husband begged the press to be merciful. Explaining how overwhelming it was for Carolyn, an ordinary person, to become the most talked about woman in America, John politely asked the press for discretion when approaching her for photographs or comments. He reasoned that she should be allowed space to adjust to her role as a wife and newly anointed celebrity.

The frenzy began despite John's gallant effort to dissuade the media from aggressive behavior. It was an infatuation that would never cease, and her image remained a paparazzi prize until that fateful day when she lost her life.

– – –

Ruby's long, poignant sigh caused Guy to rest the pages across his knees. He withdrew his toe tips from the seat edge, setting them onto the van's floor, and looked over at her, wondering what, if anything, was wrong. He cradled her mouth in one of his hands and stroked the underside of her chin with his index finger. Ruby looked up at him and blinked.

"Carolyn died in a plane crash, right? With her husband and her sister?" Stacey attempted to initiate a conversation.

"Yes, a couple of years ago," Guy confirmed as Ruby shrugged away from his petting and turned her head toward Stacey.

---

[50] Kochan, "John and Carolyn, Camelot's Golden Couple," 40–47.

"Oh, I know that. It was in July 1999. I watched the funeral on TV. President Clinton was there with tons of movie stars and famous people. It was epic, even though they were dead and all. I just loved him, you know. I mean, who didn't? Did you know that John Kennedy Junior was the third most photographed person in the world? Yes, it's true! It was him after Lady Diana and Madonna," Stacey said as Ruby hopped up into the front passenger seat beside Stacey.

Guy sat back in his seat and nodded as Stacey continued.

"And then he dated Daryl Hannah, the one from *Splash*. That was my favorite movie when I was growing up. I so wanted to be a mermaid. My mom made me a mermaid fin, and I would wear it in the pool and pretend my name was Madison. I want to go to Madison Avenue when we get to New York. You good with that, Ruby?" Stacey asked.

"I'm getting back to work," Guy announced, picking up his pen.

– – –

Over the nearly three years between their marriage and funeral, there were two sides to Carolyn so often captured through photographers' lenses. The first was the everyday Carolyn, walking, dining, hailing cabs, and living in the city. In many of these shots, she usually appeared frowning, looking downward toward the streets with expressions of annoyance and resentment. Indeed, one could hardly blame her. She was, after all, just a regular person hurled into celebrity through marriage.

But many would argue that she knew what she was getting into when she married Kennedy. He was one of the most famous bachelors in the world, the son of a former president of the United States, and

ALLISON LANG COOK

an unofficial American prince. Surely she knew their union would catapult her into the realm where the public felt entitled to know all the details of her life? It came with the territory.

With two failed attempts at the New York bar exam and a string of love interests behind him, John had grown used to the negative attention brought by being a public figure. He was used to the media and admitted having developed a thick skin to shield himself against the public's prying eye. But this did not make it any easier on the person he chose to marry.

By all accounts in the press, Carolyn suffered miscarriage after miscarriage, though there was never any admission that pregnancy was imminent or desired. There was constant speculation over when she and John would produce an heir.

Others christened her a fashion supernova, the next Jackie, and placed her on the daily style watch for trendsetting garb.

On January 24, 1997, Carolyn was captured on the frigid streets of Manhattan with John and their dog, Friday. She wore a red textured knee-length coat, belted at the waist, with ebony buttons down the front, a matching black toque, a turtleneck, blue jeans, and boots.[51] In several photographs, she appears with her arm tucked closely into John's. The coat was never seen again in public but left a lasting memory on chic wannabes who idolized Carolyn as America's newest fashion first lady.

The second side of Carolyn's photographed persona was one where she felt more comfortable. It was the world of charity balls, gala openings, and exclusive parties. There, she appeared graciously, smiling for the cameras beside her husband.

---

[51] Michaelis, "Great Expectations," 130.

The couple was no stranger to black-tie events, attending several high-profile parties throughout their courtship and marriage. As was the case for his presidential father, who accompanied Jacqueline Kennedy to Paris,[52] John Kennedy Jr. was aware of the attention given to his stylish wife.

"Let me use the same phrase that my father did when he went to Paris with my mother 35 years ago," JFK Jr. told guests at an Italian industry fashion dinner in 1997. "My name is John Kennedy, and I am the man who is accompanying Carolyn Bessette to Milan. I am honored to tell you she is my wife."[53]

A very small and elite group of up-and-coming designers created some of Carolyn's most iconic looks. This included Japanese phenom Yohji Yamamoto.

Carolyn wore a Yamamoto design at the party celebrating the renovation of New York's Grand Central Terminal on October 5, 1998. The gown was sleeveless and black, hitting midlength at her midcalf. She wore her hair tied back and very little makeup except for glossy lipstick. According to guests at the function, John asked the other guests to look at the back of his wife's gown, suggesting it was the best part

Yohji Yamamoto was born in Yokohama, Japan, in 1943. He studied law before following the truth in his heart and switching to the study of fashion. He attended Bunka College in Tokyo, graduating in 1968. During that time, he began to test his developing skills by making clothes for his mother and her friends.

---

[52] "I am the man who accompanied Jacqueline Kennedy to Paris, and I have enjoyed it" (J. F. Kennedy 1961).
[53] Staff, "Kennedy Was 'Man Accompanying Carolyn Bessette.'"

In 1968, he earned a scholarship to study in Paris and started designing clothing in 1970. He launched his company in 1974 and showed his first collection in Tokyo. His Paris debut occurred in 1981 and then in New York in 1982.[54]

Yamamoto's use of black fabrics and flat shoes with layered, loose, flowing garments seemed antiaesthetic to the Parisian tradition of pinched silhouettes. After all, he designed for Japanese women and thought of their comfort and cultural identity. This aesthetic provided a new approach to how the body wore clothing.

Yamamoto's creations were considered two-dimensional rather than directional, dramatically sculpted without compromising femininity.[55] His cuts allowed movement manipulation brought by an infinite combination of symmetrical and asymmetrical shapes that, when viewed together, formed garments of great style and purpose. In his years of practicing and perfecting his craft, he earned the reputation of a master tailor.

Carolyn was a fan of Yamamoto's balance, and the designer created some of her more iconic looks. Nothing was too tight, and nothing was see-through; understatement was the key.

In 1999, she elevated a simple white dress shirt at a benefit for the Whitney Museum. Pairing a Yamamoto Homme shirt from the Spring 1999 men's collection, she left it unbuttoned, crossing the fabric over and tucking it neatly into a ruffled black skirt from the designer's women's line. She completed her outfit with black sandal-strap heels and a small gold-chain purse. Her long hair was parted

---

[54] Menkes, "Fashion's Poet of Black: YAMAMOTO."
[55] Staff, "The Look of Yohji Yamamoto."

simply in the middle and tucked behind her ears, allowing it to fall down her back.[56]

At the same year's Municipal Art Society gala, she wore a black Yamamoto obi gown from his Fall/Winter 1998 collection with velvet opera-length gloves. The strapless creation cut across in stark contrast to her pale shoulders and upper arms. She styled her hair back in a tight bun and, once again, used a mark of red lipstick across her mouth as the night's accessory.

In May 1999, she wore a Yamamoto opera coat with a cascade of beige ruffles down the front. It was arguably one of his most avant-garde creations and a departure from the sleeker outfits Carolyn had worn before. It also wasn't completely black, which was a bit of a departure for Carolyn, who preferred wearing black to evening events. Minimal makeup and a sleek ponytail completed the look.

On December 9, 1998, Carolyn stepped out among various movie stars and the cast of *Friends* at the 9th Annual Fire and Ice Ball held in Los Angeles. She attended with several of her famous Kennedy in-laws, including Maria Shriver. The event was unique for its dressing protocol, with black ties for men and white or red gowns for women. Carolyn chose a long-sleeved white wool gown by Donatella Versace, who was making headway on her own under the Versace label after the unfortunate death of her beloved brother, Gianni.

Respect between the designer and muse was mutual, as Donatella Versace confirmed:

> When John started George, he was coming to Milan often and stopped in Gianni's office. But I first met

---

[56] Staff, "JFK JR. Captured in All His Glory," 58–65.

ALLISON LANG COOK

Carolyn about four years ago, when she came to Milan with John and spent time with me and Gianni on Lake Como. She was very similar to my brother, both entertainers. Gianni would usually go to bed very early, but Carolyn kept him up. Of course, I was a little envious of her, too—who wouldn't be? She said, "I'm never going to give up my friends, but at the same time, I will be the best wife for John." She said John had a completely open mind about her fashion friends, who were different from his friends. He adored her personality, her outlook on life.

Any entrance Carolyn made she made a statement. Apart from the clothes she wore, she had a way of moving her head and smiling, and her eyes were so expressive, she would always seem to be looking right at you. I thought that if anyone could take the place of his mother in the family, it could be her. After Gianni died, we went to a beautiful dinner at the home of Countess Crespi. You couldn't smoke inside it, so Carolyn and I went upstairs and smoked in the balcony outside, and then we couldn't get back in. The door had locked. John finally came by looking for her and he let us out.

Recently, I saw her in my shop on Fifth Avenue. I said, "Carolyn, what are you doing here?" I never saw her more happy. She was full of projects. I was making fun of her, saying, "What do you do all day, sit at home just waiting for the next party? That's not you." She said, "You just wait and see."[57]

---

[57] Roshen, "Prince of the City."

Carolyn and more than two thousand others attended the funeral for Donatella's brother Gianni Versace in Milan, Italy, on July 22, 1997. In photographs, she is seated in a prominent position in the pew behind Diana, the Princess of Wales, and Sir Elton John. Carolyn's ethereal blonde hair glowed against the sea of black worn by the mourners.

"She is the hippest person I ever met," said Hachette's Jean-Louis Ginibre. "She is totally au courant. Very bright, there is nothing she doesn't know. She can focus on one person for ten to twenty minutes and be totally involved with this person. She is very intense, very touchy-feely, and can mesmerize a person."[58]

Carolyn's style genius meant she appeared to place herself firmly in fashion, yet her singular minimalist identity put her timelessly outside it. Where Jackie gave the world the pillbox hat and tailored Oleg Cassini suit, Carolyn preferred the geometry and illusion of elongation made possible by her favorite designers. Even when dressed down, she pulled off styles from basic staples like the Gap with enviable elegance and ease. Her love of simplicity and confidence in adorning clothing, from designer to streetwear, captured the essence of the time and cemented Carolyn Bessette Kennedy as a trendsetter.

– – –

Guy put down the text. He folded it and returned it to his case alongside *Vanity Fair*.

"All done?" Stacey asked once she saw him pack away the manuscript. She looked back at him in the rearview mirror.

"For now," Guy answered as he packed his editing pens.

---

[58] Roshen, "Prince of the City."

"Good." She yawned, gripping the wheel. "Jeepers, I'm getting sleepy. I'm going to turn on the radio. That will help. You don't mind, do you?"

"No problem. I'm good to take over the wheel. Pull over when you are ready," Guy said.

"Oh I'm going to keep going for at least another hour or two, you can take a rest, Guy." Stacey announced while cracking open the can of cola Guy had watched her retrieve from her bag earlier. "This'll help!"

Stacey drew the can to her mouth and took an audible slurp. "Turning on the radio, radio," she announced like a song as she adjusted the volume to be the perfect midlevel pitch for the van. Guy noticed that since they were well into their journey, the location change meant that 88.9 no longer jockeyed '80s music around the clock. Replacing it was talk radio–style programming.

"And we're back," the voice announced. "I'm Dinah Walsh, with our guest author, Spirit analyst and animal-communication expert Sylvia Vogel. Sylvia, tell us about this theory of human-to-animal reincarnation."

"Well, Dinah, the idea is based on the belief that pets can be more than mere animals. And who knows better than famed spiritual communicator Dr. Greg Osmond, the Australian veterinarian, or Doc Aus as we like to call him because he is *awesome*." Sylvia paused and giggled. She continued, "Doc Aus studied a dozen pets whose owners felt they were trying to communicate something to them."

"How did the study work?" Dinah asked.

"By studying the animals' behavior when exposed to certain objects or places, they determined that in all but one case, the animals were trying to point their owners back to a space of great importance to them in a previous life," Sylvia answered.

"That sounds unbelievable," Dinah said.

"Indeed, but I can assure you the study results are solid. Let's examine the case of Bear. Bear was a three-year-old chocolate Labrador retriever. Bear's owner was alarmed by the animal's constant desire to dig, and he seemed to dislike men, especially men wearing heavy construction or army-type boots. Doc Aus met with Bear and observed this odd behavior. He suggested the owner place a map of the area before the animal and note Bear's reaction. Well, the dog began scratching the map in one particular place. The team took Bear to the location he was scratching on the map. It was a farm property just outside of a neighboring town. The dog recognized the area and began to whine incessantly. That was until we stopped and let him out of the car," Sylvia explained.

"What happened then, Sylvia?" Dinah asked.

"Bear took off into the woods until he reached a particular spot where he began to dig. His digging uncovered a pair of heavy black boots. The boots were attached to the body of a man. When Bear uncovered the feet of the victim, he stopped and calmly walked away from the scene. He lay down and watched our shocked reaction," Sylvia answered.

"Unbelievable!" Dinah exclaimed.

"I can assure you that I speak the truth. Doc Aus has outlined the episode in our latest book, *Living Ghosts, the Study of Human to Animal Reincarnation*," Sylvia said.

"And that idea is what we are here to talk about tonight. We have Sylvia Vogel on the line to answer your questions. Our lines are now open. So, Sylvia, I am frankly amazed by that story. Did they ever figure out what happened?" Dinah asked.

"Well, yes, it seemed that the man was a murder victim. Bear knew about the location of the body. The only logical conclusion to draw under such circumstances is that Bear was the reincarnation of this man. He came back to solve the crime of his very own death," Sylvia answered.

"Fascinating stuff, Sylvia … now we do have a caller. Joe, you are on with Sylvia," Dinah said.

"Thanks, so, ah, my question is: What if my cat is my dead grandmother? Ah, is it OK to get naked or make out with girls in front of it, or is that sick?" Joe asked.

"Joe, do you think your cat is your grandmother's reincarnated spirit?" Sylvia asked.

"Well, ah, sometimes I guess she reminds me of her. Ah, the cat likes wool, and, ah, my grandmother knitted stuff. And, ah, she looks at me disapprovingly sometimes," Joe answered.

"OK. Joe, when did your grandmother pass on?" Sylvia asked.

"Ah, about five years ago," Joe answered.

"OK. And when was the cat born?" Sylvia asked.

"Ah, well, the cat belonged to my grandmother," Joe answered.

"The cat belonged to your grandmother?" Sylvia repeated.

"Ah, yeah," Joe answered.

"Well then, you have nothing to worry about, Joe. The cat can't possibly be your grandmother, because she was still alive when the cat was born. Spirits can only enter another form once they rid themselves of their past shell. So you have nothing to worry about," Sylvia concluded.

"I guess we should clarify, Sylvia, that not all pets are reincarnated individuals. Our current estimate is 9 percent of the pet population have walked the earth in human form before being animals," Dinah said.

"That is an excellent point. If you consider my paper on this topic, "Killing Select Ants: The Study of Reincarnation and the Spirit's Desire for Release," I caution people not to look too deeply for signs in their pets. One knows when their family dog or cat is the spirit of a deceased individual. I call it "the known factor," Sylvia explained. "Like the ant that scurries away and never squishes under your shoe. Maybe there is a reason for that salvation?"

"Wow, heavy, let's get to that after the break. If you are only now joining us, we are speaking to author, spirit analyst, and animal-communication expert Sylvia Vogel. Sylvia works alongside the world-renowned Doc Aus. Our lines are currently open, and we are awaiting your calls," Dinah said.

The radio crackled as it went off to some local commercial.

"That sounds freaky," Stacey said. "I've heard of this Doc Aus guy, though. He was on Leno the other night. I think he's handsome, like Nick Nolte or Jeff Bridges, in a scruffy way. Have you heard of him before?" Stacey asked. "He is so informed. He's the hottest thing going right now. He is everywhere!" she exclaimed.

Guy was suddenly reminded of the slip of paper from the diner. He opened the attaché case, withdrew *Vanity Fair* to find the torn square in the spot marking Carolyn and John's picture, and flipped it over onto the other side to take another look. From the opposite seat, Ruby sat up and cocked her head to one side, watching Guy intently as he read the message.

Does your pet seem to have something to say?

Do you want to know their most profound thoughts?

Get answers from world-renowned spiritual and animal communicator Dr. Greg Osmond. E-MAIL ME WITH YOUR QUESTIONS.

Or visit me in my Marvel Studio in New York, New York.

Doc Aus, the Australian veterinarian.

The radio programming returned from a commercial break.

"And we're back. I'm Dinah Walsh, and tonight we are with Sylvia Vogel. Sylvia is here to discuss the matter of communications with the spirit world. Well, our hour is just about up. We can only take but a few more lucky callers. But never fear listeners—Sylvia will return with Doc Aus for our show next week." Dinah signed off.

The radio crackled, and Guy knew they were losing the local signal. "Stacey, the radio static is annoying. Do you mind turning it off?" he asked. He took the slip of paper from the diner and replaced it to mark page 130 of *Vanity Fair*. Next, he put the magazine and the manuscript back in his case. He had read enough.

Guy reclined back and closed his eyes, succumbing to the heavy nag of fatigue. It had been a long day and so much had happened. He pushed his perplexed feelings into the future. They could wait until after he had rested. He was just about to drift off when suddenly Stacey swerved the van, summoning Guy back to reality.

"Um, Guy," she said, in a panicky tone, "There is a motorcycle on our rear end, like right up the tailpipe."

Guy remained reclined. "Just one?" he asked.

"Yeah," she confirmed. "Just one and it's riding close. What do you think they want?" she asked nervously.

"Is there a rest stop up ahead?" he asked.

"Think so." Stacey nodded.

"Well," Guy was careful not to put any tone of worry or concern onto his words, "keep driving and pull into it when you get closer. Park in the back with the trucks."

"Sure thing," Stacey said.

Stacey slowed Toto to let the motorcycle pass. Guy could hear the bike's roar as the rider accelerated, revving once, twice, and three times before pulling out to pass them. The motorcycle sped along Toto's left side so close that the van vibrated violently for a moment, and Guy was worried that Stacey wouldn't be able to hold a steady course.

Guy sat up when Toto's touring hum returned to the vehicle's interior. He assumed Stacey felt disconcerted by the episode but didn't know how to explain. While the hunt was in its infancy, he hadn't taken the twitches threat seriously. Now, it appeared that the Broomsticks had found them. At some point, he would have to tell Stacey.

"Phew," Stacey expressed relief. "The tailgating emergency is over!" she announced comically.

"Sorry that you went through that, Stacey," Guy offered.

"It's all good, Guy," Stacey replied cheerfully.

Guy pointed at the sign for a rest stop ahead as Stacey signaled her intention to exit right off the highway. He observed that her knuckles were practically white; she gripped the steering wheel tight. *I'll have to figure out a way to explain*, Guy thought as Stacey eased Toto off the road on a gentle arc and stopped behind the main building, where the trucks parked, just like Guy had suggested.

CHAPTER 9

TINA

Sunday morning, Interstate 90 outside
Rapid City, South Dakota

They traveled through the night, Guy back at Toto's wheel while Stacey snored quietly beside him in the passenger seat. She was so chatty when awake, and after all the adrenaline-infused happenings, he was glad for the silence. It allowed him time to reflect, sort out his thoughts, and form a plan.

Evading the Broomsticks was the main priority. Guy only had to add up (1) the rallying email, (2) the interlude with the first solo scout, and (3) his SOS knowledge to deduce that the group was purposeful and tenacious. For reasons unknown to him, they wanted Ruby. It made him uneasy that he had yet to tell Stacey the whole truth, but Guy's instincts told him it was not the right time to disclose the evolving story.

As he pondered the predicament, the terrain had changed into forest, and the road carved a path between tall, thin pines. From above their pointed tops, stars twinkled in the dark sky. The sight was surreal, cosmic in tone, and blessed with a spiritual energy unparalleled to any felt during daylight hours. Guy noted how majestic the universe seemed from that position. He opened his window a crack to smell the night's sweetness, allowing a cool breeze to sweep across his cheek, complementing the moment's serenity.

Toto's tank was running close to low, and Guy pulled into an all-night station for gas and much-desired coffee. He asked Stacey if she wanted anything. She murmured a refusal, and Guy was unsure if she had heard him. He suspected that she was talking while asleep, unconscious and unaware. He decided to get her an orange juice and then drank half of it himself before approaching the checkout.

The man at the counter acted oddly when Guy presented at the counter to pay. At first, he thought it was due to his consumption of the unpaid juice. Sometimes, people get fussy about stuff like that, even if there is no intention of theft. He screwed the cap back on the juice and said with a gulp, "Sorry, I couldn't wait. Hope that's OK."

The man looked Guy up and down, and Guy thought he took particular notice of the dog food Guy had found on the shelf for Ruby. "It's for a friend," Guy stuttered, offering his credit card. It was only at the awkward moment when he passed the card across into the hands of the attendant that he realized the error.

"Cool van, Guy Myles," the attendant read from the Visa's face. He smiled, revealing a set of yellowed teeth.

"Thanks." Guy tried to appear calm.

The attendant snapped the Visa into the anointed compartment of a plastic copier and laid a carbon chit on top. After swiping the payment, the attendant removed the card and placed it and the chit on the counter. He pulled a pen out from behind his ear and offered it to Guy, who took it and quickly scratched his signature on top. The man ripped the top layer of the receipt and passed it back to Guy.

As Guy took the receipt and tucked it into the slot of his wallet, any optimism from the early morning hours was instantly quelled. Guy knew the carbon copy of his credit card would live inside the cash register, waiting for the Broomsticks to come and confirm his identity. He wanted to hop over the counter and steal back the receipt but knew that gesture would land him in different trouble.

"Have a pleasant day," the attendant snidely remarked as Guy turned to leave the store.

Guy hurried back to the van and turned the key in the ignition. Thankfully, Toto had no backfire. Without disturbing Stacey or Ruby, he slid out of the gas station, hoping they would get a little farther on the yellow-lined road before the Broomsticks became aware of their route. The man knew his name and had proof of his identity; it wouldn't be long before they put two and two together to realize the way they were headed.

Guy could no longer consider the situation promising but struggled to anoint it with a better descriptor. As time passed, he grew increasingly fretful, nervously looking over his shoulder for a phantom behind, anxious at every mile marker for what could come. His imagination oscillated between scenarios of capture and escape. At some point, his eyes tricked him in the dim light of early dawn, and he thought a cluster of tree trunks were motorcycles in the distance. All the while, Stacey slept, and Ruby lay casually on the back seat, oblivious to Guy's concerns.

Shortly after six, Guy witnessed the sunrise, a spectacular mélange of apricot, rose, and mauve clouds peeking over the treetops. He was pleased to be refreshed by daytime friendliness. Using the span of his hand to measure the distance driven on the yellow-lined map, he figured they were already a third of the way to New York. They only needed to evade the Broomsticks for a few more days.

Suddenly, he caught sight of something ahead, stationary at the side of the road. It reflected the sun. Now and then, electric beams would twinkle off its metallic surface, sending one directly across his line of vision. They forced him to squint, his top and bottom eyelids pressing close together. As he drew nearer, he could see that the object was a car. It was the first they had come across after miles of road and trees. He focused his attention on the broken line dividing the lanes. Even still, the blinding light caught the corner of his eye every few seconds as if to say, "You can't ignore me!"

Curious, he began to slow down until Toto traveled at half the speed allowed on the highway. On approach, he noticed the car was an expensive-model convertible with its top down. A woman was standing beside it. As he neared, he saw that she was wearing a scarf on her head. It sat folded into a flat triangle over her hair and tied at the back of her neck. The scarf was large, and the two tails flapped gently against her shoulders. She was wearing dark sunglasses in metal frames and pressed the buttons of a cellular telephone with one pointed, painted fingernail.

Exasperated with the gadget, she threw her arms up in frustration, tossing the useless telephone onto the passenger seat. The next moment, she thought the better of her hasty decision and bent down through the open top to retrieve the phone.

Guy decided to stop.

As he came off the highway onto the shoulder, chunks of gravel crunched under the weight of Toto's four wheels. Guy parked and turned to the backseat to see whether Ruby wanted to hop out. Sensing his stare, she opened her eyes, stretched, yawned, and circled on the seat to lie back down. Guy took that to mean that she was not interested. He was getting good at deciphering her moods.

Stacey woke and slowly opened her eyes to adjust to the scene. Realizing Guy intended to help the stranded woman, Stacey reminded him of a story she knew about a con artist couple.

"Guy, I swear, they purposely stranded their vehicle at the side of the road. The woman stays in the car while the man hides in the bushes. When an unsuspecting motorist comes to assist the damsel in distress, the man hops out of the brush and steals the motorist's vehicle." Stacey spoke theatrically.

"I'm just going to see if she needs any help. You stay here," Guy said to Stacey.

"Are you sure, Guy? You know how some of these stories go. Person in distress at the side of the road, a Good Samaritan comes to their aid, and then, presto, before you know it, you're dead and they've assumed your identity," Stacey continued.

"You have quite an imagination, Stacey." Guy assured her, "We'll be fine. But if you're nervous, stay here and lock the doors until I return."

Stacey agreed. "OK, Guy, you go do your hero thing, and I'll get into the driver's seat just in case," she said.

Guy left the van and walked back to the champagne-beige convertible. He wondered who the girl was and why she was in the middle of the woods. She couldn't be related to the Broomsticks, though the thought did cross his mind. It seemed unlikely they would randomly plant a girl with this type of vehicle in the middle of wooded nowhere. He felt confident that she was alone and there would be no ambush like Stacey had warned.

He noticed that she was smaller in stature than he initially estimated. Perhaps, Guy thought, it was because she had removed a pair of heeled sandals. He noticed them discarded in the ditch beside the road. He watched as she slipped on another pair of sandals, these flat, with one hand while continuing to fish for her cellular phone from its place on the car seat with the other. Mission accomplished, she stood and swore.

"Goddamn piece of crap." She looked up at him. "I hate cell phones. They don't ever work when you need them. You're lousy," she shrieked at the handheld gadget, banging away at it again.

"Do you need help?" he asked calmly, unfazed by her tantrum.

"Uh, no." She paused, if only for effect. "I've decided to make this haven my home." Stressing the word *haven*, she sarcastically threw her arms up and spun a full circle. "Of course, I need help," she said exasperated.

Guy resented her sarcastic tone but was intrigued by her audacity. "And you are?" he asked her name.

The woman did not answer immediately. She lowered her sunglasses and eyed him up and down from hair to loafers. She did so slowly, with pauses in certain places. "I'm me," she finally announced with a smirk and a light eyelash flick upward.

He repeated his offer of assistance. "We can drop you at the nearest station."

"No, I'm dumping this piece of junk." She sealed its fate by kicking the passenger-side door. "It never worked anyway." She looked at him again. "Can I get a ride with you?" Her question sounded more like a demand. "I'll pay you."

"That depends. Where are you heading?" Guy asked.

"New York," she said as if there was any other place to go.

"Funny," he began, "that's where we're going." He decided not to elaborate further.

"Perfect," she purred, delighted. "You're my new chauffeur! Got room for my stuff?"

She smiled, revealing dazzling white teeth. Guy noted that she was an attractive woman. He thought the additional passenger might help them evade the Broomsticks. No one was looking for a van with three people.

"Sure." Guy shrugged and watched as the woman reopened the car's side door and snapped the glove compartment latch, pulling out a stack of credit cards of various precious metal rankings. She held them up in a fan and aired herself by flapping the trio back and forth, nodding knowingly at Guy's expression of surprise.

"They each have a ten-grand limit," she announced, her statement laced with a hint of delight. "And," she found a roll the size of a fist underneath the armrest, "should be a thou." She tossed the wad of money at Guy, who, although taken off guard, caught it midair like a champion.

"That's me officially hiring you," she said as she popped open the convertible's trunk and withdrew one oversized bag of patterned brown leather. Guy knew the print was from a famous designer. Alongside were several matching others. Each appeared enormous, and Guy momentarily considered that there would be no space for them all in Toto's back. She thrust the most oversized bag into his arms.

"I'm going to get the rest," she announced.

Guy watched as the woman spun around and returned to the front of the car to grab a more petite yet matching bag to the one he held. Bending over the car door, she fumbled for something, found it, and followed Guy to Toto, who was parked in front only a few short steps away.

"Ace!" She sized up the vehicle. "At least we won't be squishy."

Guy made room for the bags and placed the one he carried in the back. He had to slam the trunk door twice before it hitched and closed. He noticed Stacey had moved into the driver's seat and sat defensively, clinging to the steering wheel. She seemed nervous. The new girl opened the passenger door and sat beside her, leaving Guy with no choice but to slide into the back with Ruby.

"Don't you want the rest of your stuff?" he asked, remembering the additional bags.

"Nah. I'll get them when they find the car." She seemed utterly disinterested in the fate of her possessions, and Guy assumed this meant she was wealthy.

"What's your name?" he asked again while leaning into the space between the two front seats. She had not answered when he asked before.

"Tina." She smiled and reached back to shake Guy's hand. In contrast to Stacey's vigorous three-pump handshake, Guy noticed that this woman offered an almost political two pumps before briskly withdrawing her hand.

"I'm Guy, and this is Stacey," he introduced.

"So, are you guys married or just screwing?" Tina asked.

"Neither." He set her straight. "We're just friends."

"Actually, we just met," Stacey interjected.

Stacey smiled and winked into the rearview mirror. Guy nodded back at her reflection as Stacey put the van into drive and gently accelerated back onto the highway. As they left the open-top convertible, Guy noticed that Tina paid no attention, not even glancing back at it as they drove away.

"What happened to your car?" Stacey asked.

Tina replied flatly, "It ran out of gas."

Tina flipped down the passenger-side visor and slid open the mirror. She took a small yellow tub of Carmex from her purse, considered her choice, and exchanged it for a tube of lipstick. Pulling off the top with a smack, Tina began to apply the color slowly. She withdrew a tissue, folded it, and pressed it between her newly painted lips, creating a red impression. It seemed theatrical to Guy as he watched. Frankly, he was unused to women apply cosmetics.

"So, you just met." Tina eyed them both more suspiciously than before.

"Well, yeah," Stacey replied. "But Guy's the type you feel you've known forever."

"Interesting." Tina snapped the visor mirror closed.

They rode in silence for a while. The sun was just about at its morning peak, and Stacey suddenly announced that she was hungry.

"Is anyone else hungry? I'm starving," she said.

"I could eat." Guy agreed although he was uncertain about stopping at another service station. He would use cash now that Tina had given him some. It would prevent the Broomsticks from discovering a trail of credit-receipt breadcrumbs.

"Do you want some chips?" Tina offered.

"Sure." Stacey greedily nodded.

Tina pulled out a big bag of plain Lays from her oversized purse and opened it. When Tina passed the bag over, Stacey practically dove in. She rooted, her hand wholly submerged, until she had a fistful, withdrew the chips, and pressed them into her open mouth.

"Mmm." She crunched. "These are so good."

"Please, do not talk with your mouth full," Tina scolded.

"Sorry," Stacey muffled an apology, shrugging her shoulders while tiny flakes of Lays gathered on her chin and at the sides of her lips. After swallowing, Stacey took another handful and then another. She dumped both into the lap of her skirt and began to savor each chip individually as if they were a rare delicacy. As her hunger subsided, she wiped her shirt sleeve across her mouth and concluded the chip binge.

Tina shuttered. "Ugh, disgusting."

"Hey, did you know I once invented names for the different kinds of chips?" Stacey boasted.

"You mean like ketchup, salt and vinegar, and creamy bacon?" Tina turned and looked at Guy in the backseat. She tilted down her sunglasses to roll her eyes. "I think the chip company probably did that long before you were born."

"No. Like the ones that come folded over, they're called tacos. The ones with air bubbles are the pillows and the burnt ones …" Stacey burst into uncontrollable giggles. "I call them the *assholes!*" She whispered in delight.

"Wow, Stacey, you made that up *all* by yourself," Tina chastised in baby talk.

"Yeah," she gasped as she calmed down from her laugh attack, clearly amused by her brilliance. "Isn't it great?"

"Can you pass back a couple of pillows there?" Guy asked, using a strange Western drawl. He needed to cut the building tension between the girls. He sensed it, but Stacey appeared unaware or unfazed by Tina's sharp tongue, which seemed to make Tina all the more ruthless.

"Mind if I smoke?" Tina asked as she tossed the bag of Lays back to Guy.

Stacey wrinkled her nose yet answered that it didn't bother her.

"You want one?" Tina offered the selection in an elegant silver case. In it lay a pair of slim, rolled cigarettes. In her other hand, Tina held a matching silver lighter.

Stacey declined. "I've never smoked."

"Never?" Tina seemed shocked. "Not even pot?"

"No, especially not that. My reading says it kills all your brain cells. I'm not that stupid," Stacey said.

"Ah, the ignorant voice of today's youth." Tina turned to face Guy in the backseat. "I'm sure you've smoked a splif before?"

Guy did not bother responding.

"Um, it's not that I think it's bad. It's just not what I think is the best thing to do. And we are always trying to be our best selves, aren't we?" Stacey said.

"How old are you?" Tina was curious.

"I'm twenty," Stacey announced proudly.

"Have you ever been drunk?" Tina asked.

"Absolutely not! I'm underage. That's the stupidest thing I could do." Stacey shook her head as she made the confession that seemed more like an affirmation to Guy.

Tina mimicked Stacey's prudish answer, adding overtones of mockery. "It's the stupidest thing I could do. But I could get into a car with a stranger," she said in a condescending-sounding snigger while looking at Guy.

Stacey defended herself. "I guess I'm just not like you."

Tina retaliated, "I think we're both in the same boat here, sweetie!"

Stacey corrected her. "You mean van."

Tina rudely exhaled a puff of her cigarette across Stacey's face. In response, Stacey grimaced and rolled down her window to blow away the smoke.

"What's your gig, Guy?" Tina sounded vicious.

"I'm just a guy." He shrugged.

"Career?" Tina asked.

"He's an editor," Stacey offered. "He's reading a biography on Carolyn Bessette Kennedy."

"What's the deal with the dog? Is she yours?" Tina asked Stacey.

"No, she belongs to Guy. Her name is Ruby," Stacey said with authority.

Tina turned to pose the same question to Guy. "So, Guy, what's the dog's deal?"

After carefully considering the details, he answered Tina's question with the minimum amount of information. "She's not technically mine. I'm taking her to New York."

"Any special reason?" Tina pried.

Guy again delayed his response, and Tina grew bored with the interrogation. "I'm taking it that you're not real talkative." Tina turned to face the front of the car. She paused and inhaled one last drag of her cigarette. Pursing the remainder between her thumb and middle finger, she flicked the butt across Stacey and out the driver's-side open window.

When hit by a straying spark, Stacey yelped and briefly let go of the steering wheel. Tina grabbed the wheel, rotating it sharply to the right. The wheels mimicked her motion, and the van veered onto the shoulder. Tina pressed the wheel back toward Stacey, correcting their course.

Stacey let out a small cry.

"What's the problem, Stacey? Was that a stupid thing to do or something?" Tina mocked.

Stacey looked back at Guy through the rearview mirror and then briefly turned to Tina. "You're an asshole," she alleged before looking back at the road and rolling up her window.

"Are you calling me a burnt potato chip?" Tina laughed and lit her last cigarette while unrolling her window on the passenger side.

Guy noticed that Stacey had no retaliation for Tina's latest taunt. *Clever*, he thought.

Out of nowhere, Tina shared, "I'm going to New York to see my dad." She paused to take a deep drag of smoke. "He's getting married in Vermont."

After Stacey eyed Tina sideways, Tina tried to catch Guy's attention in the backseat. "Yes, he's getting married to a dude!" Tina exclaimed as though Guy and Stacey needed an explanation. "It just became legal in Vermont, so after New York, we're heading together for him to do the deed."

"Is he the one who bought you the car?" Stacey asked.

"No, that was my mom's," Tina replied.

"Where's your mom?" Stacey asked.

"She's in Vegas," Tina said, looking out the window, not turning to face her fellow passengers.

"You came from Vegas?" Stacey sounded impressed. "I want to try gambling when I'm old enough. Vegas is on my bucket list. Have you heard that expression? It means things to do before you die." When no one said anything, Stacey continued, "Did you know that sandwiches were created in 1762 in England so that John Montagu, the Fourth Earl of Sandwich, didn't have to get up from his hand of cards? I'm dying to gamble and eat a sandwich."

Tina spoke over Stacey's story. "No, actually, I came from Montana. She has a place there too." Tina added, "She's famous."

"Famous? How?" Guy asked.

Tina removed her sunglasses and the scarf that covered her hair. She rolled her head, shaking out a mass of silky dark curls. "Can't you tell?"

Stacey glanced away from the road and took a quick peek. "Yeah." Stacey shook her finger and nodded. "I can see it. You're her daughter."

"Whose daughter are you?" Guy did not know.

Tina closed her eyes and announced robotically, "Tony- and Oscar-winning actress Jezebel Mann, a legend of her time, best noted for her seventeen movies, her four marriages, and several toxic affairs."

"I'm sensing something out of *Mommy Dearest*," Guy commented.

"Ha-ha, very funny, *Guy*." She drew out his name as though it were a threat.

"Is that why you're abandoning the car?" Stacey asked.

Tina yawned with little emotion. "She'll get it picked up once she hears it's gone. But that'll take a while. They'll have to figure out it's hers first."

"Your mom doesn't know you took her car?" Stacey asked, puzzled.

"No, Miss 'I can't break the rules,' she doesn't know." Tina added, "And I'm fine keeping it that way."

"I'm sensing that you don't want us to stop and tell the guys at a service station that it broke down?" Guy asked to confirm what he had already assumed.

"No," Tina said adamantly.

"OK, then." He settled back into his seat and closed his eyes, relieved.

Guy listened as Stacey nagged Tina, asking question after question. What was her mom like? Had she met any other movie stars? Which ones? Where? What were they like? Finally, Tina snapped. "Look, Stacey, my mom is an actress. That means that she is selfish. She always moves around. She always has a new man. She always worries about being fat. Now she thinks she's getting old. It sucks growing up with a mom like that."

"Oh," Stacey replied as she sucked in her breath.

"I mean," continued Tina, "there were perks. I've traveled to many great places and am always treated like royalty."

"Oh really?" Stacey was intrigued. "Where was your favorite place to go?"

"Probably the Amalfi Coast. It is like heaven there. It's in Italy," Tina added in a patronizing tone.

"What's so great about it?" Stacey asked curiously.

"Well, the beaches are to die for." Tina smiled.

"What's your favorite spot there?" Stacey asked.

"Easy. Conca dei Marini, which is halfway up from Postino. There's a restaurant there that makes this amazing pasta with zucchini and bacon. The place is called La Tonnarella. I loved it so much. I ordered it daily, sometimes twice, and begged my mom to make it when we got home." Tina sighed. "Of course, my mother, who, by the way, doesn't cook, never did make that dish for me."

"Well, if we are talking Italian, did you know that Caesar salad was invented in Mexico?" Stacey asked. Tina and Guy shook their heads to indicate that they did not know. "Yeah! It's true. Senor Cardini and his brother owned a restaurant in Tijuana. The story goes that it was the Fourth of July and they were almost out of food, so he took things they had already in the kitchen: crusty bread for croutons, anchovies, garlic, and egg yolks for the dressing, and voila! He just invented it! The rest, as they say, is history."

"For a young girl, you seem to know a lot!" Tina laughed. "Tell us more cool stuff, Stacey!"

— — —

Stacey felt a swell of joy in her heart. *Finally!* Developing rapport with the new van mate was a massive achievement. *Yay me!*

Stacey was aware that sometimes she read situations the wrong way, and her brothers always warned her about the consequences of her actions. *If you ask too many questions, Stacey, you may eventually get answers you don't like.* But in this case, she asked the questions, got the answers, and impressed Tina enough to warrant a compliment. Stacey was on cloud nine.

"I'll take that under advisement," Stacey added as a follow-up, using a newfound phrase she learned after completing a John Grisham novel. *God, that sounds smart.*

As a responsible driver, Stacey took a quick moment to survey the van's instrument panel. The gas gauge was half full, and Stacey knew they would have to start looking for a place to stop within a few hours. *At least I know not to run out of gas!* She assumed they could probably make it to midnight on that half tank.

Hmm, what can I tell them next? Stacey was about to launch into the story of the Spanish prisoner scam and how it supposedly made a comeback online as something about Nigerian Princes needing money when she stopped and focused. In the reflection of the rearview mirror, she noticed a swarm of motorcycles encapsulated in a cloud of dark dust emerging on the road behind them. Alarmed, she checked back every few seconds to ensure they were not getting too close.

Stacey was about to alert Guy when Tina beat her to it.

— — —

"Um, guys?" Tina murmured. "What's that?" She pointed toward a dark cloud of dust gathering behind them in the moonlit sky.

Guy peaked out the van's back window. *Broomsticks!* Immediately, he slunk into the seat to feign a sleeping position and yanked his attaché case over his head. The span of the case barely covered his shoulders.

"It looks like a gang of bikers," Tina announced without recognizing the threat. She overzealously waved at the first bike as it sped by and noted, "Ooh, they're chicks!"

Guy's neck prickled with heat, and he began to sweat. "Can you see their logo?" he whisper-yelled from the backseat. His hand was on Ruby, who lay on the van's floor. She seemed unfazed by the episode and lay perfectly still, much to Guy's relief. The last thing they needed was for Ruby to reveal herself and confirm that Toto's occupants were indeed the subject of the Broomstick's cross-country search.

"*Psst.* Why are you hiding?" Tina cupped her hand to direct her question and whisper-yelled back to Guy without turning to address him in the backseat. She continued to wave at each of the bikers as they passed.

"Don't look back. Just pretend I'm not here." Guy added, "Tell me—are they wearing Broomsticks jackets? They have yellow tassels and a big sweeping broom on the back."

"Yes," Stacey and Tina collectively confirmed.

"Keep driving, and remember that I'm not here, and neither is Ruby. Don't look in the backseat. Keep driving." Guy's instructions sounded more like orders.

Guy remained still under the cloak of the attaché case in the back of the van. Beads of sweat gathered on his face and neck, and he could feel dampness accumulating on his hairline. He heard the roar as the bikes passed, one after another, in an endless line. Toto shook each time, and Guy could tell they were close enough to see inside.

"Are they gone?" he asked after a period of quiet.

"Yes, I think so," Stacey said confidently.

Guy sat up and pulled the case from his face and shoulders. "That was close," he exclaimed, his face red and flushed. He wiped his cheeks with his sleeve and smoothed back his hair, which had started to curl from the moisture. It took him a few minutes to catch his breath and slow the rapid beating of his heart.

"What's going on?" Tina demanded to know.

"It's kind of complicated," Guy said while looking down at Ruby, who remained still at his feet. He needed a moment to organize his thoughts.

"Well, uncomplicate it," Tina snapped.

"Back home the other day, I was in this accident. It was pouring rain, and the wind was crazy," he began.

"It was probably a typhoon," Stacey interrupted.

"Could it be a typhoon? I mean, aren't those storms for Asia?" Tina wondered.

Stacey continued, "When the Pacific Northwest gets wind storms, they are called typhoons. Look it up. There was one in 1962, and there must have been one the other day back at your home in Vancouver. Right, Guy?"

"Sure," he continued. "It was a crazy storm, and I was driving home after work. Somehow, I was in an accident in the parking lot outside my apartment. It was dark, and my neighbors were looking for something using flashlights. They shone their light at me, and I accelerated by mistake and knocked over their motorcycle. I think that's when Ruby found her way into my van. Now they are after her."

"The motorcycle riders want the dog?" Tina asked.

"Yeah, sorry. I missed that part of the story. As crazy as it sounds, yeah. My one neighbor emailed the entire gang, east to west. All those bikers are out looking for Ruby," Guy explained.

"Why do they want the dog?" Stacey asked.

"Maybe she does tricks." Tina snickered.

"I'm not sure. But Ruby has this charm on her collar, and the address says to return her to New York. So I think it's only right to follow the instructions," Guy said.

"Well, I'm square with it." Tina smiled. "But if she does tricks, I'm taking her on Letterman."

Guy looked up at Stacey, meeting her gaze in the rearview mirror, and said, "I really could use your help too."

Stacey agreed without hesitation. "I'll do what I can, Guy, which right now is looking out for more of those bikers. Boy, that was wild! Twice in one day," Stacey said.

"I'll tell you what, Stacey. Pull over at the next exit, and I'll drive." He paused briefly before adding, "You can read this." He opened the attaché case and held up his copy of the manuscript, remembering his promise.

"So that's the big Kennedy novel." Tina jeered, raising an eyebrow suspiciously. "Looks wimpy," she added sarcastically.

Stacey giggled and quickly eased Toto off the highway. Guy passed the CBK text to Stacey while they swapped positions from the driver's seat to the back. "Now, Stacey," he said, "as an editor, I'm not supposed to share this. But I said I would, so I am. The stuff you read here is unpublished. Keep it to yourself for now."

"Will do, Guy," Stacey said, standing tall in a salute before she slipped into the backseat and shut the van door.

"Here, you'll need this." Guy opened the glove box and withdrew a small flashlight. He flicked it on and passed it back to Stacey, who was already deeply engaged in the first page.

CHAPTER 10

LEANNA

*Sunday, late evening, Interstate
90 outside Chicago*

"*Phew!* After all that excitement, I need a Puerto Rican bath!"
Tina broke the silence of the late evening ride as she sniffed her
underarms on both sides. "Any chance of a pit stop soon?"

"What's a Puerto Rican bath?" Stacey asked, looking up from the
manuscript.

"You mean you haven't read about that yet?" Tina asked, feigning
surprise.

Stacey shook her head to answer no.

Tina paused as a hush fell over the other passengers, Ruby included.
"Well, the story goes that John Jr. and Carolyn went down to Mar-a-
Lago, an estate in Florida owned by Donald Trump. According to a
friend of my mom who lives nearby, Carolyn was a real trash talker.
When she arrived at this one party after flying in from New York,
she announced to a room full of people, 'I had to take a Puerto

Rican bath on the way down in the airplane.' People were shocked, but that was her. She said it like it was."

"That was her?" Stacey repeated. "Wait, Tina, did you know her?"

"Not really. I once saw Carolyn at an LA party, the Ice Ball, or something like that. She was with the lady married to Arnold Schwarzenegger."

"Maria Shriver?" Stacey asked.

"Yeah, her. My mother hates her because, once upon a time, she did a hack-job interview on my mom for *Dateline*. It cost me my summer trip to Italy that year because my mom was so embarrassed that she hid my entire school break in Montana." Tina pouted.

"What about Carolyn?" Stacey reminded Tina.

"Oh, yeah. Yeah, Carolyn seemed cool but looked like a ghost. Maybe that was her thing? She was super pale, and she wore a long-sleeved white dress. It was a few years ago, and I was pretty young then, so she wasn't my jam. I barely paid attention. But when she died, I sure heard lots about her." Tina chuckled.

"What kind of stuff?" Stacey asked eagerly.

"Oh lots of its stuff that I can't repeat. I'm sure it's mostly bogus, though. You know how people talk after someone dies suddenly, especially a celeb? Like when Diana died, they just went crazy. All kinds of stories popped up," Tina said knowingly.

"Yeah," Stacey agreed. "Like the palace ordered it and that she was pregnant and going to marry that Dodi guy. Or that Prince Philip had her killed. Or that she faked her death to live peacefully in the English countryside. Or—"

"Oh my God! Enough already, Stacey. Come up for air!" Tina exclaimed.

"Sorry," Stacey replied, adding a polite, "please go on."

Tina opened her purse, searched for the Carmex, unscrewed the lid, and applied a generous lump across her bottom lip. She paused while rubbing her lips together. Finally, she spoke in a hushed tone, "That's the stuff that made it into the mainstream."

Tina sat back and cackled.

"Come on, Tina. Don't leave us hanging," Stacey pleaded.

"OK." Tina's voice became an uncharacteristic whisper. "Well, I heard that Carolyn and John broke up by the end. They were living apart, and the only reason the sister was with them was to keep the peace. Otherwise, they would have gotten physical and messed each other up badly! Plus, Carolyn was a major coke addict, and John wasn't into that, so he bullied her about it behind closed doors. And the thing that they didn't want anyone to know? His broken ankle was because he kicked a wall when fighting with her. I mean - kiteboarding? Please. Who breaks their ankle kiteboarding?"

"Oh my God!" gasped Stacey.

"Oh yeah." Tina lied. "Carolyn and John got scrappy, and things got rough when they did."

"Bullshit!" Guy muttered quietly. He was on to Tina.

Stacey frowned before saying, "But it says here that they reconciled and were going to his cousin's wedding as a fresh start." She flipped through several pages before pointing to the manuscript pages detailing the couple's final days.

Stacey quoted, "John and Carolyn confirmed their attendance for Rory Kennedy's wedding at the family compound in Hyannis Port by mailing back their reply card as Mr. and Mrs. John F. Kennedy Jr. alongside a selection of beef as their main."

"Ahh," Tina said convincingly, "that's what they want you to believe!"

"So it's true?" Stacey questioned.

"It's how false gossip gets spread, Stacey," Guy explained. "People make up stuff and then, if enough people start to say it, somehow people start to think it's true."

"How do you know what's true and not true?" Stacey asked.

"I guess you never really do!" Tina laughed. "Can we stop soon? I'm squirming here!" she announced while uncrossing and recrossing her legs.

"We'll stop at the next station," Guy said.

"Good, I've got to wee like a racehorse!" Tina exclaimed.

"And take your bath," Stacey reminded her. "What was that again anyway? Do you use the sink to wash or something?"

"No, you just use deodorant or perfume to mask your stink, and most of the time, you wind up smelling overly floral and douchey." Tina added, "It's just a joke, Stacey. It is better to have real showers."

The comment was lost on Stacey, who Guy noted had already returned her attention to the manuscript. Five minutes later, the sign for a service station appeared. Guy left the highway and pulled up at an empty gas bay. He was thankful to note that there was no sign of any motorcyclists.

"Stacey, I'll fill up." Guy decided to remain by the van, just in case they needed to make a quick escape. He peeled a twenty off the fat roll of money and handed it to Stacey, adding, "Can you go into the shop and grab us some food?"

Stacey placed the open manuscript on the seat beside her and replied, "Sure, do you want something special? I'm getting Cheetos, not the hot kind, just the regular ones. The hot kind has some weird chemical that makes them hot, and I hear it causes cancer. That, and the red dye on M&Ms. I always pick the red ones out. Any other requests?"

"I'm good," said Guy as he unscrewed Toto's gas cap and began to pump the regular unleaded while Tina slammed the door and went to find the restroom.

— — —

Meanwhile, inside the station's ladies' room, Leanna Del Rorro stood at the sink, staring at her reflection in the mirror. She turned on the tap marked with a C, releasing a flood of cool water, grabbed a handful of paper towels from the dispenser on the wall, and held them under the running tap. Then she applied the mass to the underside of her eyes, which were swollen from crying.

My life sucks, she lamented.

She dotted the wet paper cloth against her hot skin and sighed. The room was dingy, dark, and disgusting. It stunk of urine, and used paper towels lay scattered across the floor. It was so quiet that she could hear the buzz of the electric light. *How has it come to this?* she wondered. The promise of her life, her hopes and dreams, and everything else had combusted instantly after a disastrous episode caught in its entirety on video by *Inside Edition*.

And now even her most loyal supporter, her grandmother Nonna, had tired of her "rotten attitude" and essentially abandoned her a short distance from that roadside station. Leanna could find her own way home. That was the suggestion when Nonna accused her of being a perpetual hothead with an uncontrolled temper, pulled the car over, reached across Leanna's seat, and opened the door.

"Walk," her grandmother instructed while pointing to the road.

Furious, Leanna shouted back insults, calling her a wrinkled old raisin, which Leanna instantly knew was odd as all raisins were wrinkly. That realization enflamed her even more. Nonna calmly told her that she was behaving just like her father and his father before that, and, in her experience, one day, Leanna would thank her for the tough love. Nonna drove away, leaving Leanna boiling mad in a cloud of dust. She stomped the quarter mile to the nearest gas station and found the restroom immediately.

There, alone, she finally broke down.

As usual, she hadn't meant to pick a fight. But Suzanne Smyth, the stupid, snotty, stuck-up bitch had pushed her buttons, pointing out the failure that Leanna was to all those jerks at the pool hall, and Leanna couldn't help herself. She got right up into Suzanne's face and made such a commotion that it took both the cute new bartender and Joey Roberts to pull the two girls apart.

"Careful, girlfriend. *Inside Edition* called, and they are sending a crew." The taunt echoed, and Leanna felt that familiar fire igniting her gut.

It wasn't the way it was supposed to be. Leanna had once been someone on the path to glory. She attended college in Chicago and studied journalism, working summers at a local news station. When she expressed interest in behind-the-camera work, an instructor revealed a once-in-a-lifetime opportunity. With his help, Leanna applied and won an apprenticeship as Herb Ritts's photography assistant intern.

The opportunity meant relocating to Los Angeles, which was fine because Nonna's sister, Auntie Nettie, lived that way. Leanna landed and went straight to work. Her first shoot assisting Herb was for his infamous portrait entitled "Stephanie, Cindy, Christy, Tatjana, Naomi, Hollywood, 1989" for *Rolling Stone*. With the artful impression of the five intertwined in the nude but without being too revealing, Leanna decided to align her budding career with theirs. No one knew it yet, but Leanna sensed they were about to become very famous.

In no time, Leanna was the confidant, protector, and sometimes healer of the rising stars. As they grew in status and popularity, Leanna listened and offered advice. Should Linda bleach her hair platinum for the George Michael "Freedom" music video shoot? Why not? Should Cindy marry actor Richard Gere? Of course.

She was there for the 1990 Peter Lindberg *Vogue* cover shoot featuring Christy Turlington, Cindy Crawford, Naomi Campbell, Linda Evangelista, and Tatjana Patitz. This iconic image launched the five top-paid, top-booked faces as *supermodels,* a term that revolutionized the industry and substantiated the female model as a celebrity. Their rocket to fame was unlike anything seen before.

Leanna's competence caught the eye of a man who was New York's top modeling agent at the time. When he approached her, she almost could not believe her good fortune. When the Ritts internship ended, Leanna left LA and joined his Manhattan team, working with the talent as their on-set assistant and representative. Leanna brought toughness to the role, which was ideal because everyone wanted something from the supermodels. She knew when to push and when to retreat. And she could give as good as she got.

Her hunch about the famous five from her first Ritts job paid dividends as they became stars. Within a few months as a trusted player, Leanna tallied assignments with the world's top talent on shoots for fashion's best brands by its most celebrated photographers. With this fame, the ladies could demand higher pay and be choosier about their projects. And Leanna was right there beside them for it all, seemingly invincible.

"Leanna Del Rorro, you are a goddess." Her boss applauded after she convinced Claudia Schiffer to style one additional look at a shoot. Claudia had by then replaced Tatjana in the famous five as the "buxom blonde."

In a casual conversation one evening with Linda, Leanna thought aloud: "Supermodels are so culturally relevant that they shouldn't even get out of bed for less than ten thousand dollars per day." Linda loved it and was credited with a similar quote in the October 1990 issue of *Vogue.*

Leanna was there when, out of nowhere, the entire look of a fashion model changed overnight with one campaign starring a young, British Kate Moss. Kate was petite at five foot six, and her appearance was against a traditional model. She was almost waifish, coining the term *heroin chic*.

In 1993, her boss asked Leanna to do him a favor and fly to Jost Van Dyke in the British Virgin Islands with Kate and her boyfriend Mario Sorrenti. The client was Calvin Klein, whose fashion house was in the running for America's Best Designer, an award he would later win. Leanna was to discreetly keep her eye on Kate and Mario as they intended to stay alone in a beachside abode. The pictures from the trip resulted in a masterful campaign for the perfume *Obsession*.

That she was on the sideline of that piece of history propelled Leanna into the upper stratosphere of New York's fashion scene. She was expected to be everywhere, invited to the A-list parties and events. Although life in the city was expensive, Leanna lived in a decent apartment with an up-and-coming artist roommate and even amassed some savings. Since she was tall and lean, many of her model friends would pass off designer clothing, jewelry, and extra makeup. As a quick study, Leanna learned to apply cosmetics expertly to make the best of her features.

Everything was going so well. Leanna's connection to the big six (Kate Moss eventually joined the crew) gave her authority, and soon, younger models begged her for advice. But then, almost perfectly aligned with the decline of the supermodel, the thing happened that ruined it all, and nothing was ever the same.

Glory no more.

A fat tear gathered at the corner of her left eye, and Lenna watched it fall across her cheek and down the length of her neck. She had not willed the tear; instead, it came naturally. It left a wet streak, and she watched it dissipate from the surface of her face, feeling strangely pleased by the idea that it had been absorbed as those seconds and minutes passed.

Leanna grabbed both sides of the sink and stared intently at her reflection, compelling nerve. *No guts, no glory*

Her old habits were hardly charming and were not advancing her cause. *It's time to invoke courage, the courage to change.*

Suddenly, the washroom door flew open, and Leanna's heart leaped at the sound of metal on metal as the back of the door slammed against the trashcan with an alarming *BAM!* The lid relentlessly swung back and forth on its rusty hinges, and Leanna spun around defensively, fists up and ready to go.

"What the fuck!" Leanna screamed, inches from the stranger's face.

It was clear to Leanna that the woman was not expecting to be shouted at as her shiny, plump lips took hold in a perfect round *O*, and her eyebrows shot above the line of her sunglasses. Leanna hot-stepped between her sneakered feet as Tina lifted her sunglasses from the bridge of her nose and balanced them atop her head.

"Hey there, kitty. Cool it," Tina responded in a firm and even tone.

Leanna could feel her heart beating rapidly, pumping hot blood through her body in perfect synchronicity with the squeaking lid. It took her a moment to catch her breath and release her tightly knotted fists. "Sorry, you scared me." Her voice was suddenly meek, and Leanna hardly recognized it as hers. She wiped her eyes dry, not wanting the woman to notice her tears.

"Well." Tina shrugged. "The door was stuck."

Tina went into the only stall in the dim room and locked the door. Leanna could hear as she fussed with the button of her pants, wriggled herself loose, and released a steady stream into the toilet bowl. Tina coughed a couple of times in a row and then spat something into what Leanna assumed was a tissue or a piece of toilet paper. She listened as she unrolled several sheets, attended to herself, and then stood up and flushed.

The drainage noise drowned out all else that the woman inside was doing, and so Leanna was startled once again when Tina suddenly emerged from the stall. She had not estimated that she would be able to reemerge in such a short time.

"Yuck!" Tina exclaimed as she shook her hands at her sides. "This is the most disgusting bathroom ever. I don't suppose they ever clean in here."

Leanna nodded her head in agreement and moved away from the sink. Tina quickly took the spot where Leanna had stood and turned on the faucets. She paused momentarily, leaning into the mirror to inspect what seemed to be a blemish. Leanna couldn't be sure. She watched her rinse and dry her hands with a paper towel drawn from the industrial dispenser on the wall. Then she crumpled the moistened towel and tossed it onto a mountainous pile growing beside the metal wastebasket by the door.

Before moving away from the sink, Tina took a moment to assess her appearance. Leanna watched as she moved her head from side to side to view the entire scope of her face, from cheek to cheek. She paused in the middle and drew the tip of her right hand's middle finger across the bridge of her nose. Tina looked for shine on her finger pad and wiped it across the seat of her jeans. She did the same across her forehead and chin before removing a compact from her oversized bag. She flipped it open and began to apply a thin coating of powder.

"You want some?" Tina broke their silence. Leanna grew hot with embarrassment. She had not realized that she was staring so intensely. She shook her head ever so slightly to indicate disinterest.

"Come on. Come over here," Tina beckoned the woman closer. "I won't bite."

When Leanna didn't move, Tina said, "OK, I'll come there."

She took the two steps toward Leanna. "Well, aren't you a hot mess," Tina announced as she assessed Leanna's appearance. "Is everything all right?"

Leanna folded her face into her hands and shook her head. *No, everything was not all right.*

"Do you want me to get someone for you?" Tina asked.

"No," Leanna mumbled. "I'm alone."

The door opened again without warning, knocking on the metal trashcan lid. The same rhythmic creak, created as the lid turned from side to side, announced Stacey's arrival.

"Hey, Tina, I got Ding Dongs. I'm so excited," Stacey practically gushed as she swung the bag of goodies back and forth. "I love Ding Dongs." She stopped to look at Leanna, standing with her face in her hands.

"Is everything good here," Stacey asked nervously.

Leanna screamed. It was a long, even shriek delivered into the palm of her hands. It lasted for several seconds, and when it was over, she felt better. She lifted her face from her palms, wiped the remaining wetness from her eyes, and reached to still the annoying trashcan lid.

Leanna's emotional outburst startled Stacey, and she backed toward the door. "I don't have to pee that bad after all." She made the excuse while defensively pressing the bag of gas station treats against her chest.

"What's the story here," Tina demanded with authority when Leanna finally faced the women in the room. "You can't just scream, lady."

Leanna allowed her gaze to drift between the two women. The one girl seemed on edge and afraid, and the way she clutched the bag with the Ding Dongs was unusual. *What have I done?*

"Look—I'm sorry," Leanna confessed slowly, weighing her words cautiously to avoid igniting the situation further. "I'm having a shit day in a shit life. I'm nearly broke, and I've got no ride."

"Aw, honey." Tina sighed. "It sounds like you need a friend." Tina approached Leanna and put her hand on her shoulder, gently patting it soothingly. "And we've got one right here for you." Tina gestured toward Stacey.

"Be careful, Tina," Stacey warned. "She could be a scammer—the kind that robs people in gas stations."

"Hey," Leanna roared, offended. "I'm *not* a scammer!" she announced, emphasizing the *not* within a sharp expel of breath. She felt the hot prickle of fury returning to her cheeks. *Careful, Del Rorro,* Leanna warned herself not to lose her cool. That kind of stuff got her into trouble in the first place. If she wanted her old life back, she couldn't afford a repeat.

"Look," Tina said jokingly, "I can give you money if that's what you want. Lord knows I've got a ton of it!" She smiled.

"Tina," Stacey hissed.

"What? If she wants money, what do I care?" Tina shrugged and returned to the bathroom mirror. She pulled out her red lipstick and applied it, using a paper towel from the dispenser to blot the excess. Leanna watched as Tina took a moment to sniff her underarms and decided to apply deodorant.

Stacey, fixated on Leanna, asked, "Well, if you have no money and no ride, then what's your plan?"

"I don't have one." Leanna's confession met with an uncomfortable silence. Her voice, filled with despair and a genuine blend of panic and sadness, echoed in her ears.

Stacey looked to Tina, who momentarily stood away from the mirror. "Well," Tina sighed, bored, "you should probably come with us. I've paid the guy outside to drive me, so he can't care if you come too."

Stacey continued, "Yes, it's late out there, and this is no place for a woman to be alone. We are headed to New York and can take you as far as you need." She opened the grocery bag of treats and offered the new girl a bag of Cheetos and a Coke. "Here, it looks like you need these more than me. Do you want a Ding Dong too?"

Leanna declined the food offer, but the girl had said the magic words: *New York*. She looked at the two strangers, who looked back at her, waiting for her answer. Leanna noticed that the first seemed eager and authentic, while the one who loved looking in the mirror seemed irritated and indifferent to Leanna's response. She was used to both sorts of personalities.

"Thank you. That's a generous offer." She could join these strangers on their journey or return to her life, which no longer seemed worthwhile or healthy.

"Carpe diem, seize the day. I'm Stacey." Stacey extended her hand for Leanna to shake.

"Carpe diem." Leanna smiled and shook Stacey's hand with one quick pump. "I'm Leanna Del Rorro. Sometimes people call me Lea."

"Hi, Leanna, Lea. I'm Stacey Crowe, and this is Tina Mann. Outside in the van are Guy and his dog, Ruby." Stacey maintained the grip on Leanna's hand and forced two additional pumps.

"Guy's my chauffeur," Tina said dryly.

"And you said you are going to New York?" Leanna asked.

"Yeah," Stacey confirmed. "You've been there before?"

In a low voice, Leanna nodded and said, "I used to live there."

"OK, then, times up! Let's go," Tina snapped, taking one last look at herself in the mirror before opening the washroom door.

"Come on," Stacey said, grabbing Leanna's hand. Together, they followed Tina.

A return to New York it shall be.

CHAPTER 11
NOT JUST POLITICS AS USUAL

Monday past midnight,
Interstate 90 through Ohio

"Guy," Tina said with authority when they returned from the bathroom. "This is Leanna, and she's coming too."

Tina didn't care if Guy was bothered by an additional passenger. She paid him, and they had a deal. A thousand dollars was probably as much as the shitty van cost him. And Guy seemed preoccupied with the dog and the motorcycles anyway.

"Welcome, Leanna," Guy said, opening the van door and ushering the girls into Toto's back seats. Ruby lay sprawled on the front passenger side, so it made sense for the girls to take the rear seats. Stacey was deeply engrossed in conversation with Leanna, and they took seats beside one another, leaving Tina next to the door.

"So, you used to live in New York?" Stacey asked while Tina smirked at Stacey's blatant attempt to pry.

"Yeah." Leanna seemed reluctant to share.

God, the girl likes to talk. Tina rolled her eyes at the persistence of their nosy van mate but was thankful that Stacey had someone new to attack with her endless interrogations. Having nothing better to do, she noticed the manuscript opened and abandoned on the seat between her and Stacey. With Stacey absorbed in Leanna's saga, Tina discreetly picked it up and began to read.

– – –

CBK: 4

Using coy dating tactics and an undeniable mystic allure, Carolyn Bessette Kennedy cemented herself as the exclusive partner of America's prince, John Kennedy Jr. Soon, she was privy to the protocol and obligations of such a role. Public curiosity, incessant gossip, flashing camera bulbs, and constant attention came with the prize.

By all accounts, 1995 was a good year for Carolyn and John.

In early April, Carolyn moved into John's loft at 20 North Moore Street in New York's trendy Tribeca district. Many assumed they were on the fast track to marital bliss and began the "wedding watch" with ever-escalating intensity. Then they adopted Friday, a lively Canan terrier, making a union all the more inevitable.

As John's live-in girlfriend, Carolyn became a "thing" in the eyes of the public. Until then, she had been a rising star in the world of public relations at Calvin Klein, but she was suddenly a refugee in her new home. Gone were the days of freedom to walk around town, shop, or meet with friends for anonymous drinks or dinner. Instead, reporters camped out on her doorstep, eager for prized pictures to earn them thousands.

A marriage proposal came a few months later on a warm summer weekend on Martha's Vineyard. While out fishing, John presented a platinum eternity band with round-cut sapphires and diamonds, a copy of a ring his mother wore. "Fishing is so much better with a partner," he was rumored to have said. Carolyn allegedly responded with perfect *Rules*: "I'll think about it." But of course, she said yes.

Simultaneously with their courtship heating up, the couple also faced the pressure of the launch of John's magazine, a demanding and unforgiving mistress christened *George*.

John and his business partner, Michael Berman, raised three million dollars over six months to launch *George*. Under the corporate name Random Ventures, they teamed up to bring their vision of a political lifestyle magazine to the marketplace. However, the three million dollars Random Ventures raised was reportedly only one-third of what was necessary to launch their dream.

Earlier that March, French publishing giant Hachette-Filipacchi made a significant financial commitment. They agreed to spend twenty million dollars on *George* over five years or until the freshman publication began to turn a profit. Hachette-Filipacchi was already an industry heavyweight, publishing over twenty magazines, ranging from *Elle* and *Women's Day* to *Premiere* and *Road & Track*.

The inaugural issue of *George* hit newsstands on September 26, 1995. Its famous cofounder and editor-in-chief proclaimed it "a lifestyle magazine with politics at its core, illuminating the points where politics converges with business, media, entertainment, fashion, art, and science."[59]

---

[59] Kennedy, "Editor's Letter," 9–10.

George was initially released bimonthly, and circulation began at an estimated two hundred and fifty thousand copies. The issues were oversized, full of advertising, and touted as lighthearted, offering insight into the intersection where national politics met popular culture. When the magazine reduced in heft but reduced to a monthly schedule, readership grew to over four hundred and fifty thousand.

John Kennedy Jr.'s personal, in-depth interviews with Fidel Castro and George Wallace were acclaimed by news media worldwide. Celebrities such as Madonna, Julia Roberts, and Edward Norton, to name but a few, graced the covers and provided their input for articles, including an "If I Were President" feature. *George* attempted to make politics of the past, present, and future attractive to the ordinary person.

Soon after the magazine's release, John appeared as a guest on CNN's *Larry King Live*. Larry and John debated the much-discussed cover of the inaugural issue that depicted a bare-midriffed Cindy Crawford in a drag costume of the magazine's namesake, George Washington. King observed that using one of her generation's most famous fashion models seemed to some to trivialize whatever was political about the magazine. Kennedy countered that politics in the US had become intermixed with popular culture. He pointed out that the program *Larry King Live*, itself a phenomenon of mass media culture, was where serious politicians announced crucial decisions, such as running for national office.[60]

Carolyn, in a show of support to her then-rumored fiancé, accompanied John to the taping in Washington, DC, returning to New York later that evening by train.

---

[60] Kennedy, "Editor's Letter," 9–10.

The magazine business is known to be challenging to succeed in. Statistics showed a 50 percent failure rate for new magazines within their first two years and only 5 percent surviving long enough to celebrate a fifth anniversary. John was deeply involved in a pressure-filled industry where his reputation dangled on the line. Luckily for him, few would opt not to return the ambitious editor's phone calls because of his famous name and socialite reputation.

These compounding pressures contributed to the young couple's now infamous February 25, 1996, Washington Square Park brawl. John, wearing sunglasses, red shorts, and a light-green sweater, and Carolyn, who donned sweatpants, were caught on videotape exchanging heated words and gestures.

What began as a peaceful Sunday stroll on a beautiful early-autumn day suddenly turned ugly. The couple was captured shoving each other and arguing as their dog, Friday, looked on before they eventually kissed and made up.[61] "What's your problem," Carolyn was thought to have screamed as John grabbed her wrist and pulled the engagement ring off her finger.

Carolyn instantly burst into tears, burying her face into her hands as John yanked the dog's leash from her and walked the other way. She paused for a moment or two, paralyzed by the shock of the situation, before opting to chase after him, charging at him in a fit of rage. The fight continued as they left the park.

Feeling overwhelmed by the situation's intensity, John opted to sit on the street curb, where he collapsed his head into folded arms. Carolyn remained standing as she spoke to him and demanded her ring back.

---

[61] Seligmann, "Sunday in the Park with George."

"Give it to me!" she shouted.

John reached into his pocket to retrieve the ring and handed it to her. She responded by touching her head to his, attempting to make amends, as tears rolled down her cheeks. Unprepared to forgive, John abruptly rejected the gesture. He countered by pushing her away.

Carolyn flew into a fitful fury. She tried to draw Friday's leash out of John's hand, resulting in a tug-of-war over the bewildered dog.

"You've got your ring," passersby overheard John yelling. "You're not getting my dog!"[62]

"It's our dog,"[63] Carolyn reminded him, tugging to wrest the dog leash away from his grip. Eventually, John let go, and Carolyn, triumphant, set off down the street with Friday.

Left behind to watch his world walking away, John turned in the opposite direction. Soon, perhaps realizing the pettiness of their clash, Carolyn turned and chased after John, leading him to a bench where they could talk out their differences.

A little while later, they stood and departed the park, stopping only to embrace each other in the middle of the sidewalk.

Two journalists filmed the altercation and later sold the tape for a rumored $250,000.[64] It was aired almost a week later on all the prime-time gossip shows. John, who was trying to draw attention away from his private life and toward his professional career, was

---

[62] Seligmann, "Sunday in the Park with George."
[63] Jeffreys, "Blonde Ambition," 158–159.
[64] Jeffreys, "Blonde Ambition," 158–159.

mortified. Kennedy men, especially Jackie Kennedy's son, did not behave that way publicly.

Their documented emotional clash became hot public consumption. Publications such as the *Enquirer*, the *Globe*, and the *Star* splashed still shots of the argument across their front covers and distributed them to supermarkets and media outlets nationwide.

Carolyn became the villain. She was labeled as aggressive, cruel, sadistic, vicious, unstable, hot-tempered, and entirely unsuitable for John Kennedy. Those who willed a Kennedy Dynasty resurrection quietly hoped he would come to his senses and drop the flashy armpiece in favor of a demure lady like his mother. *On the verge of breaking up!* other headlines promised to the millions of John's admirers.

Some thought that John chose the fashionable and well-spoken Carolyn because she was like his mother, a woman he had admired for his entire life. Others felt the opposite: that his attraction to Carolyn was physical. She was a similar type to his prior love, actress Daryl Hannah. They both were statuesque and blonde.

Before the year was out, the couple mended their differences and married in a private ceremony on tiny Cumberland Island, just off the coast of Georgia. The date was Saturday, September 21, 1996, and news of their marriage made national headlines by Monday. John Kennedy Jr. was married, and American women collectively mourned the loss of their chance at a date with the country's most eligible bachelor.

On returning from their exotic honeymoon, three days in Turkey followed by a ten-day Aegean cruise, many began to speculate about what Carolyn would do with her time. She had already given up her profession as a publicist with Calvin Klein before the wedding, quitting the fashion house before her marriage.

Once the media discovered the relationship, Carolyn began receiving daily harassing phone calls at the Calvin Klein workplace. She knew this attention would worsen once they married, and privacy to perform her job would be too great a challenge. It made sense to withdraw from her role as a publicist when all the press wanted to know was the details of her private life.

Others indicated that she was ready to give up this career path. As Mrs. John Kennedy Jr., Carolyn knew that her life was evolving away from her New York party girl days. Her new role would be charity work, black-tie events, and supporting her husband in his magazine endeavor.

Carolyn served as an unofficial hostess at many of *George*'s functions. She was interested in the cover design and layouts of some of the magazine's features. John sanctioned Carolyn's involvement, which upset his partner, Michael Berman, who believed she had no expertise or authority to make such decisions. Unfortunately, this led to the inevitable spectacular dissolving of Kennedy and Berman's partnership and friendship just a year later.

In the fall of 1996, *George* passed their first birthday, celebrating in almost perfect synchronicity with the newlywed's wedding. But trouble loomed for the sophomore publication, and some would say the Kennedy and Bessette union.

Of course, the Kennedy name and pedigree meant that John did not have to support the magazine financially. Rumor had it that he inherited more than one hundred million dollars from his mother's estate on her death in May 1994, but he did not need to use his own money to fund *George*.

The partnership with the French publishing company Hachette-Filipacchi enabled Kennedy and his partner, Berman, to realize their dream of taking politics to the masses. People were eager to see how the son of a beloved former president would make his mark on the political landscape. Many hoped that John would take the same route as his father. Some even said they would vote for him without hearing the young man's platform on relevant political issues.

Over what seemed like overnight, *George* would intrigue enough audience to become America's largest-circulation political magazine. Yet despite its success, *George* was losing money.[65] Whispers of losses of up to $4 million per year could not be quieted.

In February 1997, sensing trouble and eager to use his beautiful new wife's talents, John sent Carolyn to meet with top European designers. Many suspected he hoped Carolyn would persuade them to buy ad space in *George*, while others whispered that Carolyn demanded her husband put her to work. She was becoming bored in the role of housewife, with nothing more than shopping, lunches, and charity work to keep her occupied.

Regardless, it was then that John and Berman split,[66] and John took on Berman's *George* responsibilities. John could hire Carolyn without a business partner to tell him otherwise. It was also seen as a constructive way to get Carolyn out of hiding away in their home, which many reported she did to avoid the merciless paparazzi.

There were rumors around that around this time Carolyn had increased her intake of and dependence on drugs—particularly cocaine. Where once this habit may have been one of occasional

---

[65] Hirschkorn, "JFK Jr.'s Magazine Salutes Its Fallen Leader."
[66] Staff, "Messy Split, Bye George."

social dabbling, observers feared that the pressures of life inside the constant fishbowl pushed her toward more frequent chemical escapism. The press speculated that her weight loss and gaunt appearance were drug-related without acknowledging any stresses their prying had on the new bride.

To others, John appeared to take public life in stride and preferred exercise, like riding his bike, and healthy living as his release. Carolyn, on the other hand, did not. Whenever seen out, she appeared increasingly fearful. Her appearances outside their home became rare; she was seldom seen on the New York streets. The lack of sightings fueled the assumption of aggravated drug abuse.

Those closest dismissed this portrayal of Carolyn as the victim of addiction. They would cite the ever-present eye of the media as being primarily responsible for her misery. They indicated that she fell into a depression, unable to cope with the constant scrutiny of her movements.

Unless she was at a public event, dressed accordingly, she resisted all media and public curiosity by offering very little of herself. Many criticized her for being uncooperative and cold, an ice princess. When photographed on the streets, her face often frowned with resentment. She would hold her hand to shield her face. She hopped into cabs to avoid the attention.

This unfriendliness somehow resulted in accusations of abuse. Carolyn provoked fights with John, some headlines read. She was unstable and needed therapy. After John sought treatment at a local hospital, some speculated that Carolyn had angrily attacked him. John required emergency surgery for a severed nerve in his right hand. The only statement on the incident came from *George's* spokesperson, who called the incident a "kitchen mishap."[67]

Because of her cold demeanor, the press overreacted by portraying Carolyn as the aggressor in this and other similar situations. They wanted to capture her in an imperfect form because it sold more papers and was a better story. It got to the point where Carolyn could have felt the media was stalking her, hoping to capture her in a distressed state. For example, when she tripped while carrying a load of packages on the step of her front entrance, photographers snapped picture after picture instead of helping her.

A friend recalled that the paparazzi were obsessed with Carolyn. She sometimes had to leave hours early for appointments, often before 7:00 a.m., to escape being trailed as she went about her day. They camped outside her home on North Moore.

"She was like a hunted animal; that was no way to live," this friend observed.

Though Carolyn loved the idea of her husband running his magazine, *George* was becoming a significant obstacle in the couple's relationship. With his increased responsibilities, John grew more stressed by the constant battle to keep the magazine afloat. While he was out working to make *George* a success, Carolyn remained at home, growing increasingly disconnected each day.

When the conversation turned to children, Carolyn naturally hesitated, wondering about bringing little Kennedys into a life where they would be constantly harassed and followed. She wanted to move away from the city and set up a home in her native

---

[67] N. Services, "JFK JR. UNDERGOES SURGERY ON HAND."

Connecticut, where she felt their family would have a better chance at leading a more normal life.

On the other hand, John was desperate for children but reluctant to leave the city. He argued that his mother was able to raise him and his sister, the children of a popular former president, in New York under what he felt were pretty happy circumstances. They could make it work.

Eventually, the couple committed to entering counseling in March 1999.

The media saw this move as a step toward divorce, and the nation's press relished the prospect of having a long, drawn-out, and dramatic breakup. They enhanced their coverage of the more negative particulars, embellishing even the slightest details. Of course, something was wrong with Carolyn, and therefore, they needed therapy.

An anonymous friend says, "Carolyn struggled. She loved John, but he had work commitments and wasn't always available for her. She turned to a few of us as confidants, and we grew close, often hanging out at her place because she could never go anywhere. The number of times I caught her in tears looking out the window was sad. And on top of everything else, they were so upset about Anthony." *Citation?*

Alongside the pressures of their public life, John and Carolyn faced sadness invoked by the impending death of John's cousin Anthony Radziwill. Radziwill suffered from metastasized cancer, a prolonged battle he would eventually lose in August 1999.[68] For John, it was unbelievable that his best friend was about to pass away.

---

[68] Nemy, "Anthony Stanislas Radziwill, 40, Award-Winning TV Producer," C21.

The boys were born only a year apart. Anthony arrived on August 4, 1959, to Lee, the younger sister of Jackie and Polish prince Stanislaw Radziwill. John Jr. followed in 1960 on November 25. The cousins enjoyed a close relationship brought closer by Anthony's 1989 diagnosis of cancer. They were each other's best men at their respective weddings.[69]

While Anthony's initial treatment permitted several years of remission, cancer returned after his August 1994 marriage to Carole Ann DiFalco. This upset followed the death of Jackie in May and, one speculates, forced John to take a long, hard look at his own life and the choices he was making. At the time, he was almost thirty-four and had yet to settle down.

Carolyn entered the scene at that opportune time and became integral in assisting John and Carole through the challenging roller coaster of Anthony's cancer treatment. She was said to have spent hours at the hospital, offering bedside support and encouragement. Whereas John's duty at his magazine did not permit the luxury of much spare time, Carolyn found purpose in being present, often for several hours.

This emotional complication certainly added to the pressure the couple faced. Carolyn and John were modern people, mature enough to understand the work required for a business to be successful and, in parallel, the energy it took to maintain a harmonious marriage. Things could have been tenable if it hadn't been for the media's attention.

"Not just politics as usual" was the slogan for John's beloved *George*. It would appear that this could also be the tag phrase for

---

[69] N. Services, "Anthony Radziwill, JFK Jr's Cousin," 99.

the relationship of a couple who weathered their ups and downs under the microscope of the world press.

— — —

"Heavy stuff," Tina whispered to Ruby, who had somehow joined her in the space vacated by the manuscript. Tina allowed Ruby to rest her head on her lap, tucking the manuscript under her hind legs.

Tina was used to media attention, having lived with her mother's fame all her life. Reading it like that made her feel kind of sorry for Carolyn Bessette. It was one thing to want to be in the public eye, like becoming an actress, but it was another to not aspire for or want the attention but be forced to live with it. As described in the CBK manuscript, Tina understood what Carolyn went through.

She also knew all about counseling, having been enrolled in therapy since she was five. It started when her father left her mother for another man. The story led the gossip circles for weeks on end. At that time, no one in Hollywood had come out publicly as gay, especially no one as high profile as Tina's father. Jezebel was inconsolable.

Tina hated her therapist, a middle-aged know-it-all with thick-rimmed glasses, a bowl cut, and brown clogged shoes. In those sessions, Tina sharpened her skills of rebuttal and sarcasm. When delivered correctly, retorts made her feel good. Her quick wit enhanced her artistry, and she was a full-fledged expert by her midteens.

She could shock a room with one lash of her tongue. This power was intoxicating, and her quips were often off-color or offensive.

Tina knew and didn't care. The more furious her mother became, the more successful Tina felt. It was fun.

At first, Jezebel hoped Tina would outgrow the phase. They switched therapists a dozen times as Tina entered her late teens and early twenties. Each quit one by one, like a triggered row of dominoes. Their weakness only emboldened Tina, who relished power.

Then there was the latest one. Tina was in Montana at her mother's ranch when a call came through the front gate announcing a guest. It was a younger man this time, and he was cute in a nerdy way. Tina tried her usual tricks, sensing the purpose of his visit. None worked. Then he said to her, "Tina, you are twenty-five. It's time for you to forgive your parents for the past. Grow up and move on." He then stood up and left without the pleasantry of a goodbye.

Nothing like that had ever happened to Tina before. Most service people took what she dealt them; some engaged because it meant more billable hours. This man was different. She sat for a while, digesting. Then she packed her stuff and stole away in the champagne convertible she knew was her mother's favorite.

CHAPTER 12
POPPY'S MAGAZINE SHOP

Early Monday morning, Interstate
80, Pennsylvania

It was a comedy when Guy, from the driver's seat, verbally coached the girls through the steps to reorganize Toto's rear seat. When all folded together, the combination made a bed, and the girls wanted to sleep. Stacey, Tina, and Leanna made three attempts before finally succeeding. Even still, there was a small gap where there should have been none. Exhausted, they lay on the assembly of cushions, and their giggles faded until there was silence. They were well into the second half of the yellow-lined route and would arrive in New York later that day.

The night passed slowly, and Guy combatted boredom and fatigue by sipping on Red Bull and listening to the radio's programming. The station played the hit music of the new millennium, and the current selection was "Survivor" by Destiny's Child. It ended, and the DJ segued into a funky hit, "Lady Marmalade." "Yeah, yeah, yeah," he sang along to the song until he caught Ruby staring at him in the rearview mirror.

Although it was dark, Ruby's eyes shone vividly. Guy could see she was awake, watching from her place beside Tina on the folded bed out onto the stretch of road. After a prolonged exchange through the rearview mirror, he realized he could not be sure if she looked out the windshield or at the reflection of his eyes as he scanned the road behind the van. Every time he glanced back, she was there, waiting to connect.

At some point in those early hours of the day, Guy understood that she was not simply looking out at the world going by. Ruby's gaze was undoubtedly intentional. Guy knew it sounded preposterous, but he sensed that Ruby was trying to communicate something to him. He wondered what it could be. It wasn't as though she could speak and tell him what was on her mind. Somehow, he would have to figure out the message.

Once the sun was up, "Ride wit Me" by Nelly began to play, and almost on cue, the girls woke. Everyone was hungry. The "where to stop" debate abruptly concluded with the sight of the golden arches.

"Yay, McDonald's." Stacey clapped happily.

"I hate to admit it because I don't usually eat that crap, but even I'm excited," Tina agreed as they pulled into the parking lot at the next exit.

Guy took the long way to the restaurant's tree-lined rear, telling the girls that the shade would help keep the van cool. He took a minute to pour Ruby a sip of water and offer a bowl of food, explaining that they were going inside for a short while but would return soon to finish the journey. Ruby seemed to understand, and Guy thought he had seen her nod before she jumped into the driver's seat to wait.

He followed the girls through the back door and immediately noticed how the thick aroma of the deep fryer and vanilla shakes filled the restaurant with delightfully familiar smells. Soft elevator-style music played in the background while an illuminated menu boasted images of steaming cups of coffee and perfectly styled Egg McMuffins. On the counter, a glass-enclosed box protected the latest Happy Meal toys from the clasp of engaged youngsters. Guy took in all of the fine details, marveling at the consistency of each McDonald's experience.

There was no line, and an overly friendly girl stood behind the counter smiling. She donned a blue uniform and a visor-style hat. A giant button pinned above her heart announced the Employee of the Month. In her usual way, Tina was already making small talk laced with petty insults.

"Hello and welcome to McDonald's. I'm Erin, and I'm here to take your order," Erin chirped.

"OK, Erin," Tina played along, "we are here to eat your food. This relationship will be mutually beneficial, don't you think?"

"Yes, ma'am," Erin replied happily.

"I'm a Miss, not a ma'am, Erin. That's insulting." Tina snorted.

"Sorry there, ma'am. I mean Miss." Erin stammered, blushing.

"Good, you are a quick learner," Tina said with a snide undertone.

"Thank you, Miss. How can I take your order?" Erin proceeded.

"How?" Tina could have extended the retort, and Guy was surprised when she did not. He was even more shocked when Tina ordered everyone breakfast, including extra hash browns, orange juice, and coffee. She even smiled when she asked Erin for additional ketchup packets as she passed over a gold Amex to pay.

The food was not long, and they devoured their meals once seated. Guy held his stomach, leaned back, and groaned contently.

"Guy, you remind me so much of my brother Dwight. He always groans like that after a big meal!" Stacey exclaimed.

"Is that the brother with the motorcycle?" Tina asked dryly, clearly irritated by all the talk of Stacey's brothers.

"No, that's Frank," Stacey replied. "He's the fearless one who loves to attract trouble. Dwight is my sensible brother. He likes to keep the peace."

"How many brothers do you have?" Leanna asked.

"She has four," Tina announced while holding up four fingers. "She's the baby." She continued as she collapsed her four fingers, pointed her thumb toward Stacey, and flipped it downward to indicate displeasure.

Guy noticed a wave of delight spread across Stacey's face. She positively stuck the thumbs of both hands into the air and continued using counting gestures as she explained, "Yup, four brothers. Herb, Frank, Harry, and Dwight. And then me!" Stacey started. "Herb's my wise brother. He goes to Columbia. He's a planner, very organized, and *super* dedicated to his studies. Frank's the rule breaker. He means well, but he just makes suspect choices sometimes. Harry is the adventurous one, very charismatic with a *ton* of friends, and Dwight is my dutiful brother who always keeps us in line. He's like the glue of the family."

"And Stacey says Guy is a little bit of each of them," Tina told Leanna. "A little nerdy, a little naughty, a little daring, a little steadfast. Am I missing anything, Stacey?"

Stacey changed the subject. "Guy, why Carolyn?" Stacey asked. "From what you told me about BlackJack being all no-nonsense, why are they interested in her story?"

"My boss, M, has a thing for the Kennedys, and I guess she thinks Carolyn got a bad rap when she died." Guy added, "M once worked with Jackie Kennedy, so there's that. She was M's mentor."

"Are you talking about Carolyn Bessette?" Leanna asked.

"Yes," Stacey confirmed. "Guy is editing a biography about her life."

"I once worked with her sometimes boyfriend." Leanna's voice trailed off. "Well, her ex, a model named Michael Bergin."

"Wasn't he on *Baywatch*?" Stacey asked.

"Maybe, actually, yes, I think so. But I knew Michael as an underwear model. I worked on set for the shoots," Leanna said. "The pictures were in Times Square for a long time."

"Oh wow, Leanna. I had no idea you had such a great career. Do tell!" Stacey said giddily.

"It was a long time ago," Leanna said, standing with the trays to empty their garbage.

The trio took Leanna's lead and followed her toward the exit. Guy turned back to ensure nothing was forgotten on the table just in time to witness several motorcyclists pull into the McDonald's front parking lot. One by one, they arrived until about a dozen were gathered idling outside.

How do they know we are here? he wondered.

Guy was interrupted by Erin, who tapped lightly on his shoulder. "Would you and your friends like some free sunglasses, mister?" Erin asked.

"Free?" Guy wasn't used to being offered anything for free.

"Yes, free! It's a happy day today here at McDonald's, and we want to reward our loyal customers. Here, take them!" She thrust four individually packaged sets of glasses. Guy accepted and distributed them to the girls as they exited from the back doors beside the washroom. Toto was parked conveniently at the rear of the restaurant, hidden behind the building. Guy applauded his foresight.

"Free sunglasses! Wowee! My mother always said, 'It's better to be born lucky than rich or good looking,'" commented Stacey as she slid her pair on.

"How true," Guy agreed, putting on his glasses as he started Toto with the usual rev and pop. He adjusted the rear-facing mirror and found Ruby staring back at him intently. There was no time to see what she wanted, as the threat of the Broomsticks was imminent. Guy was able to slip the group away undetected. It was better to be born lucky, and he crossed his fingers that their luck would not run out.

As they sped closer to New York, Guy loved how the scenery filtered through the new sunglasses and felt premature remorse when he eventually would lose them. The world exuded brilliance from behind their tinted lenses. Everything held an unmistakable sublime hue. Guy almost felt a leprechaun could even pop out of the woods on the side of the service road. They were that close to being in a rainbow.

Toto was driving like a dream, and their forward propulsion lulled the group into harmonious contentment. For a while, there was silence, save for the hum of Toto's wheels spinning on the road, which was soon interrupted by the suggestion of a road trip game.

"Does anyone want to play eye spy?" Stacey asked.

"Sure," Tina agreed, newly distracted by petting Ruby on her lap.

"I'm in," Leanna said while staring out the window.

"OK, you go first," Guy said to Leanna. He was driving and really couldn't play.

Leanna seemed to scan the scene outside the car for something important until Stacey correctly reminded her to select an object inside the vehicle. She made a valid point that the item needed to be available to the others who were guessing. Anything out of the van would be in the distance if missed.

Leanna decided on her clue and announced, "I spy something that starts with the letter *B*."

"Ruby's eyes," Guy answered, ending the game after only a second. It was unfair since he wasn't even supposed to be playing.

Through the rearview mirror, Guy observed Ruby's reaction to his answer. When he looked back, she stayed in the same position on Tina's lap, gazing intently at him as though in a trance. *Why is she*

178   ALLISON LANG COOK

staring that way? he wondered as he alternated between the road up ahead and Ruby through the rearview mirror. This back and forth continued until he noticed something in the distance that was equally distracting.

What's that building? He was curious. Oddly, the instant he noticed the place, Ruby released her intense eye lock with Guy, refocusing on what he saw ahead. The next second, she looked back at Guy in the mirror and reconnected her fierce gaze. Then, back at the place ahead, then back to Guy. *She wants me to stop,* Guy thought as he pumped Toto's brakes to pull off the road.

"I spy a scary-ass creepy house," Tina said, Stacey's eyes widening as they pulled off the road into the circular driveway of the mysterious structure.

"We're stopping here?" Stacey asked.

Behind a low hedge, a building about the size of a barn stood to the right. It was painted dark green and had a shiny-red metal roof. There were no windows to see inside, only a lone large door. Attached to the door was a sign, but Guy couldn't see what it said as the typeface was too small to read at that distance. He needed to get closer.

"I spy a scary-ass creepy house," Tina repeated slowly.

"Where are we, Guy?" Stacey asked.

"That we are about to find out." Guy parked Toto in front of the building. He wanted to go inside, but he wasn't sure why. When Ruby refocused her stare toward the entrance, Guy assumed she wanted him to investigate.

"Trust me," Guy said, ensuring the girls.

"Trust you! Well, let me tell you something, Guy. I, for one, would never have boarded a plane on a dark night, especially one piloted by an amateur aviation apprentice recovering from a broken foot. Carolyn trusted her husband that night. Look where it got her." Stacey huffed.

Tina snatched Guy's *Vanity Fair* from Stacey's hands and gave it to Guy. "Stacey, you're getting way too involved in the story," she said curtly.

Guy had no idea that Stacey had the *Vanity Fair*. He was engrossed in Ruby and their strange attraction to the green building with the crimson roof. He picked up the publication and set it on Toto's dashboard.

"Let's just go inside." Guy turned off Toto's engine. He exited the van and walked up to the bottom of the stairs leading to the door, where he finally could make out the words on the sign. It was rusty around the edges, and red letters sprang from a floral background.

"Poppy's Magazine Shop," he read aloud.

"Guy, did you not hear us? Tina and Leanna both agree this place is a bad idea," Stacey said as she opened the back door, allowing Ruby to hop out. Guy watched as Ruby wandered away to the side of the building and sniffed the air until she found a patch of grass in the sun. She lay down, stretching long, and looked up at Guy as if to say, go on inside, and I'll wait out here.

"Guy …" Stacey cautioned as she poured a water bottle into Ruby's bowl. She opened the waxy wrapper of a leftover McMuffin and placed it in front of Ruby.

He interrupted her midsentence, saying, "I'm going in with or without you."

"Oh, Guy, you sound like such a renegade. That's a lot of naughty!" Tina cooed from the backseat as she swung her legs out the van door, "OK, I'll play. I'm always up for an adventure."

"Yeah, now you're a lot like my brother Frank. Bad news," Stacey muttered as she petted Ruby's head.

Taking Tina's lead, Leanna met Guy at the base of the steps. Shrugging her shoulders, Stacey reluctantly joined along, grumbling that a magazine shop in the middle of nowhere was hardly reasonable business practice for whoever the owners were. Further, the stop seemed to have little else to supplement income. "There is no gas pump, no restaurant, and no motel," Stacey noted as Guy approached the door.

The girls trailed Guy up the steps, and together, they proceeded through the entry of Poppy's Magazine Shop.

Inside was dark; it took a moment or two before they could adjust their eyes and survey the building's contents. The store was, as advertised, an emporium for weekly and monthly glossy publications. As far as they could see, racks of magazines were packed full. At least six long metal shelving units spanned the room's width, with the top of each aisle marked with the letters *A–C*, *D–G*, and *H–Mc*, in library style. Guy swore he had never seen so much printed material in all his life.

"Wow." Guy began to laugh, awed.

At that moment, a woman with an enormous bosom came rushing into the foreground of the shop. Guy's first thought was to wonder how the woman kept upright as the weight of her chest appeared more than what he would have called substantial. He forgave himself for staring. He had never seen anything quite as monstrous in proportion to a woman's regular body.

She jiggled over to where the four of them stood and invited them to look around in a loud voice that filled the shop. "I'm Poppy. I'm the owner. Please, be my guests," she gushed as she huffed to catch her breath. "I believe we have most issues ever printed and several duplicates in my other storage out back. Some are not for sale, but most are. But I must warn you to be careful. People become so engrossed in these materials that they lose hours from their journey."

"Thank you but we're just passing through. We won't be long," Stacey announced to the woman.

"That's what they all say," she said wryly. "Well, enjoy! I'll be in the back. Let me know if you need anything," she responded before disappearing into the rear of the shop.

Guy took a moment to survey the situation, unsure where to begin. The room carried the musk of old paper and ink, and he closed his eyes, taking in a nose full of the unique scent. It certainly did not smell boring. Beside him, Tina selected a magazine covered in a blanket of dust. She lifted it to the level of his face and blew a stream off its cover. The filth rose as a thick cloud until it dissipated past Guy, over the rack, and into the neighboring aisle.

Guy felt a tingle building from a place high up in his nostrils. He tried unsuccessfully to suppress the urge. *Achoo!* His sneeze reverberated as if in an echo chamber around the space. In that instant of release, an idea awoke like a light bulb in his head. It was so profound that he wondered how he had never thought of it. A

ALLISON LANG COOK

compounding series of thoughts began to flow, leading Guy to the ultimate conclusion. He had a workaround solution for the CBK project.

"Bless you," he heard Stacey say from the next aisle.

The three girls scattered to various points around the store, exploring. Guy had yet to move away from the front door, the site of his sneeze, and the idea that would change everything. He spent a few moments formulating a plan.

While stories based on speculative information were considered a cardinal sin at BlackJack, quoting other sources on such stories already in print could not fall under this category. It was like a loophole.

If he curated a collection of as many already printed media articles featuring the late Carolyn Bessette Kennedy as possible, they could augment the CBK text. Published articles, even from smutty sources, were reference materials, and Guy saw reason to include them as long as they were correctly cited. He was confident that his concept would not only pass BlackJack's standards but would undoubtedly thrill M, propelling his career in a new direction.

He walked toward the far section of the middle aisle marked *Mc–P* and selected an issue of *People*. He searched for the date. From what he already knew, the publications of prime importance would be in late September 1996, around the wedding, and early August 1999, after their deaths.

The first issue he pulled from the *People* stack was dated January 18, 1982. On the cover was a picture of Brooke Shields getting a shoulder ride from designer Calvin Klein. The header read, "Brooke & Calvin. Her bottoms-up commercial made Klein the best-known name in U.S. fashion." The irony of that find was apparent to Guy, who took the discovery as a sign that he was onto something. He guessed the space required for a decade, assuming six inches per year, paced it out, and went to the end of the aisle to search through the racks.

He found his desired time frame quickly. It covered nearly the entire end portion, with issues stacked by year. Soon, he had the "Well Done!" wedding issue and August 2, 1999's "Charmed Life, Tragic Death." He tossed them to the floor, the start of what he hoped would become a giant tower.

A surprise find came with the discovery of a newer magazine, July 24, 2000's "JFK Jr. & Carolyn, Scenes from a Marriage." After thumbing through one hundred pages, he found the article "To Have and to Hold" and scanned it, notably retaining its highlighted points.

> "When everybody is watching you, every problem is magnified," says Kennedy biographer Laurence Leamer of the couple (in '98). "Of course they were having problems. Who doesn't?"[70]

> John loved her desperately. He really worshipped the ground she walked on. She was a creature with a lot of "weather," and you had to be ready to ride the storm. John loved it that way.[71]

> Contrary to the ice-queen image that dogged her throughout her short marriage, friends paint Bessette as a warm person with a wicked sense of

---

[70] Smolowe, "To Have and to Hold," 100–109.
[71] Smolowe, "To Have and to Hold," 100–109.

humor. "She could make fun of herself," says (Lynn) Teroso. "Once when a magazine put her on the cover and called her a 'Style Icon', Carolyn called me and joked, 'Six months I was nobody, and now I'm a style icon!'"[72]

Whenever there were downtimes, you could rely on Carolyn.[73]

Close friends dispute any talk of divorce—as does Raoul Felder, the high-price divorce lawyer, who flatly denies a newspaper report that he was approached by Carolyn. Similarly, few close to her believe she was wary of flying with Kennedy. "She wouldn't have invited her friends [to fly with John] if she didn't think it was safe."[74]

"For some reason, there's this desire to constantly demean them," says a friend, "I don't know why. Theirs was a beautiful love affair."[75]

Guy was soon seated cross-legged on the floor, engrossed. Page after page told him little new, yet it cemented his project as being of viable interest to others. He found images of Carolyn with celebrities and political icons and many photographs of her with John. There was something about seeing her life that way, accompanied by pictures and snippets of detail, such as dates, places, and times, that genuinely brought her story to life.

---

[72] Smolowe, "To Have and to Hold," 100–109.
[73] Smolowe, "To Have and to Hold," 100–109.
[74] Smolowe, "To Have and to Hold," 100–109.
[75] Smolowe, "To Have and to Hold," 100–109.

Guy knew he was on to something and worked uninterrupted to find more. After exhausting the *People* section, he tucked the six magazines about Carolyn under his arm. The *OK!* magazine section yielded two issues; he found an additional five in the *US Weekly* area. By then, Guy was carrying thirteen Carolyn specials and was feeling motivated.

Around a final corner, he discovered the supermarket tabloid zone and ventured into the realm of extreme gossip: *Globe, Enquirer,* and *Star.* It was the kind of world that Guy rarely visited. Sure, he scanned the headlines relating to Michael Jackson in grocery lines, but he never purchased or read them.

First, he found the *Globe* tabloid's October 15, 1996, issue. Published only three weeks after their marriage, it boasted the alluring title of the top twenty-five things no one knew about Carolyn.

She colored her hair every three weeks to avoid the shock of roots, loved to drink white wine (#20), and hated insincerity. Her favorite ice cream was maple walnut (#11), and she had a cat named Ruby. When she worked at Club *29* in Boston in the spring of 1987, she was known to play *Let's Go* by Wang Chung and *Funky Town* by Pseudo Echo on the jukebox (#5). As a teen, she loved cork-soled sandals and rooted for *Babe* to win the 1996 Oscar. She was five foot ten and wore a size six dress (#7). She turned down several marriage proposals from Saudi princes.[76]

In these magazines, there were a plethora of pictures. Guy noticed that the images seemed grainy and repeated over the various media. It occurred to him that some seemed to have been obtained without consent. Unlike the regular weekly glossies, the tabloid headlines

---

[76] Staff, "25 Things You Didn't Know about Carolyn Bessette," 36.

were cruel and accusatory. Issue after issue dealt with rumors of pregnancy, miscarriage, drug abuse, and marital woes.

JFK Jr.'s SECRET: BRIDE IS 9 WEEKS PREGNANT[77]

JFK JR BABY HEARTACHE,
New blow for rocky marriage as Carolyn loses baby.[78]

WIFE CATCHES JFK WITH EX-LOVE DARYL,
Marriage Hits Crisis! John F. Kennedy Jr.'s wife Carolyn caught him red-handed with his ex-lover Daryl Hannah, exploded in anger and dealt the biggest blow yet to their short, tumultuous marriage. And furious Carolyn retaliated by giving her hubby a taste of his own medicine. The blonde beauty was spotted out with a mystery man.[79]

JFK JR. HEARTBREAK: BRIDE HATES BEING A KENNEDY,
Depressed Carolyn is losing weight, goes on crying jags & is afraid to go out in public. Dispirited Carolyn is a shadow of her lively former self. "I'm trying my best to change, but it's taking a toll on me," she told a pal.[80]

Guy tossed them atop his growing pile until an article caught his eye, causing him to stop and read.

JFK's BRIDE IS A TRAGIC ANOREXIC!

---

[77] Staff, "JFK Jr.'s Secret: Bride Is 9 Weeks Pregnant," 3.
[78] Charlton, "JFK Jr Baby Heartache," 29.
[79] Solomon, "Wife Catches JFK with Ex-Love Daryl," 4–5.
[80] Staff, "JFK JR. Heartbreak: Bride Hated Being a Kennedy," 8.

> Gaunt, haggard Carolyn refuses to eat anything but salads and veggies, say pals, and her weight has plunged to 110 pounds.[81]

The article described how the pressures of her new public life were taking their toll on Carolyn, forcing her into a strict diet where she ate very little. Her starving body could no longer complete basic day-to-day tasks and was wasting away. Everyone was frantically worried and trying to help.

As Guy read the article, something puzzling entered his consciousness: he had never seen Ruby eat.

They had offered Ruby food. He tallied the count: the bacon in the Styrofoam container from Glinda, the dog food from the gas station, Cheetos from Stacey, and leftover hash browns from Tina. But the dog had snubbed them all.

"Guys, can a dog be anorexic?" Guy asked aloud.

"Are you conscious, Guy? Cause you're acting like a bozo," Tina said from behind a row of magazines.

"Is that about Carolyn?" Stacey snuck up behind him and took the *Globe* from his grasp.

"She sure was skinny," commented Leanna, who wandered toward Guy from the end of the aisle.

Tina crept over to see. "Ah. She's the *thinspiration*," she offered with a sorry shake of her head.

"What does that mean?" Stacey wondered.

---

[81] Staff, "JFK's Bride Is a Tragic Anorexic," 3.

"The inspiration for people to diet. You know, magazines do it all the time. All the stars starve for days before award shows and then they appear on the covers wearing whatever designer, making the rest of us feel bad about ourselves." Tina was so accustomed to this behavior that she was surprised to witness Stacey and Guy's expressions of disbelief.

"Wow, you know so much, Tina." Stacey seemed sad as she turned back and rooted through shelves.

"But Ruby doesn't eat," Guy reminded her. "Ever," he added firmly to make a point.

"She probably eats her shit, Guy. She's a dog," Tina said.

Leanna went closer to Guy and said, "Guy, I'm certain that Ruby is not anorexic. I used to work with a lot of people who were that way. She's probably just not used to being on the road. She probably feels uptight or worried or something. She'll be fine, I think."

"Thanks, Leanna." Guy felt somewhat comforted.

"Um, Tina, Guy, Leanna, do you feel that? It's freezing in here!" Stacey suddenly cried.

"*Brrrr*, you're right." Leanna chattered, prompting Guy to offer his arm around her shoulders. She accepted and tilted her head comfortably on his shoulder. They stayed like that for a minute until Poppy's sudden return.

"Sorry about that. Just a little house trick," Poppy exclaimed as she jiggled back into the room. "I turn on the old A/C whenever folks like you stay past their prime. I warned that you may let the day slip away."

"It's already one thirty!" Stacey exclaimed as she peeked at Guy's watch.

"Just why I thought 'twas time to snap you off. After all, as a good song once wisely sang, 'All you touch and all you see is all your life will ever be.' I suspect that you folks have more living to do than what's on offer here." Poppy explained.

Leanna bent down and helped gather the magazines on the floor. Guy's new plan yielded a grand pile, almost three inches tall. They split the stack into two and proceeded up to the register.

"My stars!" Poppy exclaimed when she saw Guy's accumulated volumes. "That's quite the bundle."

"Thanks, I'll take them all," Guy confirmed, pulling out his wallet to pay.

Tina bought something too and then she and Leanna left the shop. They held the door for Guy, who went to find Ruby. He found her sitting on the passenger side of the van, seemingly content even though the group had left her alone for several hours. She hopped down and sniffed at Guy's findings, trailing him to the van's rear, where she sat and watched as he arranged the stack of magazines amid Tina's bags.

Stacey stayed to pay last, hiding her purchase from the others until she was sure they were gone from the shop.

"Ooh," Poppy cooed when she saw the source of Stacey's secrecy. "He's a special one. I've seen him on Maury Povich. He's quite the sensation."

"Yeah, I find his studies fascinating. We heard his interview on the radio the other night. He's so smart. I read his book. It was very, um, enlightening," Stacey said.

"That'll be ten seventy-five," Poppy said. After which she added, "These are newer publications, so they cost a little more."

Stacey did not seem bothered as she handed the woman the exact change from the pocket of her jean skirt. Poppy scooped the payment from the counter, depositing the money into her cash register while counting aloud. "That's five and ten and twenty-five, fifty, seventy-five. And he's yours!" She slid the magazine into a thin paper bag and handed the package to Stacey.

Poppy ushered Stacey toward the door and opened it. "Bye now," Poppy called out, waving to the group. "Safe travels to you!"

"Wait a minute," Stacey suddenly said. "Tina has a camera. Would you take a picture of us, Poppy?"

"Why, of course!" she exclaimed, delighted to linger a little longer with the customers. "*Ooh,*" she squealed once she saw Ruby. "I didn't know you were traveling with such a beauty!"

Tina handed Poppy the camera while they lined up in front of Toto. Guy stood in the middle as the tallest, with Tina and Leanna on his right, and Stacy quickly joined him on his left. Guy called Ruby over from beside Poppy, and she came obediently and sat at his feet.

"Should I use flash?" Poppy wondered since a thick cloud cover was setting in.

"It's on top," Tina said. "It's the button with the lightning bolt."

"Say, 'Whiskey!'" Poppy sang.

"Whiskey," they cried out in unison.

Poppy snapped the camera, triggering the flash, which went off in a burst. At that moment, Ruby jumped, clearly startled by the unexpected occurrence. She looked at Guy, eyes wide in alarm, darted back to the van and hopped up to the front seat. Guy noticed that she curled into a very tight ball and tucked her head underneath her paws as though attempting to appear invisible.

Poppy passed the camera back to Stacey and bid them a final goodbye while Tina followed Ruby to Toto's front seat and proceeded to pet the trembling dog lightly. "Good girl," Tina said soothingly.

CHAPTER 13
ENDINGS AND BEGINNINGS

Monday afternoon, Interstate 80
through Pennsylvania

"What did you buy, Tina?" Guy asked as he started Toto's engine in the usual way.

"It's nothing. It's just an old *TV Guide* with my mom on the cover," Tina said. She was buckled into the passenger seat, sitting on her side to accommodate sharing it with Ruby.

"Here, let us see." Stacey squealed for permission from the backseat. "I want to see what your mom looks like."

"No. I'm going to destroy it." Tina spoke in a calm, flat tone.

"Tina, why?" Leanna leaned up and asked.

"Why? Because she looks appalling. I don't want anyone to remember her like that," Tina explained. "This is from when my mom did a stint working on a prime-time soap opera. I don't think she would appreciate knowing that this magazine still exists. I mean, it's a *TV Guide*!"

"Well, let us see it before you torch it," Guy said.

"Yes, come on," the girls pleaded.

Tina rolled down her window, causing a gust of air to howl through Toto's interior. She hesitantly lifted the magazine close to the open gap as though she were going to toss it from the van.

"Tina, you can't throw it out the window. There are fines for littering!" Stacey protested.

"Who is going to give me a ticket out here?" Tina challenged.

"Hold tight," Guy suddenly cried, swerving the van to turn abruptly down an industrial side road. In the rearview mirror, he had caught the glint of a motorcycle headlight amid the darkest storm cloud and detected a cluster approaching from ahead in the distance. They faced a dreaded ambush from both sides if he stayed on the road. Guy brought Toto to a stop next to a truck yard and flicked off the headlights.

"Is it them again?" Stacey asked.

"What, who?" Leanna asked, alarmed. "Who are *they*?"

"Don't you worry your pretty little head, Leanna. It's just a terrifying motorcycle gang. Have you heard of the Broomsticks? They want Ruby for some reason, but Guy doesn't know why." Tina filled her in on the details while nonchalantly rolling up the window.

"I know why," Stacey suddenly revealed, much to the shock of the other passengers.

"Go on, girl. Don't stop now!" Tina said.

"Guy, pass me *Vanity Fair*. It's up there on the dashboard." Guy reached up and passed the magazine to Stacey in the back seat.

Stacey flicked on the small flashlight. "I was flipping through the magazine and found this picture." She held up the magazine, shining light on it for everyone to see. Leanna took it first, passed it on to Tina, and then back to Guy in the front seat. When he received it, one glance was all it took. He understood what Stacey was saying. In a safari-inspired advertisement for St. John, there was a dog in the perfect likeness of Ruby.

"You see, I'm guessing Ruby is a dog model. Those bikers probably make a lot of money off her, and they want her back," Stacey began. "It just makes sense. I mean, why else would they want her? She's a small dog!"

"She's a Broomstick dog," Tina added, her tone implying there was something more sinister about the chase.

"What is that supposed to mean?" asked Guy.

"Really? What planet do you live on, Guy? The Broomsticks are badass. They are supposed to be worse than the Blood Angels and the Crazed Monkeys combined," Tina said, referring to two other notorious groups.

"I don't know about that," Guy answered with uncertainty.

Guy knew the twitches were mean, but he never thought they were criminals. After all the hours he spent exploring the group on their online platform, he had not made the connection to any illegal intent. His research confirmed the group as do-gooders for animals, not badass as Tina thought. When he got to New York,

Guy would look into this accusation, wondering if he had missed something in his initial SOS.

"Hey, what's this?" Leanna asked, showing Stacey a scrap piece of paper. "It fell out of the magazine when you opened it."

"What does it say?" Stacey asked curiously.

Leanna read the writing on the paper aloud.

Does your pet seem to have something to say?

Do you want to know their most profound thoughts?

Get answers from world-renowned spiritual and animal communicator Dr. Greg Osmond. E-MAIL ME WITH YOUR QUESTIONS.

Or visit me in my Marvel Studio in New York, New York.

Doc Aus, the Australian veterinarian.

"Let me see that." Stacey held her hand out to Leanna, who placed the paper in Stacey's palm. After a glance, she held the paper up to show Guy and asked, "Guy, why do you have this?

It took him a second to figure out what Stacey was asking. He was still in conflict about the Broomsticks. He looked at the slip she dangled in his peripheral view. "Oh, Glinda, a waitress at the diner suggested I take it."

"She thought you should go to Doc Aus?" Stacey asked.

"No." He laughed. "She tore it out for me because of what was on the other side," Guy recalled Glinda's words. *Here. Take it with you to remind yourself when things get a little unclear. You may be feeling lost and misplaced for now, but there is no need to worry; your journey will be enlightening, I'm quite sure.*

"It was the daily quote a few days ago," Guy explained.

Stacey flipped over the paper and read the quotation aloud. "It's lyrics from a Pink Floyd song. Weird because didn't Poppy recite something like that back at the shop?" Stacey wondered aloud as she shrugged and tucked the paper into her pocket.

"I think so," Leanna agreed.

"You're pretty astute for connecting those dots," Guy told Stacey.

"Stacey, our favorite dot connector," Tina said snidely.

"Have you guys ever watched the movie *The Wizard of Oz* to the soundtrack of Pink Floyd's 'Darkside of the Moon'?" Stacey asked, ignoring Tina.

"Seriously?" Tina said, surprised. She added, "Miss I-don't-smoke-pot, that seems like a pretty stoner thing to do."

Stacey turned to Leanna, who confirmed that she had heard the rumor about the sync to the film but had never tried it.

"I know. It's true," Stacey agreed. "You start playing the album at the third roar of the lion. That is the third roar of the MGM lion in the opening credits, not the cowardly lion. You must start it right at the movie's beginning, or it will not work. Right, Leanna?"

"As far as I know," Leanna said.

"I thought that was all urban legend, and the band denied writing the music specifically for the film." Guy had read something about it.

"Of course they are going to deny it!" Tina exclaimed. "It's Pink Floyd!"

"Do you think we should get going, Guy?" Leanna asked. "It looks like it's going to start pouring any minute."

"I guess we should." Guy surveyed the sky.

"Looks like the coast is clear. And besides," Stacey said, "I'm guessing motorcycles don't like riding in the rain!"

"Let's hope you are right," Guy said as he reversed Toto and turned out of the industrial parking lot. He had enough of traveling on the side routes and decided to find the highway. If Stacey were right, the Broomsticks would be taking shelter from the rain anyway.

"Can we please see the picture of your mother?" Leanna leaned forward to Tina and asked with a whisper. "I promise not to laugh if you are worried about that."

"Fine, I guess." Tina groaned and reluctantly handed back the brown paper bag.

Leanna pulled out the publication, switched on the small flashlight Stacey handed her, and surveyed the 1983 *TV Guide* cover. She smiled and reached out to squeeze Tina's shoulder. "She is beautiful," Leanna said aloud.

Leanna passed the *TV Guide* to Stacey. "So this is your mom!" Stacey exclaimed. "Wow, your mom was sure the Cher of her day!"

"What are you talking about?" Tina protested. "Cher is the same age as my mother."

"Different hair and eyes," Stacey commented, noting the feathered bangs and heavy makeup. "But you look just like her."

"Who is this?" Leanna pointed to a man in a picture alongside Tina's mother. Tina glanced at the photo. The man was her father. "That's who I'm going to see," she announced while holding Ruby tightly.

"We should be there by eight tonight," Guy announced as he found the interstate entrance and accelerated onto the highway.

– – –

Despite the soothing hum of the van against the pavement and the soft sounds of the Eagles on the radio, Leanna could not quiet the feeling of nervous irritation. As they crept closer to New York, blasts of unwanted, repressed memories invaded her consciousness, making settling it all the more difficult. She fidgeted by crossing and recrossing her ankles underneath the back of the front passenger seat, which she could tell was annoying Tina.

Leanna inhaled a full breath through her nostrils and closed her eyes. It was time to reflect on the past. The first thought that came to mind was time spent in a gloomy church basement in group therapy. After her meltdown, they mandated that she take anger management classes. Although it was embarrassing and what she considered unjustified, it saved her from receiving a more severe punishment.

She pictured the other members of her group seated in a circle in uncomfortably designed plastic chairs. They had all seemed surprised that she was there, that a thin woman would require counseling to harness the power of her emotional strength. They had no idea about the infamous Del Rorro temper.

Yeah, yeah, yeah, Leanna had thought while nodding at the counselor as if to agree that she needed to listen to the lesson. The counselor was preaching about cognitive reframing, which meant they needed to control their emotions before acting. She advised everyone to practice what she called "meditation," which may involve visualization or actual objects. She made everyone circle the room and share their meditation and their plans for coping.

Leanna wasn't stupid, and she knew that she at least had to appear interested. She formed the concept of a good meditation, a bracelet from her Nonna. She smiled and shared it all with the others through clenched teeth, feeling nothing but hatred for her predicament. After they went around the room and had their chance to share, the group clapped for her, and when it was their turn, Leanna put her hands together for each of the others.

After passing the attendance-based course requirement, she rang up her boss at the talent agency to see what was happening work-wise. He didn't answer and never returned any of her voicemails. Some days, she even wondered if she had called him at all. It was like she didn't exist, a ghost. Not ready to give up, she tried again and again.

After a week of calling without a response, she went to the agency's main office on Fifth Avenue. She looked polished in a pencil skirt and matching blouse, had her hair tamed into a top bun, and wore heels. When she arrived at the front desk and asked for her boss, the man who gave her a break, and to whom she had brought so much success over the years, Leanna was shocked to discover they wanted her escorted out by security.

Expulsion from her former workplace caused pulses of fluid anger to overtake her slight being. Leanna yelled, swore, and threw her purse and shoes against the building's revolving door. It was a proper meltdown. Unbeknownst to her, a camera crew from *Inside Edition* was parked outside the building, hoping to get pictures of talent as they met with their agents. Leanna's rant was captured on camera, and just like that, *boom!* She was over.

She only had the stomach to watch the video once. In it, her neat hair became an unruly mess of wild curls. Somehow, the top button of her blouse came undone, revealing the slight hint of her bra, and the garment became untucked from the band of her skirt. Her face reddened as she hollered while removing her shoes. Then, driven by the strength of her shoulders, Leanna angrily tossed the heels one by one, followed by her purse. When she realized what she had done, she grabbed her hair at the site of each temple and screamed before stomping toward the building to collect her items.

If she had been anyone of importance, her video would have made bigger headlines. Instead, it was just a personal humiliation that, in tandem with a professional snub, meant the end for Leanna in New York City. She packed her bags and went home, increasingly resentful about how her exile had evolved.

After hearing from friends on a catch-up call several months later, she was incensed to learn she was being called a bully. She indeed developed thick skin working with Kate, Christy, Linda, and Cindy. She had needed to. Handlers had to set boundaries since everyone always wanted something from the supermodels. She did a good job. She participated in and observed many yelling matches because part of working was pushing back, especially during the high-stress environment of a runway show.

Leanna was known for speaking up in these situations. She had gained the label because of her tight friendship with the top six, some of whom had troublesome reputations. As they became more powerful, they demanded more money, shorter working hours, exotic shoot locations, specific photographers, and the covers of only the best publications. Eventually, the top editors took notice and felt the need to quell their dominance. It only took Renee Zellweger, a petite actress, to be featured on the cover of *Vogue* for the supermodel's reign to waiver.

By then, Leanna was working with a new crop of hungry younger models whom all sought the fame and fortune enjoyed by their maturing predecessors. The talent agency paired Leanna with a gorgeous French ingenue, Xanthe. At first, the relationship seemed promising. Xanthe booked important shows and gradually became a muse for a critical photographer who booked her for several Prada and Longchamp campaigns. Leanna held her hand throughout the process.

And then Xanthe called Leanna at three in the morning, crying and borderline hysterical. Leanna knew where she was staying: a luxury midtown hotel since she had arranged for the room on her corporate account. When Leanna arrived, she found Xanthe's suite in disarray. At the time, it was a thing to trash hotel rooms. The most notable example was Johnny Depp, who caused ten thousand dollars of damage to the twelve-hundred-per-night presidential suite at the Mark Hotel. Xanthe's wannabe musician boyfriend, a French national named Pierre, was the culprit of this show of destruction.

Xanthe was sobbing and shaking, and Leanna suspected they both had taken various drugs and alcohol. Drunk, high, and scared, Xanthe made the plea. She begged Leanna to take the blame for destroying the room. Pierre was working in the country illegally, and Xanthe would lose her new contract as the face of Dior if the scandal became public. She would pay for the damage, but Leanna had to do her this favor.

Against her better judgment, Leanna ferried the couple down the stairs to the street, loaded them into a cab, and went upstairs to make the call. She booked the room in her name as Xanthe's handler, so no one doubted she caused the chaos. To her shock, she was charged with a crime and forced to appear in court. Lawyers recommended a guilty plea, leading to a fine and anger-management sessions. Recalling the event made Leanna's blood boil with resentment. Doing her job cost her a career, and that lone fact made her so angry that she felt she would explode.

Once back home, her resentment festered, and she spun wildly out of control. When someone made her mad, she reacted with that hot, De Rorro, untamed aggression. That was why Leanna practically went for the throat when Suzanne Smyth said what she had the other day.

Nonna knew that Leanna was not expressing her true self and would constantly remind her granddaughter not to take the bait so readily offered by the jealous contemporaries of her hometown. She was better than that, Nonna would remind her. But whatever it was, it was wired into her DNA. Leanna could not avoid succumbing to the beast of anger that dwelled within.

Having dealt with a similarly passionate husband and son, Nonna was patient with Leanna. She always spoke calmly in the face of shouting and remained expressionless in explosive frustration. "Leanna, calm yourself. There is no need for this anger." Leanna heard Nonna but found it impossible to switch off. The lessons she reluctantly learned in group therapy, like cognitive reframing, became essential.

Leanna opened her eyes and noticed Guy's manuscript open on the folded-down bed between her and Stacey. Stacey had abandoned her place in the text and had fallen asleep, snoring softly. Leanna needed the distraction, so she picked it up and decided it could be a meditation to read one chapter.

– – –

CBK: 5

Friday, July 16, 1999, was a typically warm New York summer day that drew into a sultry night. The day's highs topped 95 degrees, forcing many New Yorkers inside with their air conditioning on high. John, Lauren, and Carolyn went about their last moments from opposite sides of the city.

Earlier that afternoon, John had checked out from his suite at the Stanhope Park Hyatt Hotel, a pricey Fifth Avenue establishment close to where he grew up. It seemed a logical choice as *George* maintained a corporate account. He commented jovially to the desk clerk that his wife had thrown him out of their Tribeca loft. Of course, a knowing wink ensured the joke was not fact.

Many would forever speculate about the reasons for the couple's separate sleeping arrangements. On the one hand, rumors of an impending split gathered strength. Carolyn was at a breaking point from intense curiosity about her life. She felt stalked in the streets, and there were moments she feared for her safety. She was frustrated that John seemed flippant to her concerns. He was used to the public's prying eye, but it was all new to her. It was a constant theme in their couple's therapy sessions.

Others suggested that Carolyn wanted to give her husband the space to sort out *George*'s woes. The magazine's survival was reaching a critical stage, and John had to make every effort toward its success. If he had the time and space to focus entirely on the business, he would eventually return home as a more attentive partner. It made sense for him to stay uptown, closer to *George*'s offices, and devote 100 percent of his attention at this critical time.

There were other reasons why moving into the Stanhope made sense. John's broken ankle was in a foot cast, making his preferred bike transportation impossible. Also, work stress made him an insomniac, and Carolyn preferred that he paced elsewhere in the early-morning hours. Regardless of the reason, the couple was living apart, which was concerning to friends and family.

Earlier that week, Carolyn and her sister Lauren Gale Bessette, a thirty-four-year-old investment broker at Morgan Stanley Dean Whitter & Co., joined John for lunch at the Stanhope's Café M. The trio dined on sea bass and salmon while discussing their upcoming weekend. Carolyn and John were due to attend the wedding of his cousin Rory Kennedy at the compound in Hyannis Port. Lauren would accompany the couple only as far as Martha's Vineyard, where she would meet up with friends.

Lauren was on the fast track at Morgan Stanley. She was fluent in Mandarin, having spent four years working in the Hong Kong office, and held an MBA from the University of Pennsylvania's Wharton School of Business. Colleagues described her as brilliant and astute, with many wanting her on their team when making deals.[82]

---

[82] Kelly, "Friends Remember Lauren Bessette, Who Was Thriving at Morgan Stanley."

Lauren transferred to New York in 1998 and earned a promotion from vice president to principal, a step below the title of managing director.[83] She purchased a million-dollar loft on White Street in Tribeca, close to where her sister lived with John.[84] She and Carolyn shared a love of fashion, especially Prada, and many noted that Lauren was just as stylish as her more-famous sister. The two would often meet for brunch on the weekend or drinks after work and maintained a tight bond.

Early into lunch at the Stanhope, there was an evident strain, and observers noted the severe tone of the table's conversation. Eavesdroppers suggested that Carolyn was on the fence about attending the wedding with John. She did not want to fly with her husband in his Piper Saratoga, and she was significantly nervous about his ability to fly after his recent foot injury.

In May, John broke his ankle. It took six weeks to heal. The cast would come off on Thursday, the day before they would fly. Carolyn felt it was too soon, but John was eager to get back into the skies and enlisted Lauren to help persuade her sister.

Lauren, rumored to be dating John's cousin Robert (Bobby) Shriver,[85] wanted to mend her sister's fragile marriage, which was strained by tremendous public scrutiny and personal stress. At a moment of high tension at lunch, Lauren joined hands with John and Carolyn and asked them to grasp each other's hands to form a circle around the table. She kept the conversation light and reminded John and

[83] Kelly, "Friends Remember Lauren Bessette, Who Was Thriving at Morgan Stanley."

[84] Kelly, "Friends Remember Lauren Bessette, Who Was Thriving at Morgan Stanley."

[85] Kelly, "Friends Remember Lauren Bessette, Who Was Thriving at Morgan Stanley."

Carolyn of their love for one another and their family's love for them both. Besides, it would be fun to fly together!

On Friday, July 16, the plan was in place. At 6:00 p.m., Lauren left Morgan Stanley and walked to meet John at his *George* headquarters. She was excited about the weekend and her sister's reunion with her estranged husband. She carried a black garment bag with her business card tucked into it as a luggage tag.

Earlier that afternoon, Carolyn went shopping for an outfit for the wedding. She purchased a two-thousand-dollar, black, off-the-shoulder silk crepe cocktail dress from the fall Yves Saint Laurent Rive Gauche line by Alber Elbaz. While searching for the gown, she expressed her worries about flying that night to the Saks Fifth Avenue saleswoman, complaining that John had only just gotten his cast off the day before.

Whatever her concern may have been, Carolyn packed for the couple back at their Tribeca loft. At 6:30 p.m., she entered a black Lincoln Town Car and made the forty-five-minute journey to the Essex County Airport in New Jersey. There, she met her husband and sister, who drove together in his white Hyundai convertible.

John's flight plan had the group departing the airport at approximately 7:15 p.m. He would fly under visual flight rules, which meant he wanted to take advantage of as much daylight as possible. Given Piper's cruising speed of 180 miles per hour, he estimated they would land in Martha's Vineyard at 8:30 p.m., just before nightfall.

It would seem that time was not on their side. The two cars became seriously delayed, arriving within ten minutes of each other; John and Lauren first, and Carolyn, dressed in black pants and a black blouse, emerged from the town car second. At 8:38 p.m., twelve minutes after sundown, the tower at Essex Airport cleared John for takeoff. The tower operator would be the last to converse with him alive.

After their fate became known, there were questions about why the trio departed so late. Though Manhattan's relentless Friday-afternoon traffic was an easy scapegoat, many dismissed it as the official reason. After all, they *could* have left the city earlier, arrived at the airport before traffic set in, and placed themselves at their destination for sunset.

Some suggested that Lauren Bessette was tied up in meetings, pushing the group's departure time. However, her colleagues denied this theory, saying she spent the afternoon hanging out rather than doing official work and could not be held accountable for the delay. Others indicated that Carolyn was late arriving due to a beauty appointment. Unsubstantiated rumors were that she made a pedicurist redo her nails several times to reach a particular shade of lilac.

Whatever the cause, the responsibility inevitably lay with the plane's pilot, John Kennedy. He was a novice pilot taking off in conditions of haze that caused poor visibility. Perhaps the daredevil in him got the better of his common sense. John took the chance and lost his life, along with that of his wife and sister-in-law, shortly after 9:40 p.m.

Around eleven that Friday evening, the family was alerted by a driver who was due to pick up the couple at the nearby airport. After midnight, they grew increasingly worried about John and Carolyn. By 2:15 a.m. on Saturday, July 17, the Kennedy family notified the Coast Guard that the plane was missing[86]. As was

---

[86] Grunwald, "JFK Jr. Feared Dead in Plane Crash," A1.

protocol, the Coast Guard told the Federal Aviation Administration (FAA), who contacted other local airports to see if the small plane had landed elsewhere.

At first light for the following morning, the Coast Guard and Air Force launched a massive search-and-rescue operation. The agencies allotted two ships and twenty aircraft to survey the Atlantic Ocean between Long Island and Martha's Vineyard, over 1,500 square miles.

By 8:06 a.m., NBC broke the news: JFK Jr.'s plane was missing and feared lost.[87]

The world woke that early July day to the news that Kennedy's plane was gone from the radar. Was it another Kennedy tragedy? The story dominated early Saturday broadcast across the major networks. Scenes of helicopters and boats scouring the waters of the northeast coast played while news anchors tried their best to remain optimistic. Instantly, the focus was on John, the son of a beloved former president and the prince of a nation.

Households across America clung to the hope that John, Carolyn, and Lauren had survived an assumed crash. Perhaps the plane lost course, went off the radar, and they had yet to connect? But as time ticked by without confirmation of life, the focus turned to what was the most obvious outcome.

As per the *Washington Post*: "There is always hope," Coast Guard Lieutenant Gary Jones said yesterday. "But unfortunately, when you find certain pieces of evidence, you have to be prepared for anything."[88]

---

[87] W. P. Staff, *The Life of JFK Jr: Crash and Search.*
[88] Grunwald, "JFK Jr. Feared Dead in Plane Crash," A1.

Soon, bites of unconfirmed yet ominous information trickled across the airwaves. Debris from the plane, including the fuselage and luggage bearing Lauren Bessette's identification tags, was spotted. Another had a prescription bottle belonging to Carolyn wash ashore. The epicenter of these discoveries was Philibin Beach in the town of Aquinnah, a part of Martha's Vineyard popularly known as Gay Head.

What started as a mystery turned grim. Around 2:00 p.m., Philibin Beach was closed, and the search narrowed to 550 square miles nearby. Later that evening, the National Oceanic and Atmospheric Association deployed the *Rude*. This research vessel used multibeam and side-scan sonar to scour the ocean floor for the missing plane.[89]

The Coast Guard cutter *Willow* arrived at the search area early Sunday morning. The group had been missing for thirty-six hours. Coast Guard HH-60J helicopters and the Air Force HC-130 flying command post joined the expanded search. Around noon, a second Piper headrest, similar to the one found on Philibin Beach, was discovered three miles to the south. Then, at 2:00 p.m., a cluster of plane cockpit insulation was found floating in the water.

At 4:00 p.m., an air force HC-130 detected a "ping," or electronic transmission, from an underwater transponder. Believing it was from the plane, Coast Guard Rear Admiral Richard M. Larrabee shifted the search area and sent the *Rude* to this new site. Unfortunately, the ping turned out to be a false lead.

The mission changed from search and rescue to save human life to search and recovery by 9:00 p.m. on Sunday. Conceding the slim chance of survival after more than eighteen hours in the

---

[89] Staff, "NOAA Ship *Rude* Has Wreck-Finding Expertise.

sixty-eight-degree waters off the coast, Larrabee declared this shift of focus and supported a federal investigation into the cause of the crash.

Police divers set out in three twenty-eight-foot Coast Guard boats from Menemsha Harbor in Chilmark, Martha's Vineyard. The 163-foot *Whiting*, another research vessel, and the *USS Grasp*, a navy salvage vessel, joined search efforts. The remarkable recovery combined the expertise of the Massachusetts State Police Underwater Recovery Team, the Coast Guard, the US Navy, and the National Oceanic and Atmospheric Administration (NOAA), an unprecedented set of resources for private citizens.[90]

After another agonizing thirty-six hours, the *USS Grasp* located the wreckage of the Piper Sarasota just before midnight on Tuesday, July 20, four full days after the crash. It had sunk 110 feet below the surface and lay in a mess of twisted and tangled debris spread over ten meters on the ocean floor.

The *Grasp* repositioned over the site, and at six thirty the morning of Wednesday, July 21, thirty divers collectively from the navy and the Massachusetts police entered the water. Senator Edward Kennedy, John's uncle, flew to the *Grasp* with his two sons and was briefed on the efforts to resurface the victims. Visibility was at six-to-eight feet, but the recovery team identified the bodies of John, Carolyn, and Lauren by ten thirty that morning, still strapped in their seats.[91]

Later that afternoon, the bodies of John, Carolyn, and Lauren were recovered and placed into individual sleek metal caskets. Their

---

[90] Allen, "Rescue Search in Kennedy Crash Ends; Coast Guard Tells Family There Is Little Hope," A1.

[91] Duke, "Bodies of Kennedy, Bessettes Brought to Shore," A1.

remains were returned to port and transported to the county medical examiner's office by motorcade. The coroner determined that they had all died on impact five days prior.[92]

The Bessette family issued the statement, read by family friend Grant Stichfield:

> Dr. and Mrs. Richard Freeman and William J. Bessette would like to thank the many individuals and governmental agencies that have assisted in the exhaustive search for their beloved family members.
>
> Each of these three young people, Lauren Bessette, Carolyn Bessette Kennedy, and John F. Kennedy Jr. was the embodiment of love, accomplishment, and passion for life.
>
> John and Carolyn were true soul mates and we hope to honor them in death in the simple manner in which they chose to live their lives. We take solace in the thought that together they will comfort Lauren for eternity. We are especially appreciative of the privacy and support provided us by our friends and family and community. Nothing in life is preparation for the loss of a child.[93]

At 9:00 a.m. on Thursday, July 22, seventeen family members from the Kennedy and Bessette families arrived at Woods Hole. The group boarded the cutter *Sanibel*, which took them to the *USS Briscoe*, a navy destroyer with a crew of three hundred sent up from Virginia overnight by special request of the secretary of defense. At

---

[92] W. P. Staff, *The Life of JFK Jr: Crash and Search.*
[93] Family, "Statement of Grief by Wife's Family," A20.

a place about three miles from shore, the families committed their loved ones to the sea, along with three flowered wreaths.

Meanwhile, back in Tribeca, mourners from all parts of the city placed tributes of flowers, candles, and pictures alongside the entrance to the couple's loft at 20 N. Moore St. A fan created an enormous painting of Carolyn, a replica of a published photograph of her at a charity function. It showed her luminous face, highlighted in angelic pastel strokes, and she stood prominently among the offerings.

An invitation-only memorial service was held for John, Carolyn, and Lauren on Friday, July 23, at the 126-year-old church of St. Thomas Moore on Manhattan's Upper East Side.[94] It was the same church John had attended on Sundays with his mother as a young boy. Jacqueline was a regular parishioner and offered a mass for her late husband each year on the anniversary of his death, November 22.

The structure, located only blocks from Central Park, was made from sandstone blocks imported from Nova Scotia in the Gothic Revival architectural style. It resembled traditional English churches, including an asymmetrical pinnacle at the top of the tower, and became revered among the Catholics of Manhattan.

Preparing for the memorial service on July 23 was a massive operation, complete with armed snipers, police guards, and sawhorses. Metal fences and police on foot patrol surrounded the blocks of the small stone church and restricted access to East 89th between Madison and Park. Only those on the 350-person guest list were allowed to be within this perimeter.[95]

---

[94] Pyle, "Eulogy Speaks of Unfulfilled Potential."
[95] Pyle, "Eulogy Speaks of Unfulfilled Potential."

Scores of regular New Yorkers assembled around the limited space to pay their respects to the son of their former president. They stood together, mostly dressed in casual attire, some in silence while others chatted with one another, pointing out the famous as they arrived at the church steps. Many wore sunglasses and hats since the sunny day was expected to reach a high of over 85 degrees.

Scores of media camped out along the streets, broadcasting live. Kennedy and Bessette's family members, friends, and dignitaries came by limousine, taxi, car, and some by foot. Each presented an invitation the size of an index card to the organizers to gain access to the church. The cameras captured the noteworthy attendees' arrivals as they assembled shortly after 9:00 a.m., even though the service would not commence until eleven.[96]

The invited mourners dressed mainly in black formal attire—including sitting President Clinton, his wife, Hilary, and daughter, Chelsea—made their way into the service. John's sister Caroline Schlossberg arrived by limousine with her husband, Edwin, and young family, daughters Rose and Tatiana and son Jack.[97] The media was not permitted access to the inside of St. Thomas Moore church, but the official transcript of the eulogy was released to the public after the service concluded.

In his eulogy to nephew John, Senator Edward Kennedy referred to Carolyn:

> And for a thousand days, (John) was a husband who adored the wife who became his perfect soul mate. John's father taught us all to reach for the moon and

---

[96] Duke, "Family Memorializes Another JFK," A1.
[97] Duke, "Family Memorializes Another JFK," A1.

the stars. John did that in all he did—and he found his shining star when he married Carolyn Bessette.

How often our family will think of the two of them, cuddling affectionately on a boat, surrounded by family—aunts, uncles, Caroline and Ed and their children, Rose, Tatiana, and Jack, Kennedy cousins, Radziwill cousins, Shriver cousins, Smith cousins, Lawford cousins—as we sailed Nantucket Sound.

Then we would come home, and before dinner, on the lawn where his father had played, John would lead a spirited game of touch football. And his beautiful young wife, the new pride of the Kennedys, would cheer for John's team and delight her nieces and nephews with her somersaults.

We loved Carolyn. She and her sister Lauren were young, extraordinary women of high accomplishment—and their own limitless possibilities. We mourn their loss and honor their lives.[98]

A friend and fashion-industry executive Hamilton South eulogized Carolyn. He praised her for "her graceful being, her special allure" and for being the "physical expression of an inner fact."[99] He noted that she could be a generous listener and that so often, after a lengthy conversation on the phone, she would apologize for talking so much about herself, which was untrue. Carolyn was a stylish and unique member of New York society and would be missed dearly by friends and admirers.

---

[98] E. M. Kennedy, *American Rhetoric Online Speech Bank*.
[99] Carlson, "Farewell, John."

Hip-hop band The Fugees lead singer Wyclef Jean was chosen as the soloist for the ceremony and sang the Jimmy Cliff reggae song "Many Rivers to Cross."

Strangers stood silently outside the church to pay respects to New York's golden couple: gallant John and the glamorous Carolyn. The shock of their loss brought overwhelming sadness. Cameras captured the tear-streaked faces of mourners as the service concluded and they left the church.

It was over. After an agonizing search, a heartbreaking recovery, and burial at sea, the lives of John and Carolyn Bessette were history, a footnote in time. There would be no children for the couple to share with the world. They would not grow old. Everything written about them and their achievements lived in the past tense. There would be nothing more.

As time progressed into the next century, the lens of focus on the 1990s New York fashion scene celebrated Carolyn as the face of the minimalist movement. She embodied the sleek, muted palate, the unfussed uniform of the decade. Carolyn's special allure would transcend the length of her life, and she grew even more revered in death.

The short moments of her public and private life, images captured in photographs and video clips, summarized Carolyn Jeanne Bessette Kennedy's eternal "cool" persona.

– – –

Leanna flipped off the mini flashlight and returned the manuscript to the seat beside her. She had already left New York when John and Carolyn died. For the longest time, people back home would ask her if she ever knew Carolyn and if she had worked with her. The answer was no, but the questions persisted. It always irked Leanna as she tried to put the past in the past and forget about New York.

Leanna considered that she had many past mistakes to make right, but at least she had the opportunity to make those amends. The fact that she was granted a second chance invited a shift in mindset to one of gratitude. Instead of fueling her heart with perceived injustices, she would push that anger away and permit its space to fill with other, long-buried emotions: sadness, empathy, and grief. It was finally time to return, and Leanna hoped she was ready.

Feeling much calmer, she tried to stretch her legs underneath the passenger seat and realized there was an obstruction. She bent down and discovered a shoe box without a lid. She withdrew it from under the seat and placed it on her lap. The box contained a stack of what initially appeared to be silly notes, but as she read them one by one, a familiar feeling of outrage began to build.

Your van is so slow that it has a calendar for a speedometer./ Get the hint, hippie: your hunk of junk belongs in the dump! / Note to Guy's van: you're smelting! We will escort you personally, flatten you, and return you to your original form. You are a wasted space, road hog. / Guy, your van is so stupid that its manual is written in crayon. It does not deserve to drive. / We will enjoy crushing your van into a million tiny pieces, Guy Myles. Goodbye.

CHAPTER 14

THE CITY

Monday nightfall, New York City

"Is that it? Are we there?" Stacey asked eagerly.

They arrived in time to take in the full splendor of the city against the darkened sky. After driving through a maze of winding roads congested with toll booths and commuters' noxious fumes, the million lights of New York City twinkled an impressive welcome to the foursome. Collectively, the brightness lifted upward, creating an orange dome that encapsulated Manhattan's tall buildings like a protective force.

Tina had a lot on her mind and needed the hush that fell over Toto as each passenger took a moment to appreciate the awe-inspiring sight of the city by night. She noticed Stacey's left cheek and nose pressed against Toto's left window in the backseat, fixated.

You twit, Tina thought when Stacey commented aloud: "It's amazing!"

"Oh! I can see the top of the Empire State Building," Stacey gushed with renewed energy as they neared the Holland Tunnel. "Did you know it is 1,472 feet high with 102 floors and 74 passenger elevators? Well, it is. I'm not sure where I heard it. Maybe it was from *Reader's Digest* or possibly Ms. Sutherland, my seventh-grade teacher. Hey guys, when did we learn about cities in school? I can't remember. But, boy, oh boy!"

Tina considered different scenes of how she would feel when she saw her father. She never spent much time with him except for a brief stint in the early nineties. Jezebel was devastated by the divorce and responded by moving Tina far away from New York to escape humiliation. They landed in Las Vegas, where Tina was raised in a suite at Caesar's Palace while Jezebel sang and danced in a Broadway-style show.

It was there, alongside prostitutes and bachelor party drunks, that Tina became a teenager. Jezebel worked all night and slept until four, just in time to sit and sip a slow martini while Tina ate dinner. That was their time together as a family. It lasted an hour, and when it was over, Jezebel went to her side of the suite, leaving behind an empty glass and a lingering waft of her Parisian perfume.

Tina wanted to know her father, but her mother made that impossible. Even mentioning his name made her huff. Friends or handlers of her mother would hush Tina, ferrying her off into another space so Jezebel could rant and rave about her ex. "I am an award-winning actress!" Tina once heard her say. "Why doesn't he want me?"

As time passed, Tina got used to being primarily in Jezebel's custody. She stopped mentioning her father's name, and things settled into a calmer coexistence. Jezebel ensured that her daughter received everything her heart desired in exchange for the lack of a father. Jezebel sent for a green one if the shade of a blue dress was not to Tina's liking. Or when Tina wanted ice cream from Ben and Jerry's, Jezebel chartered a jet to San Francisco and back to please her whim.

Spoiled Tina grew used to the life of a star. It was natural since her mother was experiencing a career revival. Her show sold out months in advance, and she was Vegas royalty. The Tenors, Streisand, Paul Anka, and Debbie Reynolds were considered Jezebel Mann's special friends. Christmas was spent with her uncles Siegfried and Roy in their animal wonderland. Sometimes, they even brought in snow.

Under these conditions, Tina grew wild. She knew no self-control and threw clever fits of conniption at will. Her best was when she was thirteen, and her mother punished her for the only time. Tina was out for dinner at the grand opening of the Mirage Hotel with Jezebel and her lover de jour, a hefty Greek shipping tycoon with a halo of thinning hair. Tina remembered that the man always wore sunglasses, even indoors.

Dying from boredom as Jezebel and the tycoon exchanged French Riviera stories about Ari Onassis,[100] Tina concocted a memorable prank. She promised herself that the next time the tycoon said, "Ari and I," she would pull up her top in the middle of the restaurant and formally announce her prepubescent boobs. He said it, and Tina reacted with one exaggerated lift overhead. Tina would always recall the stunned silence of the room as she playfully said, "Ooh, Ari?" as she rubbed away at her bee-stung nipples.

Unfortunately, that day was the one year anniversary of Ari's daughter, Christina, being discovered dead in her bathtub from a heart attack, leaving the family's billion-dollar fortune to her

---

[100] Aristotle Onassis was the second husband of Jacqueline Bouvier Kennedy Onassis.

preschool daughter. The room was horrified by Tina's disrespect, as was Jezebel, whose mouth hung open and froze strangely in a horrified gape.

Only the tycoon found the occasion amusing as he watched the woman-child. He stood and offered his jacket. Tina reluctantly accepted it over her shoulders while Jezebel snapped her fingers for the nanny. Tina was promptly ushered back to the suite at the Palace, leaving Jezebel and the tycoon behind.

Her mother never came home that night. She sent for a few of her things and instructed the nanny not to let Tina leave the hotel suite for a month. Two muscled friends of the tycoon guarded the doorstep and would not let her out, no matter how forcefully she complained. On day six, Tina had escaped by hiding in a hotel laundry cart and hitchhiked to New York. She arrived at the doorstep of her shocked father. She was, after all, barely thirteen at the time.

He did not send her back right away. Instead, he treated her to shopping trips and introduced her to slurping oysters at the bar in Grand Central. Tina noticed that no one looked her way when she was with her father. He could live an anonymous life in a city as big as New York. She loved the time spent together, and they agreed it would become an annual thing.

The following year, she arranged her visit and returned. This time was different. Her father was dating a man seriously, and Tina was exceptionally jealous when she discovered they were living together. She wanted her father all to herself and made many attempts to separate the couple. Her father's boyfriend was annoyed by Tina's schemes and confronted her one day in the kitchen.

He told her she had to get used to her father being in a relationship. He was not going anywhere. If Tina wanted to visit, she would have to accept him as a part of her father's life. Tina was too young to understand the complexity of love. She called her mother, who was happy to provide an exit, and ended the visit early. She had not been back since.

In Montana, before the latest intervention, Tina's father called to share the news of his impending nuptials. Of course, Tina would attend his wedding, she promised, intending to make some excuse at the last minute not to show up. Then, when she left in the convertible, she decided she would go.

"It's too late to turn back now," Tina whispered softly to Ruby before picking her up from her lap and passing her to Leanna in the back seat.

— — —

With a tight grip on Toto's wheel, Guy drove. The traffic quickened after emerging from the tunnel's darkness, and the drivers swarmed and swooped aggressively in and out of his lane. Toto lacked agility for multilane maneuvering, so Guy was the target of many angry horns. He focused, determined to keep up with the flow of yellow-cab experts in this navigational game.

He was managing Toto through it all when, almost comedically, he suddenly saw a Broomstick approaching in the opposing westbound lanes of Canal Street. He briefly glanced away and lightly shook his head to clear the image before looking back. An uneasy feeling accompanied the visual confirmation.

Oh god, Guy thought, *there she is.*

He recognized her instantly: the twitch. As they passed by one another, they made eye contact and the twitch lifted her gloved fist and shook it threateningly. Time seemed to slow, and Guy noted that the tassels of her jacket danced in an exaggerated accent to the gesture.

"I'll get you," Guy thought she mouthed.

How on earth did they find us? he wondered.

"Do you know where we're going, Tina?" Guy asked hurriedly.

"Of course I do! Stacey," she demanded with the snap of her finger, "the map." Stacey passed the map up to Tina. "I know this place like the back of my hand."

Tina unfolded the yellow-lined map and relayed instructions. "Guy, stay on this street for another few minutes. I'll tell you when to turn."

Well, Guy thought as he saw the lights of other motorcycles poking in and out of the oncoming traffic, *better make it the first opportunity, Tina.*

Guy barely had time to expel his remaining breath when Tina suddenly pointed and said, "There!"

In response, Guy gripped the wheel with both hands and forcefully swung the van across the next lane. Horns blew viciously behind them as they zipped through and turned abruptly onto a one-way side street. Guy noticed that Ruby, sitting under the protection of Leanna's arm, flopped onto her lap as they all leaned to the right from the force of the curve.

"Are you trying to get us killed!" Stacey screamed.

"Yeah, Tina, a little notice next time would be nice." Guy grinned as he drove Toto in behind a black town car. From what he could tell, they had lost the Broomsticks. "That was a close one," Guy murmured under his breath.

"Yeah," Tina agreed, energized.

"What are you guys talking about?" Stacey wanted to know.

"More Broomsticks," Tina told them.

"Why won't they just leave us alone?" Leanna wondered as she stroked Ruby with her left hand. "It's got to be about more than just this dog. Look at this box of notes." She picked up the box of notes from the floor by her foot and passed it to Stacey, who began to read.

"This hunk of junk … wait, Guy …" Stacey started. "Were you having trouble with the Broomsticks before Ruby?"

"Well, yeah," Guy confessed. "Two of them are my neighbors, and ever since I got this van, they seem to hate me."

"Oh that makes sense, Guy. Everyone knows that bikers and hippies have a bad thing," Stacey said.

"I've never heard that," Tina said skeptically.

"Well, it's true. The rise of the hippies started in early 1960s San Francisco, and the story goes that the two groups initially got along because of a shared dislike of police and authority and love of a good party. Still, there was eventually a power struggle because, as my dad used to say, you can't mix oil and water. Things fell apart for good when Meredith Hunter was killed at the free Altamont concert in 1969. During a Stones performance, he tried to get up on stage, but the Hell's Angels were hired as bodyguards, and one stabbed him to death. The biker who killed him was found innocent by self-defense for that crime but died a few years later under some pretty suspicious circumstances. If I'm not mistaken, I think his cousin was one of the founding members of Your Tornados, the group that eventually became the Broomsticks." Stacey explained.

"OK, turn at the next street," Tina interrupted Stacey, pointing to the right.

"Here?" Guy asked for clarification.

"Yup," Tina confirmed.

Guy maneuvered Toto onto another one-way street where traffic had stopped, creeping only inch by inch in a frustrating expression of gridlock.

"OK, Stacey, you need to elaborate on this theory," Tina refocused her attention.

"Right, yeah, back to the story. At the end of the sixties, both groups wanted some paradise piece of land north of San Francisco. The hippies were beginning to derail and wanted to live more communally. In contrast, the bikers wanted privacy away from the scrutiny of the police force after the unfortunate events at the concert. The way my dad tells the story, the hippies sneakily outsmarted the bikers and got the land. It used to be a VW van park, but now it's an RV park. You may have heard of it. It's called Eden's Apples."

"Maybe," Tina sounded slightly confused. "You need to get to the point."

"The VW van became a symbol of the hippie, which is why the biker neighbor must have left all these notes," Stacey concluded.

"But Guy isn't a hippie," Tina stated the obvious.

"What's your take on it, Guy? Did you do something to justify these notes?" Leanna asked.

"Not to the best of my knowledge. They've always been mean, but after Toto, they became super nasty." Guy shrugged.

"They just harass you all the time?" Leanna asked as her cheeks began to flush.

"It's been about a month since I got Toto," Guy said. "And now they want Ruby."

"It's a witch hunt," Leanna muttered, rounding her hands into tight fists.

Guy noticed that as they lingered in the traffic, Ruby became increasingly alert. She sat with one paw on Leanna's lap, looking out the window. Leanna moved her arm around Ruby rather tightly, which caught Guy's attention, although he was too preoccupied to say anything about it. He would ask Stacey later if Leanna was OK.

"Why don't you roll down the window?" Guy said. A little fresh air always worked to quiet his nerves.

Leanna complied. With a flick of her wrist, she rotated the dial clockwise, lowering the glass. As she did so, a blast of moist, temperate wind enveloped the van. It held the scent of the city, acridly sweet and heavy with exhaust. It was choking yet not disgusting. With all the buildings acting like a heightened shield, there was little escape from the byproducts of its population.

Guy noticed Ruby's reaction. At first, she leaned across Leanna's lap and held her nose up high until the window opened enough to stick her entire head out, where she basked in the odorous wonder of New York City. After a few blocks, Ruby withdrew, pulled her body back into the van, and jumped awkwardly back into Tina's lap in the front seat. From there, she peered out the windshield in anticipation of their destination.

Tina scooched and made room for Ruby on the passenger seat while verbally guiding Guy toward her father's apartment in the heart of Manhattan. "Turn here," she said. As a Broadway producer, her father's home was large enough that they all could, as Tina put it, crash. She boasted that the suite had a whirlpool hot tub in the living room. Soon, they would all be soaking up the health benefits of treated Hudson River water.

A block from their destination, Guy pulled in beside the managerial booth of a parking garage, noting the dozens of vehicles stacked on elevated platforms, one on top of the next. They came to a stop, and all doors flung open simultaneously. Having little use for Toto in the upcoming days, they agreed to store the van and split the cost with Guy.

The parking attendant approached the group, and Guy arranged to store Toto until his business in New York was complete. He wouldn't need the van back for a few days, which pleased the attendant. Finding storage for a van the size of Toto was not easy in downtown Manhattan. He would have to rearrange the lot to tuck the van in the back.

Guy showed Leanna how to fashion a leash for Ruby out of his tie by knotting it around the dog's collar, and she clasped it tightly between her palms while Guy moved to pull Tina's bags from the trunk. Sporting a light load, Stacey assisted Tina by carrying the heaviest of her cases. Tina flung the remaining one over her shoulder and motioned for the group to follow her, pointing, "That way."

They marched in single file along the uneven, gum-stained sidewalk, trailing Tina as she crossed the street by jaywalking and headed down another block until they reached a door beside the pink-striped awning of a Victoria's Secret.

"Here we are," she announced as she buzzed to the apartment by pressing the top black button on a small panel beside the door.

The response came an instant later. The joy of a heavily accented Spanish woman vibrated through the adjacent speaker, a sign Guy took to mean that Tina's presence was welcome and eagerly anticipated. A louder buzz, followed by multiple mechanical clicks released the lock. Tina entered first while Guy held the door as the other ladies passed through with Ruby before he followed them inside.

Unexpectedly, the foyer smelled dank and looked dirty. The black-and-white checkered marble flooring was chipped in places and missing in others, and it seemed unnecessarily grimy. One could hypothesize that the building was once lovely and well cared for, but it gave the impression of neglect. Even Tina seemed surprised, murmuring that the building must be under new management or something.

Together with their baggage, they filled the tiny space of the elevator. Leanna held Ruby's leash while Tina pressed the button for the highest floor. They stood huddled together, waiting for the elevator doors to close. When they did not, Stacey hit the close door button, which brought the two panels together, and they started their upward journey.

Guy began to feel a little claustrophobic. It was hot in that tiny space, and the ride seemed to take forever. Finally, the elevator stopped to jerk a funny way, pausing for an uncomfortable amount of time before the doors eventually parted to reveal the loveliness of an elegant fourth-floor hallway.

The hallway was short, boasting only one door and the elevator. The walls were papered in a regal white-and-gold pattern, and the carpet was black, with a gold band running around its perimeter. Ornate crown moldings raced around the ceiling to complement a baseboard of similar proportions encircling the floor.

Tina practically pushed the others out of her way to be first to the apartment door. She did not need to knock, as the cheerful voice from the street greeted her with a high exclamation.

"My little Constantina!" The owner of the voice, a short woman with dark hair and small smiling eyes, grabbed Tina into a smothering hug before releasing her and kissing her on both cheeks. "How you've grown! Your papa will be so pleased to see you."

"Thank you, Giselle." She smiled. "It's good to see you too."

The woman's attention turned to the others behind Tina. "This is the gang," Tina announced, introducing them individually.

Giselle seemed delighted to have more people to greet and did so with gusto, grabbing the strangers into affectionate hugs and kisses on both cheeks. When she got to Guy, who stood last in the row, she grabbed his face in both hands and remarked on how adorable he was. Then she turned to Tina with a questioning glance.

"We're just friends, Giselle," Tina cautioned as she passed through the doorway into the apartment.

One by one, they followed Tina inside.

Guy noticed the entry was even more impressive than the hallway. It was as though it were right out of *Architectural Digest*. Everything was positioned and laid out in perfect aesthetic order. Guy estimated the ceilings to be high, at least twelve feet, offering that lofty look he knew was popular in the area. Tina explained that the living spaces had once been industrial. The bare windows, void of drapery, were similarly large, and because they were on the fourth floor, one could view the rooftops across the street and beyond.

The floors were dark-stained, wide-plank wood covered by area rugs of various geometric designs and vivid colors. On the walls hung oversized art, much of which was contemporary, even experimental. Ditto for the furniture crafted in unadorned, stark, white leather. There were statues scattered here and there, and an entire book shelving wall was complete with a ladder. The corner formed a dining area with a round glass table and an enormous crystal chandelier. Finally, Guy spotted the pièce de résistance, the famed hot tub.

Even it was different than expected. It sat on an elevated platform on the opposite side of the room, concealed partly by Japanese-style screens and a jungle of plant life. A fountain of a young cherub whistled a constant water spray into the tub, causing an endless trickling sound. The entire look resembled a museum or a gallery of sorts.

"This is quite the crib," Guy complimented aloud.

They stood admiringly in wonder when a man entered the room. Tina turned to face him, and Guy noticed the swell of a thrilled blush creep across her cheeks. "Daddy!" She flung her arms around the man's neck and hugged him tightly.

"Darling, darling," he exclaimed while he grasped her shoulders, holding her at arm's length. "Let me get a look at you."

Anton suddenly took Tina into a ballroom dance position and leaned her back into a dip so profound that, for a moment, Guy thought Tina's head grazed the floor. She snapped up quickly, embracing her father again for another hug.

"You have become a woman," he congratulated her. "And a fine one at that."

Tina smiled at the compliment.

"And who do we have here?" Tina's father surveyed the trio with an artistic flair, tossing a long black trench coat from his shoulders to the ground. Giselle scurried behind him to pick it up, hanging it in a closet beside the front door. Underneath, he wore the uniform of a creative guru: black turtleneck, matching wool slacks, and loafer-type shoes. Guy assumed a famous designer, likely Armani made them.

"Dad, this is Stacey." Tina pointed at Stacey, standing with her hands clasped behind her back, grinning broadly.

The man went to Stacey and indicated she should place her hand in his. Stacey reddened as Anton bowed and lifted her hand to his lips to graze her skin with a polite kiss. "A pleasure, Stacey." He nodded at the unusually tongue-tied girl.

Anton moved on to Leanna. "And this great beauty is?" He paused for dramatic flair.

"I'm Leanna," she said quietly.

"Ah, Leanna." He repeated the same response to the introduction, but this time, Guy thought Anton paused a little longer with her hand in his.

"And this is Guy." Tina introduced him last.

He came face-to-face with Guy, who was of equal height. "Pleasure," he said as his eyes sparkled, and an assuming smirk emerged from underneath an elegantly groomed mustache. "Allow me—are you a friend of Dorothy?"

"Dad, please leave him alone!" Tina grabbed her father's arm to turn his attention away from Guy.

"Constantina," he began, "you look more and more like your beautiful mother. How is she? Still caught up in that Hollywood nonsense?" Anton folded his arms across his chest.

"No, actually, she's been living in Vegas. She has her own show," Tina said.

"Oh yes, I heard that. Jezebel is still doing it, then?" Anton asked.

"For another year, I think," Tina said. "She's under contract until early next summer."

"Well, bravo for her!" he exclaimed. "She is well?"

"I suppose," Tina answered, sounding vague.

"Nice to hear. You must send Jezebel all my best." Anton was sincere.

"Where's Gustav?" Tina asked.

The color drained from her father's cheeks at Tina's inquiry. From the corner of his eye, Guy saw Giselle shaking her hands across her face, silently attempting to end the conversation. It was too late; Anton made it only as far as the nearest couch before he collapsed in sadness. "He's gone." The confession came as a murmur.

"Gone?" Tina echoed, clearly surprised by the revelation.

Giselle came to Tina's aid, pulling her aside to explain the situation. "He called off the wedding and returned home to Europe," she whispered in a hushed tone. "His mother is sick, so he went to be with her. Your father has not taken it very well."

"I'm taking it about as well as anyone would after giving someone your best years, only to have it flung in their face." Anton overheard them, adding, "There is no loyalty."

"Are you sure he's not coming back? I mean, surely his mother will improve," Tina suggested.

"He is not returning." Her father said the last sentence with such affirmation that Tina did not press the issue further.

"I'm so sorry, Daddy," Tina said sadly.

"What's to be sorry? Life is full of love. It is what makes magic. And we all know that magic is what makes everything interesting. Now you are here and have made your father a happy man! I feel better than I have in days, weeks, or years!" Anton claimed.

With that, he stood abruptly and snapped his fingers. Suddenly, the mood, which had become rather sullen, lifted. "Giselle," he called for his maid, "set these gorgeous creatures up in their rooms. And then bring us a bottle of the seventy-six Dom."

"Of course," she said, leading Stacey, Leanna, and Guy down a long hallway toward two generous guest rooms, one with a king-sized bed and one with two singles. Stacey and Leanna took the king, and Guy and Tina shared the room with the singles. There was a slight argument about who would sleep with Ruby, but after sensing Leanna's strong desire to be near the dog, Guy suggested Ruby stay in the king. When they returned from settling, Gisele presented the four with flutes of champagne.

"Come on, Stacey," coaxed Tina. "This you have to try. I don't care how old you are."

— — —

Not wanting to be the odd man out, Stacey accepted a glass and took a quick sip. It was like nothing she had ever tasted, like liquid gold. She downed her share and was thrilled to find it replenished repeatedly. Soon, Stacey felt lightheaded and fabulous.

Joining Guy is the smartest thing I've ever done, she reckoned.

And tomorrow, she would show them all how clever she was.

CHAPTER 15

MARVEL PRODUCTIONS

Tuesday morning, New York City

"It's just up here a bit farther," Stacey said fervently. "Come on."

"Where exactly are we going?" Guy felt the need to ask. Yet something compelled him to follow. It was Stacey's insistence earlier that morning back at the apartment.

Some of the previous night was a blur. He recalled opera music playing in the background. He remembered eating exotic cheese and drinking port after their third bottle of champagne. He knew Stacey slunk away before the others, and Guy thought it was because she had had too much to drink. She was, after all, only twenty and unused to imbibing wine or spirits, let alone the finest champagne.

Feeling hungry and lazy that morning, Tina asked Gisele to prepare them breakfast. Within minutes, steaming hot coffee rich with double cream and sugar, tart orange juice, hot bagels with lox and cream cheese, a fresh fruit salad with the sweetest melon, the juiciest pineapple, and big red strawberries came delivered on a silver tray. Along with the food, Giselle appeared with some square, glazed-clay stoneware, matching jumbo-sized coffee mugs, and ironed gray-linen napkins. On closer inspection, Guy noticed Anton's monogram.

"These are new, his special order," Giselle confided in a hushed tone. "When Gustav left, your dad got rid of the old stuff."

Guy unfolded the napkin over his lap and helped himself.

Afterward, they took turns showering in the most fabulous bathroom Guy had ever seen. He went last, insisting that the girls went first. Down a short hallway, he opened the door to find a windowless space with pale marble wainscoting that circled the room at hip height. The floor was made of a similar marble but cut into twelve-inch squares. Where the marble ended, a tile mosaic began. It extended upward, covering the entire domed ceiling in a Michelangelo-inspired design.

Along the back wall stood an enormous soaker tub with faucets as slender as bamboo stalks. Ivy cascaded from a tier of stands in one corner while the other boasted a series of candles. There was a shelf across the back, and Guy noticed it contained such extravagances as an ice bucket for cold wine. To the right of the tub was built-in cabinetry, complete with a full-length mirrored door. Guy opened the door to find shelves filled with white, impossibly fluffy spa towels. He held one up to his face, admired its softness, and sensed the faint hint of lavender.

Opposite the cabinet on the left side of the room was the sink. The faucet was slim and extended with a spout like an out-turned tulip. The basin sat on an oversized square pedestal that stood securely, as though rooted in the floor. Beside it was a glass-enclosed shower with a towel bar across the front. Guy felt it and noted that it was warm. He removed a towel from the cabinet and hung it on the bar.

The shower shot a zealous spray, and Guy stepped into its vigor. An assortment of fragrant shampoos and conditioners stood like soldiers in a special alcove. He vigilantly followed the directions inscribed on the back of their plastic bottles. Lather, rinse, repeat! It never felt so good to be clean. A soft bath mat greeted his feet as he stepped out of the glass shower door. The warmed towel awaited his body.

Guy found shaving cream in a glass cabinet, a razor, aftershave, and even an exfoliating scrub.

Behind it all, there was a tube of gel in the cabinet, and Guy took a large squirt and rubbed it between his palms. He used his hands to tame his bangs, which took the new style. He dressed in black jeans and a button-down shirt that he left unbuttoned at the top. As a final touch, Guy rolled up his sleeves.

There, Guy thought while admiring his reflection in the full-length mirror. *Mr. Insipid no more!*

When he returned to the living room, Guy discovered the girls filing and painting their nails in the shade Tina saved for special occasions. While their nails dried, Leanna applied eye shadow and mascara on Tina while Stacey watched. Ruby found a spot on a chaise by the window and spent the morning looking at the rooftops across the street.

When it was nearly eleven o'clock, Stacey jumped up and announced with sudden urgency the need for them to go out somewhere for a meeting. "Come on—get your shoes on," she insisted. "You're coming too, Ruby."

"Why? Who was that on the phone earlier," Tina prodded.

"What? Oh nobody." She avoided eye contact by shifting her gaze to inspect her nails.

"Stacey," Tina said, "Fess up!"

"Oh, all right." Stacey frowned. "It is that somebody on the phone. But it isn't who you think. You have to trust me."

"What? Trust you like Carolyn trusted John?" Tina said to Stacey in a mocking tone.

"Look," sighed Stacey. "You'll find out soon anyway. If you want to know, get your stuff and come with me. I'm getting Ruby's tie leash."

Guy was the first to stand and join Stacey at the door. Leanna took the tie from Stacey and attached it to Ruby's collar while Stacey returned to the bedroom to grab her knapsack. Leanna put on her McDonald's sunglasses; Guy fixed the spike in his hair; and Tina applied a new coat of lipstick at the front hall mirror.

"Are we going far?" When she returned from the guest room, Leanna took note of Stacey's bag.

"No, I've just got some stuff." Stacey grasped the bag tightly to her chest.

"Stacey," Tina moaned. "We're not going tacky tourist sightseeing, are we?"

"Just come on." Stacey ushered them out the door.

"We are off," Tina called out to Giselle.

They were a half hour into their journey by foot, and Guy was enjoying the hum of the city. The New York midmorning air was thick with fumes of fuel and grime, yet the scent of the most petite flowers from street-side bouquet stands or the pretzel vendor's yeasty dough penetrated the industrial aroma and brought soul to the concrete jungle. As a foursome with a dog, they were forced to duck in and out of passersby on the shared sidewalk, and Guy was reminded of the expression "keeping on one's toes." The city was certainly not a place for meandering.

Manhattan did not disappoint. It was what Guy had anticipated yet entirely different from any predetermined image he had once held. He never expected to feel a part of it so instantly. There was so much action, so much bustle and noise. Dudes with massive earphones listened to their Walkmans alongside women power walking in suits and sneakers. They were old, they were young, and they were representatives of everything in between.

They turned the corner down a tree-lined street whose structures were surrounded by mini wrought iron fences with circled tops, arriving at a gothic-style building. Stacey consulted an address scribbled out on a torn piece of paper. She glanced up and down, matching the numbers between her note and the building several times before confirming their arrival.

"This is it. We're here," Stacey announced.

At street level, the unassuming place seemed nothing more than a green glass door obscuring whatever was inside. Curious, Guy pressed his nose close to peer past the glass as Stacey pressed the bell twice. For somewhere within, the front latch unlocked with a buzz that hummed a moment longer than it took for the group to pass through the entrance.

They arrived in a narrow first-floor lobby with an elevator in the middle and a wire-clad black door at the far end. The ceiling was high, and every inch of the walls came tiled in forest green. Guy noticed the tiles gleamed as though they were polished. He thought it was almost too much, bordering on tacky.

"What have you got us into here, Stacey? Are we in Jolly Green Giant land?" Tina complained.

Leanna pointed out the sign. It was taped to the elevator door and read, "Lift out of order. Please walk." A hand-drawn arrow pointed them to the black wired door leading to a set of back stairs.

"Now, don't be mad, Guy." Stacey turned to face him, ignoring Tina. "I set up this meeting without your permission, but I thought it was for the best." From her backpack, she withdrew the two items. First, she held up a copy of *Newsweek*. On the cover was Doc Aus, the famed Australian veterinarian flanked by two assistants.

"Doc Aus? The crazy guy who talks to animals? *That*'s who we're here to see? This is stupid. Let's go. Being here is a waste of time." Tina was irate.

"But you have to come," pleaded Stacey. "I made the appointment in your name. With your parents being so famous, it was the only way we could get in to see him on such short notice."

Tina punched her fists to her hips and stood heatedly tapping her foot against the green-tiled floor, her anger palpable. Leanna smiled weakly back at Stacey as Stacey pouted her bottom lip, hopeful. All three looked to Guy, waiting to see what he would do.

Guy thought for a moment while looking down at Ruby. She gazed back up at him, and her tail began to wag slowly until it gathered momentum and enthusiastically swung fully left and right. He turned toward the black wire door with intention.

"Come on." Guy turned to the girls and announced over his shoulder. "We're going up."

"Oh I'm positive you won't regret it. This guy's known for his ability to communicate with the spirit world, especially with animals. I've read his book. You'll see." She grabbed Tina and Leanna's hands and pulled them toward the stairs. "This way. He's on the top floor."

They climbed what felt like a mountain of steep steps up what Tina counted as at least ten flights. It certainly was not four. A woman greeted them at the top. She had a shapely figure and a flawless olive complexion. She wore a deep-green velvet ensemble, and her dark hair shone as though brushed the *Cosmopolitan*-recommended one hundred times per day.

"Le party Mann?" she queried in a French accent. Guy recognized her as one of the two women who flanked the doctor on the *Newsweek* cover Stacey revealed at the base of the building. Stacey nodded to indicate they were the Mann party, and the door behind the woman opened widely.

"Bienvenu." She invited them to follow her inside. Guy moistened his lips with a parched tongue.

"Quelque chose à boire?" the woman asked while miming drinking from a glass in case they did not understand her.

"Yes, please." They all seemed to pant in unison.

She motioned the group to sit in a lounge area of dark velvet-covered banquette couches. The space reminded Guy slightly of the internet café where he had met Stacey. The ceiling was painted midnight blue and illuminated by a twinkle of lights, set up in some cerebral arrangement. It gave the impression of being suspended and surrounded by the universe's stars.

"Where are we again?" Leanna asked, awed.

"At the doctor's office." Tina picked up a pamphlet lying on a glass table in the corner and handed it to Leanna. "He's an animal communicator." Tina lifted her eyebrows suspiciously.

The assistant returned with a tray of greenish-hued water in miniature hourglass-shaped tasters. She passed the beverage and announced, "Oui, this is not water. C'est le Doc Aus bon jus." She stood back to watch as the liquid was consumed. Guy took a sip and noted it tasted like exotic-fruit Kool-Aid, perhaps kiwi. It was neither bad nor good, rather something squarely in the middle of his palate's usual enjoyment.

At that moment, as though pumped freshly from another room, a waft of fragrant incense drifted gently among them in an exaggerated swirling fashion as they succumbed and sipped the sweet refreshment. The assistant watched while they drained their glasses and, one by one, felt relief as the moisture took into their parched throats. None had any idea they were so thirsty. Once done, the assistant collected the glasses and placed them on a tray.

"Madame Mann, attendez ici." Her expression was void of any emotion. "Si'l vous plaît."

With a slight forward bow, the assistant extended Stacey a clipboard full of paperwork and a sharpened pencil with a pink eraser tip. She then faced the rest of the group and curtseyed. Without further instruction, she picked up the tray of empty glasses, turned, and left.

"What is this?" Stacey asked as she handed the clipboard to Guy.

"Some sort of a waiver, I think," Guy said as he scanned the top page.

"Why?" Leanna wondered why a contract was necessary for an animal communication session.

"Basically," Guy concluded on reaching the end of the page-long document, "it just states that we, 'the party,' will not take pictures or videotape Doc Aus while he works. We can all live with that, right?"

The girls nodded. "What's happening with the other forms?" Stacey asked Guy. "Want to pass them back to me?"

Guy flipped the top page to review the documents underneath. The following two pages were a type of survey, and Guy returned the clipboard to Stacey so she could fill in the details. Getting right to work, under "name," Stacey wrote Ruby. Under "city of birth," unknown. The next questions were answered by canine, female, and she scribbled a question mark on the age space. As Stacey put down the pencil, personality definers / habits were left without data population.

"There are too many unknowns here, Stacey," Guy concluded when Stacey showed him her work. "We need to provide more detail."

Guy passed the clipboard to Tina, who demanded Stacey's pencil with the wag of her finger. She used the eraser end to rub away the word *unknown*, changed Ruby's city to New York, estimated her age as two before the existing question mark, and confirmed Ruby's habits as sleeping and eating.

"You can't put eating," Stacey protested. "Remember what Guy said. Ruby doesn't eat. You have to cross that one out."

"Right, the anorexic dog," Tina remembered and drew a line through the word. "Good one, Stacey. Clever! I'll also add fear of flashbulbs. We all saw how she reacted back at Poppy's place." Tina surveyed Leanna and Guy for their agreement while Stacey beamed at the compliment and offered a hurried nod.

"OK, that about does it." Tina placed the clipboard and the pencil down on the table. "Ruby," she addressed the dog directly, "you like road trips, staring out windows, sighing, and sleeping. Your dislikes are food and flashbulbs."

A second assistant entered the room, sensing the completed paperwork. Guy recognized her from *Newsweek* cover as well. She appeared and announced, "He will see you now. But before we begin, you must relinquish cameras and recording devices. None are allowed." She looked at Stacey, pointing to the knapsack, and said, "I must inspect your personal belongings."

She took the knapsack from Stacey and peered inside, using the tips of her nails to separate the contents. Once satisfied, she returned it to Stacey, spun on her heels, and led the group from the lounge down a dark hallway illuminated with a light pattern that mimicked the lounge. Leanna felt they were on a Disney ride that simulated the future and commented in a whisper to Tina, who agreed as she passed ahead of Leanna and Stacey to join Guy at the front of the line.

Leanna, leading the leashed Ruby, followed behind Stacey until Stacey stopped abruptly in the hallway and told Leanna to go ahead of her. She stood back and rooted in her knapsack for something while Leanna and Ruby slipped by to catch up with Guy and Tina.

At the end of the hallway stood a big black door that swooshed in its hinge as the female assistant pushed it open to reveal Doc Aus's magical studio. At first glance, the room mainly appeared empty, except for a large velvet banquette against the left wall and a shelf of objects on the right. If the room had windows, they were darkened and undetectable. The woman gestured for them to sit on the banquette and pointed to another oversized door opposite.

"He will come from there when he is ready. You shall not be kept waiting for long." Her tone was so ceremonial that it felt contrived.

Tina entered first, followed closely by Leanna with Ruby and Guy. Stacey joined last, and Guy noticed that she handed Doc Aus's assistant one final item, Guy's *Vanity Fair* magazine, unfolded at the St John's advertisement page, where the dog looked like Ruby. He watched Stacey point to the dog to ensure the assistant understood the connection. The assistant took the issue from Stacey with a nod and hurried her through the door.

It took Guy a moment to get a feel for the room. It was quite an ample space, though windowless and dark. New age music played from several speakers embedded in the walls. Tina commented that she felt like she was at some gothic Aveda spa. The room felt chilly and carried the sulfuric aroma of recently extinguished matches.

Guy noticed shadows but could not identify various objects against the far wall. One item seemed large and round, and he wondered if it was a crystal ball. Beside the door where the doctor would appear was a tall mirror in an ornately scrolled frame. The mirror looked murky, almost sepia, and Guy thought their reflections looked like eerie, spooky versions of themselves.

The promised appearance in minutes ran into double digits before the doctor finally announced himself in a startling burst of incense-perfumed smoke. It came right when Guy least expected it, as he began feeling antsy and bored. Though theatrical, the event caused Leanna to scream out in surprise before pressing her hand to her mouth.

Doc Aus arrived adorned in a green velvet outfit similar to his assistant's. It was a tailored tunic, full length to the floor, though fitted through the torso. On his head perched a giant hat with rhinestones or some other glitter sewn into its fabric. Lights followed the doctor as he strolled toward the big square of a regal plush pillow. He sat on the cushion and crossed his legs in a yogi style, taking time to acquaint himself with comfort. Once achieved, he cleared his throat and surveyed the group without speaking. It was an odd silence, and Guy felt relieved when, at last, the doctor finally offered greetings.

"G'day, mates." His arms opened widely, fingers outstretched. "And welcome. Do come a little closer." He beckoned them toward him while smiling a slightly crooked, toothy grin.

Slowly, a soft light lifted the darkness, and Doc Aus invited the group to notice several cushions the assistant had arranged on the floor in a circular pattern. He gestured to which seat each should take by pointing his index finger first to them and then to their spot on the floor. He did so without speaking, so the only sounds in the room were those of waterfalls and chirping birds.

One by one, they took their places in an arc around the spot where the doctor was rooted. Stacey and Ruby sat to the doctor's left and

Guy directly across. Tina and Stacey were placed to the doctor's right. From his viewpoint, Guy could see that the man was wearing eye makeup. It was so overdone, so ostentatiously applied, that he wanted to laugh but suppressed the urge.

"Give me Ruby," he announced boomingly, rolling the *R* of her name.

Tina reached across with both hands to show the dog like an item on a game show. *Voila!* It seemed absurd since Ruby was the only dog in the room and located only an arm's span from Doc Aus's position in the circle. The doctor nodded formally and reached out to Ruby. He did not make contact but held his palms several inches away like she was a fire that emitted warmth.

"We are searching for Esprit," the doctor whispered in an Australian twang, practically sighing the final word as though it were sacred.

The assistant emerged from behind the doctor, holding the *Vanity Fair* Stacey had slipped her privately before. She knelt and placed the magazine between four candles on the floor before she turned to offer Doc Aus a book of matches. The doctor ceremoniously lit the candles, using a different matchstick for each. "Behold, the power of fire," he said aloud after the final candle was lit, dismissing his assistant with a nod. She curtsied as she left the room.

"Doc Aus …" Stacey began, reaching to flip the cover to the page with the dog that looked like Ruby but was silenced by the man as he held up his hand.

"What is the birth sign?" he boomed.

"For the dog?" Stacey asked.

"For Esprit, the dead woman," Dr. Aus scolded, sounding annoyed.

"What dead woman?" Stacey was confused.

"You are here to find the connection between this dog and this woman, right?" The doctor moved a candle toward the magazine, illuminating the cover.

Although he had seen it many times before, Guy could not help but feel surprised as the doctor pointed to the magazine's image: the face of Carolyn Bessette Kennedy. Her wistful gaze and strong profile came into his view.

"I think there's been some mistake, Doctor," Stacey began as she reached to turn the magazine cover. "If we flip through these pages, you'll find a dog resembling Ruby."

"Silence!" The doctor interrupted her. "I can assure you the dog and this woman are connected. Now, does anyone know the birth date of the dead woman?" Doc Aus demanded to know.

"January 7 so that would be Capricorn," Guy recalled from his readings.

"Capricorn, yes, of course. They are practical, prudent, ambitious, disciplined, patient, careful, humorous, and reserved. I can see it all now. Oh but there is also a dark side to the person. Pessimistic and fatalistic, miserly and grudging."

Guy leaned closer to understand more of what the doctor was saying. He seemed to speak more softly as he continued.

"In their relationships, they are often ill at ease, if not downright unhappy. They are somewhat self-centered but not excessively so, cautious around people they do not know very well, preferring not to meddle with others and, in turn, not allowing interference with themselves. They attract people who do not understand them. They treat casual acquaintances with diplomacy, tact, and, above all, reticence. They make few good friends but are intensely loyal to those they do make, and they can become bitter and powerful enemies. They sometimes dislike the opposite sex and test the waters of affection gingerly before judging the temperature right for marriage. Once married, they are faithful, though inclined to jealousy."

The doctor smiled at the dog. "Does any of this sound familiar, Ruby?"

Ruby did not respond.

"Doctor, we are confused. Are you suggesting that Ruby aligns spiritually with Carolyn Bessette Kennedy?" Guy asked.

"Silence!" the doctor commanded. "All of your talking is getting in the way of my connection with Esprit. I am just getting started. Bring the dog closer."

Stacey leaned in and scooched Ruby a foot closer so she was inches away from Doc Aus. Doc Aus put his hands on the dog, this time making contact with the sides of Ruby's waist. He closed his eyes and began to hum. The sound that came from him was a long, flat tone and lasted for what Guy felt was an excessive amount of time.

Just as that hint of doubt entered his thoughts, a strange breeze swept through the room. It was not a strong wind, just enough to extinguish the light of the various candles scattered around the perimeter, except for two of the four on either side of *Vanity*

Fair. Those candles burned vehemently, possibly with even more intensity than before.

The overhead lights flickered on and off while bombs of smoky incense erupted in a circular sequence around the room's perimeter. Doc Aus's humming grew louder and more rhythmic, climaxing in lengthy guttural groans that seemed to fill the entire space. The doctor suddenly stopped, flipped his eyes open, and met each participant's gaze individually.

"I am sensing a great deal of energy in the room. Someone here is very close to the late Kennedy bride," the doctor said, using a commanding tone.

"Guy is reviewing a manuscript based on her life," Stacey offered.

"I'm an editor," Guy confirmed.

"Tell me about her, the Kennedy." Doc Aus probed Guy for details.

"Well," Guy began, "from what I can tell, she was a career woman who gave up her private life to marry the world's most eligible bachelor."

"Yeah," chimed Stacey. "She used *The Rules* and got her prince."

"She died a couple of years ago in a plane crash," Guy continued, "with her husband and sister."

"Yes, I see that now." Doc Aus nodded. "And Ruby? She's yours?"

"Not really," Guy confessed. "She found me."

"She found you because you are connected." The doctor clenched his teeth tightly and held up a single finger. "Your editing of the book is the first connection. Tell me," he continued, "when did the dog find you? Did the timing coincide with your review of the manuscript?"

"I suppose," he began. "Actually, to be truthful, the first time I saw her, I was reading that issue of *Vanity Fair.*"

"This publication?" He held up the magazine and flipped its pages, one after the other until he settled on the article about Everest. Guessing correctly, he stated, "You were reading this, the story of the missing mountaineers."

Guy could not help but feel impressed. That was the article from when Ruby came to his apartment window. Doc Aus continued, "And now I sense your connection has deepened."

Guy had to admit that Doc Aus was correct. It was a secret he could no longer keep. For the first time, he spoke aloud of their unique communication style. "I can't explain it. It started a few days ago and is becoming more intense daily. We don't use words; it's all through eye connection."

"Of course!" the doctor responded gleefully. "And of Ruby herself, tell me more. Please include anything you may feel is relevant. What is she saying to you?"

"Well, she's pretty gentle in spirit, shy. Come to think of it, though, there are a couple of things," Guy said as he stroked his chin.

"Go on ..." the doctor coaxed.

"Well, the first day I started to read the manuscript, I was finishing chapter one, and Ruby suddenly hopped into the van through the back door and landed on the front seat where I had the magazine. Here it was on this page." He opened the magazine to page 130 and pointed to the photo of John and Carolyn together at a gala in Grand Central Station.

"Yes, yes, this is brilliant. Stage it for me!" Aus ordered.

Guy called Ruby toward him. Without instruction, Ruby recreated the scene with uncanny precision. She sat with her paw on the picture and looked up at Guy. Guy could not help but notice how Ruby cocked her head in the exact position Carolyn held in the picture.

"Is this the gesture?" Doc Aus asked.

"Yes, it was exactly like this!" Guy shared, "This is how I knew she was truly from New York. She was pointing out the picture of Grand Central Station."

"Interesting." He looked around the room. "And what is your connection to Ruby?"

The three girls shrugged their shoulders, never considering any connection. Doc Aus squinted his eyes and began with Stacey.

"You! You like to read and gather knowledge. This dog has made you interested in learning more about Carolyn."

Stacey nodded.

"And you." He spoke to Tina. "You are troubled. Some may even call you heartless. You need love and have found love through adoring this dog."

Tina raised her eyebrow.

"And you." He spoke last to Leanna. "Something truly awful has happened to you. And you find the courage to face it in the company of Ruby."

Leanna smiled.

"It is now time." Doc Aus motioned for the dog to come back beside him. Ruby obliged. She sat facing Guy, staring, while the doctor held his hands to hover over her body. He explained that the technique would withdraw Esprit. The girls closed their eyes as the doctor instructed, and they all began to hum a low vibration.

"Ripper! I have it!" The doctor suddenly had the idea, and his eyes opened widely. He paused, smiled the crooked grin, and announced, "Ruby's feeling a little clucky, aren't you, young lady?"

When the group did not understand the slang, the doctor picked Ruby up and lifted her to the ceiling to reveal a rounded belly. He cried out, "Here, she's got a joey!"

It took a moment for the four of them to digest the news. Even Ruby seemed startled and gasped as Doc Aus set her down.

"What? She's pregnant?" One of the girls murmured.

"Pregnant?" Guy repeated incredulously.

"Yeppers, and she's close, I sense. And something about the Kennedy bride is meaningful to this creature." He plucked a hair from Ruby's coat and placed it between the two burning candles on the *Vanity Fair*. "Let us all take hands, and we will make contact with the other side."

The circle linked hands. When the doctor closed his eyes, Guy noticed that makeup created some design on his lids. It appeared to be some geometric pattern, all twisted and fractured, like a kaleidoscope. Guy felt his eyes grow heavy until it was almost impossible to keep them propped open, and he succumbed to darkness.

The energy in the room changed. Fragrant incense danced in the air seductively. Guy noticed that Leanna and Stacey's hands grew limp at the exact second as his own. The doctor began to chant in some strange tongue language while a tingling sensation of wind crept up Guy's back, tickling his neck while warming his ears. It almost felt like a hot breath blown through a straw.

"Spirits, we ask you for permission to enter your kingdom. We seek a sister who has unfinished business in the world of flesh and bone." The doctor navigated the group through the entry process. "We call on your sister Carolyn Bessette Kennedy. We call on those who know her. We seek answers to the puzzlement of this fair creature, Ruby."

Doc Aus began to chant in tongues again. It lasted for what seemed a while. Then, abruptly, he stopped and was silent. When he eventually spoke, it was with a voice that sounded like a strained, hoarse whisper, not quite ghastly yet enough that it matched the overall mystic atmosphere. Guy noticed that Doc Aus's voice was void of any trace of an Australian accent when in this trance.

"I am hearing from the other side. It comes from a good source. Yes, Carolyn was expecting at the time of her unfortunate death. Her abrupt end did not quiet her eagerness to produce offspring. She chose this delicate creature to live out her final desire. Ruby, the wondrous canine warrior, will deliver soon. Until that moment, the spirit of Carolyn will inhabit this body so that she may fulfill her last desire," Doc Aus explained. "Our role is to ensure success. This spirit seeks a safe and sacred place to bear the fruits of her womb. Indeed, Carolyn Bessette Kennedy wants to give birth right here in the heart of New York City. She will only find eternal rest once she has transitioned this sacred blessing," Doc Aus concluded.

With that, the doctor made a strange gasping sound, and his body flung toward the floor, extinguishing the two candles by knocking them over on their sides. Guy opened his eyes to find the man sprawled face-to-face with an image of Carolyn peeking from the underside of his gaping mouth. Within seconds, Doc Aus returned to his cross-legged position. He dabbed his brow with a small handkerchief, careful not to disturb his makeup. He sat silently for a moment, pausing for effect, as he looked to Ruby and then around the room at each circle member.

"Did you get that?" Doc Aus coughed, and his accent suddenly returned.

"Yes," Guy answered, "but I'm a little confused, Doc Aus. What are we supposed to do?"

"It's simple, Guy. Ruby is Carolyn, the maternal. Ruby will have her baby thus allowing the deceased's spirit the occasion of the experience. It's a miracle!" He grew suddenly upbeat. "We will all witness a miracle! Yes! Yes! I can see it all now. Lights, cameras, and a blitzkrieg of cameras to witness the last hurrah of the John

Kennedy Dynasty! We must hurry in the preparations!" Doc Aus exclaimed.

He called for his assistant by pressing a button on a pager clipped to the belt of his tunic. A few seconds later, she arrived, a pad and paper in hand. Doc Aus began his list of orders, which she transcribed without blinking.

"We need a birthing altar with fine fragrant linens, a tent for privacy, and a water sponsor. The media will have to be alerted, and the police will have to barricade the street. Call Commissioner Kerik; he owes me a favor. See which top photographer is available for black and whites, and order Veuve and sushi. Yes, let's do sushi. Lots and lots of sushi—it is perfect!" The doctor snapped both fingers and stood to exit the room, the spotlight guiding his path toward the door.

"Wait a minute! What's going on here?" Stacey asked, confused.

Doc Aus turned back and looked Stacey in the eye. Next, he spent a few minutes on an unnecessary rehash of the séance's outcome, almost speaking to the group as if they were children. They listened as he explained that the tasks ahead were urgent and that he and his team needed to set everything in motion without hesitation. The group should wait there with Ruby, and Doc Aus would return shortly to prep them for the big event.

"Relax and trust me." Doc Aus smiled the familiar crooked grin. "I am a professional."

"And he's *awesome*," lauded the assistant as she followed him out the door.

CHAPTER 16

TWENTY NORTH MOORE

Tuesday after the séance, Tribeca

A strange story out of New York today …

Spiritual guru and animal communicator Doc Aus, who recently gained fame by lobbying for a canine category in the Boston Marathon, has announced that a dog called Ruby is the reincarnation of the late Carolyn Bessette Kennedy.

The dog is expecting puppies, which Aus believes is the reason for Ruby's "possession" of sorts. Doc Aus is touting the upcoming big event, which will transpire tonight, as an epiphany for all Kennedy lovers.

Of course, Bessette Kennedy was JFK Jr.'s wife, revered for her good looks and tremendous personal style before her untimely death in July '99.

No word on which designer Ruby will be wearing.

From her home in Upstate New York, Lydia held the television control in her left hand and her cordless phone in the other. Expertly, she simultaneously muted the television and called her best friend, Donna, using speed dial. Her friend picked up after one ring.

"Oh my goodness! Oh my goodness!" Donna exclaimed. "I just saw!"

"It's crazy!" Lydia exclaimed.

"Does your sister know?" Donna wondered. Lydia's sister had adopted Sweetie's last puppy and moved her to San Francisco over a year prior.

"I just hung up with her. We're both boggled. Ruby's been missing from her dog walker's van for over two weeks and then appears on national television. It's unbelievable!" Lydia said.

"We should go down to New York," Donna suggested.

"Let's do it. The drive is just a few hours. Look—the story is back on CNN." Lydia unmuted the television, and the two friends watched the coverage unfolding in the heart of Manhattan.

CNN:

We're following this one for you folks.

A crowd is assembling outside the Tribeca loft of the late JFK Jr. and his late wife, Carolyn Bessette Kennedy, to witness what they call a modern-day miracle. Doctor Greg Osmond, commonly known as Doc Aus, the Australian veterinarian, has issued the following statement. And I quote:

"Today is a great day in the study of human-to-animal reincarnation. We have discovered that our canine friend Ruby has a spiritual connection, transcending this world and the next to the late, great Carolyn Bessette Kennedy. Sometime this evening, Ruby will birth a treasured litter, and we will witness the passing of Carolyn's soul into the next world."

The doctor promises a spectacle if you dare to believe.

Of course, Doc Aus has written several books on human-to-animal reincarnation and boasts a client roster of some of the most famed celebrity pets, including the president's three cats.

– – –

Word spread across the city like a virus. Doc Aus's public relations machine worked on overdrive to pump out the message. All the major networks broke the story shortly after 3:30 p.m., with CNN and MSNBC running the headline across their ticker tapes in short rotation. It was mass hysteria, and anyone established in the broadcast world scrambled to the scene.

By six, a mass of onlookers, camera crews, and police surrounded North Moore's short block between Hudson and Varick. NBC sent Katie Couric, ABC sent Diane Sawyer, and CBS sent a live camera crew, but Dan Rather remained in the studio at the anchor's desk. *Entertainment Tonight* sent Mary Hart and *Extra* sent rival Leeza Gibbons. The producers jockeyed for prominent positions alongside the industry heavyweights. It was like a *Who's Who* with America's best-known on-screen talent lining up one beside the other to bring the story live to the nation's living rooms and kitchens.

Carolyn Bessette Kennedy reincarnated as Ruby!

Ruby is birthing a litter of puppies on the Kennedy doorstep!

Carolyn is home to have her babies!

Shortly after seven, Guy and the girls sat in a private tented space constructed to shield Ruby from the curious public. Unfazed, Ruby lay on a big cushion, her head resting on a small pillow. She seemed not bothered by all the fuss, lying lethargically relaxed. Guy thought she was remarkably calm for a creature about to endure a significant physical undertaking.

Outside their tent, a fluster of production coordinators, lighting, and sound technicians scrambled to complete the set before the big moment. As they did so, Doc Aus stood on the front step of 20 North Moore, a ten-story-high brick-and-concrete structure. He took questions from various media, ranging from the *New York Post* and *Entertainment Tonight* to the major networks and student documentary filmmakers.

Doc Aus arranged for Guy and the girls to be transported directly from his studio to the event stage, but not before coaching each of them through a brief media training session. He did not want them to give away his "trade secrets," so he instructed the foursome on the how-tos of granting interviews. He told them what to say, what not to say, and how to say everything carefully.

The doctor spoke individually to each of the girls, enlisting them with a strategy to deal with what he explained would likely be a media circus. "With my reputation, this will be huge!" he boasted.

"Not to mention the star power of Carolyn herself," Stacey reminded.

"Yes, of course," the doctor agreed briskly.

Doc Aus began with Stacey. She was not to elaborate on any of her answers. He drilled the motto into her head: say nothing. She could, however, take notes as the event unfolded. He felt it would benefit the group if someone were to be the official diarist of the occasion. He gave her a green leather notebook with a black fountain pen.

Doc Aus instructed Tina to be gracious to the media. As she was the daughter of such prominent personalities, the public would naturally be curious about her involvement with Ruby. Her best approach would be to befriend them and make them love her. The doctor gave Tina a small bottle of lip ointment that, when applied, resulted in the most glorious shine.

The doctor's attention then rested on Leanna. She stood eye to eye with the man, letting out a small gasp as he revealed his plan. Leanna was to be the official hostess of the event. Her long hair and lithe figure showed physical similarity to Carolyn, and the press would love it. Doc Aus assured her he would remain at her side the entire time. He gave her a pin connected to an earpiece, similar to one he wore, and demonstrated how she could contact him in a second by pressing a tiny jeweled button.

Finally, Doc Aus arrived at Guy. Calling him the Carolyn Bessette Kennedy expert, Guy was to be Ruby's handler. He would be beside her through it all. The doctor handed Guy a long glittering leash.

The French-speaking assistant returned to inform the doctor that the press release was live. The networks were already calling for interviews, and she booked him with ABC for five, CBS at five-fifteen, and so on. One network even recalled their newly retired anchor. The Marines were flying him up from a golf course in Myrtle Beach.

After the prep session, an army of stylists from Saks and Barneys arrived and pulled Guy, Stacey, Leanna, and Tina into separate corners of the séance room. Four sets of two junior stylists held up sheets, creating makeshift change spaces. At the same time, their counterparts unzipped large garment bags and handed selected outfits to Guy, Stacey, Tina, and Leanna.

Barneys dressed Guy in pleated brown and blue plaid trousers, a Henley shirt, crocodile shoes, and a matching belt. Stacey wore a tailored crème knee-length dress with tiny puffed sleeves, while Tina sported a red pantsuit with an exaggerated, oversized blazer. Leanna emerged in a sleek black Prada skirt, kitten heels, and a turtleneck. Her hair was swept back into a smooth ponytail against her scalp, but her abundance of curls cascaded down her back.

They presented their looks simultaneously when the senior stylists nodded, and the cover sheets dropped to the floor. The four stood at opposite sides of the room and marveled. Everyone looked so good, so polished, so different, so refined! They barely had a moment to digest their new appearances when Doc Aus's two assistants appeared and hurried them from the space and down the staircase toward an awaiting limo.

Guy watched the news coverage from the limo's tiny television while Tina raided the minibar. "Who wants what?" she asked while dangling miniature liquor bottles between the fingers of both hands. The driver announced their travel time as twenty minutes and closed the divider to the back passengers, leaving them alone.

"Are there any bubbles?" Stacey asked, sounding swept away by the excitement of the situation.

"Maybe," Tina replied as she searched through a second compartment.

"Goodie, I hope so. I love champagne!" Stacey said giddily.

"Aha!" Tina withdrew a magnum of midlevel sparkling wine. She cradled the chilled bottle between her thighs and worked out the cork with her thumbs. After a short while, it blew out of the bottle, narrowly missing Leanna.

"Careful!" Stacey scolded.

"Sorry," Tina replied, smiling as Doc Aus had encouraged.

While Tina poured the fizzing liquid into four glasses, Guy turned up the volume on the television. As promised, a phone segment with Doc Aus was about to begin before the channel went off to a series of commercials. Images of Carolyn flittered across the screen as the announcer began the story.

> "Welcome back. Renowned Australian animal communicator and veterinarian Greg Osmond joins us on the line for this story. Doc Aus, you'll do much better explaining—just what is going on?" The announcer led.
>
> "Well, it's an amazing thing. Today, I became acquainted with a group of companions to a lovely canine named Ruby. The owners brought Ruby to my attention because they seemed to have some insight into the dog's psyche, giving them the impression that she was trying to communicate an attachment to the late Carolyn Bessette Kennedy," Doc Aus replied.

"Sorry to interrupt Doc Aus. Of course, Carolyn Bessette Kennedy was the wife of John Kennedy Junior, and they died almost two years ago in a plane crash. How did you come to this conclusion?" the announcer asked.

"Well, I'm not entirely at liberty to disclose all relevant information on the case at this early date. An overwhelming aura and physical and spiritual evidence link the two," Doc Aus replied.

"But this is not all. Is it, Doctor?" the announcer prodded.

"No. When a person decides to return to our world in whatever form, it is most often because they have unfinished business to take care of before the spirit can find release. I've had many cases like this, but none quite as unique as what will transpire later this eve," Doc Aus teased.

"I'm assuming you are referring to this rumor of Ruby's puppies, Doc Aus?" the announcer asked.

"Oh, it's no rumor. Ruby is expecting; I can assure you that. We're throwing the world's biggest baby welcome tonight! And then more!" Doc Aus bragged.

"Wow. Keep in touch as the night progresses." The announcer wrapped up the segment.

"Will do," Doc Aus replied.

When the interview was over, the glass window separating the driver from the limo passengers slowly rolled down, revealing that Doc Aus was a front-seat passenger. He turned to face the group in the back and spoke. Guy noticed his look was also refreshed, with more exaggerated eye makeup and glitter. He had also lost the jeweled turban and wore his hair slicked back and sprayed into place like a helmet of waves to his shoulders.

"You must follow my instructions very closely when we get there. After this big announcement, everyone is going to want to see Ruby. Of course, it is our advantage to shield her from the public until the opportune moment. Right now, let's promise everyone the same photo op. Does that sound right, mates?" Doc Aus announced the plan.

"Sure does," Guy answered confidently.

Guy looked down at Ruby on the limo's curved seat. It wouldn't be an easy night for her, but he was committed to making it comfortable. He thought that Ruby's fear of flashbulbs made it best for her to be exposed all at once to the media, preferably late into the evening once the puppies had arrived. That seemed like the best plan. Guy connected his gaze with Ruby's to communicate his dedication. *I've got you, girl.*

"Great. Let's talk more when we get there, Guy. Leanna, you're my hostess, babe. You look fabulous. Tina, don't forget to smile and give lots of interviews. Stacey, get out that notepad! You are not the diarist after the event is over. Be present!" Doc Aus ordered.

"So, I should be tracking it now?" Stacey inquired.

"You bet!" Doc Aus returned to speak to the driver, raising the division.

As suggested, Stacey withdrew the pen and opened the notebook. "So, Guy," she began, "tell me about Ruby."

"No offense, Stacey," Tina began, "but I think the idea was to have you write down your impression of all this. He wants your ideas, not a bunch of other people's."

Stacey sat back to consider before scribbling in the notebook.

The limo arrived and parked outside a Fire Hall on Varick Street. A group of bodyguards and uniformed police officers lined the vehicle as it came to a complete stop. One of them, an expressionless bald man with a goatee and mustache, opened the limo door, offering each of the ladies his muscled arm as he escorted them out onto the street.

"There you are." He gestured toward North Moore as he helped Tina out of the limo.

Tina was a natural, smiling at the men while waiting on the sidewalk. Leanna emerged second and was slightly more cautious as she followed Tina's lead. Wide-eyed, taking in all the details, Stacey gaped at the spectacle of so many men armed with guns before returning to her assigned task, furiously scribbling words in her notebook as she joined the girls on the sidewalk. Guy exited the limo last with Ruby, who seemed weary yet content to be on the streets of New York.

Four police blocked traffic, escorted them the short distance across the street, and stopped at the corner marked by the street sign of N. Moore. Both sides were barricaded and guarded by armed police sporting full riot gear, creating an enclosed space only accessible at that spot on Varick. Midheight buildings, which Guy assumed once were warehouses, lined the street on either side. Scaffolding stood alongside a building on the right, obviously for some restoration project, making it difficult to see the street numbers.

A giant tent covered the street between the buildings on North Moore. A stage was under construction on the west end of the block at Hudson Street. Lighting technicians ran cords from various establishments and trucks in the scramble to assemble the set. One of Doc Aus's assistants seemed to be in charge as she used a clipboard to check off deliveries and pointed the service members in the correct direction.

Stacey discovered the street numbers. "There it is, Guy," Stacey announced while pointing to an unassuming entrance with industrial-style steel double doors. Above the doors was a pane of glass that displayed the number 20. Guy carefully led Ruby to that doorway. Before entering the tent, he assumed she wanted to sniff and familiarize herself with the surroundings, apparently her possible former home.

Guy went toward the building entrance, towing Ruby behind him. When Ruby suddenly stopped, he was just yards from the metal steps. He turned back to see what the problem was. Ruby was sniffing the neighborhood's silver fire hydrant. She did this with such intensity that the others also became fixated. *Is it a sign?* Guy wondered.

"Look! She remembers," Stacey noted.

"Ladies and Guy." Doc Aus's second assistant suddenly appeared, clapping for their attention. "You must come with me over here." The foursome had no choice but to follow the insistent assistant.

She led them inside the main tent, a lofty white contraption that seemed larger inside than it did from the out. A long table extended almost half of the length of one side of the tent. On it was a towering feast of various foods, from fruit to meats and freshly baked rolls—and the promised sushi. A waitress dressed in catering attire was unpacking champagne flutes onto an empty table while another dumped a bag of ice into a series of large Veuve Clicquot buckets. The assistant guided them past the refreshments and into a cordoned-off area with privacy walls covered in gauze.

Guy noted the proximity to the stage, which wasn't quite complete but nearly so. Men on ladders worked on stringing a set of white Christmas lights across the back fabric panel while others tinkered with the microphone equipment. "Ici." She parted the makeshift gauze door, revealing a grouping of white faux leather couches and a large pillow for Ruby, which seemed similar to the one Doc Aus used at his studio.

"The VIP section," she announced, ordering them to stay there until Doc Aus completed the primary interviews.

There were undoubtedly many behind-the-scenes elements of the last-minute production, and the assistant's job was to ensure everything ran smoothly. After giving instructions, she left them and walked away while speaking to someone through a microphone attached to a headset. She also carried a clipboard, and Guy watched as she darted here and there around the tent to greet the suppliers, like Evian and Pepsi, as they arrived at the Varick entrance.

Guy listened to the audible increase in collective buzz as people assembled for the event. Some were lucky enough to have scored passes inside the tent, and they were beginning to trickle in to help themselves to the bounty of the buffet. Since the walls of their VIP section were only so high, Guy could hear news reporters as they taped their stories for that evening's early-edition news.

"This is Elizabeth Beaupre for *Fashion Now!* Dr. Greg Osmond's startling revelation earlier today that a dog called Ruby is the reincarnation of Carolyn Bessette Kennedy has set this secluded Tribeca side street on fire. Not since that fateful day in July 1999 have there been quite so many fans and curious spectators assembled at this address.

Carolyn was an icon.

Now, we all are eagerly awaiting Ruby's appearance.

Later, we will return to our vault for a special on Carolyn's style. We will speak with some of her favorite designers and ask: What would she have worn while pregnant?"

The girls were taking Doc Aus's recommendations to heart. Through her role as a diarist, Stacey focused on the details of the scene. Rather than asking her usual million questions or babbling about something aloud, she was surprisingly quiet and reflective. Leanna spent the time practicing her lines for the unveiling of Ruby, slated for nine o'clock that evening. Tina, meanwhile, sat on the couch in the VIP area, assessing the shine of her lips by attempting various smiling poses in a small handheld mirror.

Doc Aus appeared at the VIP tent to grab Tina. "Tina, darling, you're on. Smile, and don't forget to be kind and gracious. It's your moment to shine."

With a quick spray of peppermint breath mist and a wink back at the group, Tina exited the VIP area, only to be swarmed by the overeager press, who took picture after picture, shouting for her attention.

"Tina Mann! Tina Mann!" they called out at her.

Unrattled, Tina smiled brightly as the flashbulbs went off. Doc Aus led her to the front of the stage, where the cameras and reporters stood in a semicircle. They took their positions in the center.

"Tina Mann, tell us about Ruby," CNN asked.

"Well, she is an adorable dog," Tina replied.

"Over here, Tina. Yes, does Ruby resemble Carolyn Bessette?" asked a student reporter.

"As I mentioned, Ruby is a dog, so no. Or no comment." Tina dismissed the question.

"Tina, does your mother know about your involvement in this?" NBC asked.

Tina answered with a muted smile. "Next question."

"Tina, what about the rumor that Ruby is a kidnapping victim?" a Canadian CBC reporter asked.

Tina furrowed her brow. "Come again?" she asked.

"Are you a part of the conspiracy, and did you steal your mother's car to assist the kidnapper?" CBC continued.

Tina gulped and could not answer.

"Enough! Enough!" Doc Aus came to her rescue. "We will answer your questions at the official press conference happening right on this stage at nine tonight. Thank you."

He motioned for his two assistants to help Tina back to the VIP section as the reporters repeatedly shouted their questions.

"That was fabulous, Tina," Doc Aus gushed as he joined them in the VIP area. "Just what they needed, a little teaser."

"Yeah, at whose expense?" Tina muttered quietly.

"What happened out there?" Leanna asked.

"Nothing that you should worry about." Tina sighed. "You look fabulous, Leanna, very chic!"

"Thanks." She blushed. "I think I have my lines down."

"I'm guessing you will knock 'em dead," Tina said. "You have a lot of balls to get up in front of all those people. I hope you have an easier time than me."

Guy looked down at his watch. "We have a little under an hour."

Doc Aus turned from speaking to his assistant and walked over to Ruby. He put his hand into his pocket, withdrawing a small jeweled case. He flipped the lid using his thumbs and removed two giant capsules filled with a dark green gelatinous substance.

"These are for Ruby," he announced.

"What are they?" Stacey asked eagerly, pen and paper in hand.

"Oh just something to get the process started. Don't worry," the doctor added to repeal the group's expression of concern. "It's perfectly safe. I am a veterinarian, you know."

His assistant raised a small plate, and Doc Aus fumbled a slab of brie off it and stuck the two pills inside. Then he went toward Ruby, offering her the treat from his hand. Ruby resisted, as Guy was expecting.

"I already told you, Doc Aus. She doesn't eat." Guy reminded the doctor.

"Ahh, yes, the anorexic dog." He considered the options. "Well, in the interest of time, which is running low, the solution is to squeeze these into Ruby's throat. Guy, do you care to assist?"

Guy held Ruby still while the doctor pierced the capsules and squeezed the contents into the dog's mouth. Ruby shuddered in disgust, disliking whatever magic serum Doc Aus dispensed. Guy unscrewed the top of a bottle of Evian and held it up to Ruby's mouth to help wash away the taste. She retired back to her cushion.

Forty minutes passed as darkness fell, and Guy could hear the swell of the enormous congregation. It wound around the block on both ends, and its enthusiasm tested the police's patience. Endless taxi horns honked, revelers shouted and laughed, and occasional sirens and whoops came from the law enforcement vehicles. At a quarter to nine, Doc Aus returned with an assistant on each arm, ready to start the show.

"Leanna, you know your lines?" Doc Aus asked her.

"Yes, Doc Aus, I do," Leanna replied.

"Tina, Stacey, you know what to do?" Doc Aus looked between them for an answer.

"Yes, we do." Tina smiled.

"Absolutely, Doc Aus." Stacey snapped to attention, placing her pen on an empty notebook page.

"Guy, can you handle Ruby?" Doc Aus asked Guy last.

"Sure can," he affirmed as he ran the tips of his fingers through his still gel-styled bangs.

"Great, then it can begin!" Doc Aus exclaimed with a thunderous clap of his hands.

Doc Aus's assistant pressed a button on her earphones and announced to the phantom person on the other end that the doctor was ready to start the show. The lights flickered on and off three times as a hush fell over the mass of media and spectators. Music from an enormous speaker was suddenly lowered and replaced by the voice of the evening's emcee, a trendy MTV VJ named Justice Holliday.

"Welcome one, welcome all," she began. "I'm MTV's Justice Holliday, and we are live here on the doorstep of 20 North Moore Street in the heart of New York's Tribeca. Did you know Tribeca coined its name from the phrase triangle below Canal? Well, tonight, that triangle seems a bit like the Bermuda Triangle: quite a mystery!

"We eagerly await the first glimpse of the dog that has tails wagging. Young Ruby, as we have come to know her, is undoubtedly a dog full of tricks, and tonight, we will witness one of the most incredible events known to man- and canine-kind alike.

"Here to explain more is the marvelous, talented, and *awesome* Doctor Greg Osmond." Justice Halliday stepped back and pointed her microphone toward Doc Aus, who stood on the VIP side of the stage.

The crowd roared in delight as Doc Aus and his two assistants made their way up to the podium, the three girls not far behind him. Guy and Ruby hung back inside the VIP area and waited for their cue.

"G'day to you all," Doc Aus began as the rowdy congregation calmed enough for him to speak. "This is an amazing evening for me and you. In my field, Ruby is the kind of specimen that makes me want to continue my studies in animal communication. Over the years, I have received criticism for my work. I have met all kinds of skeptics. But I assure you what you witness tonight will make you a believer!"

It was Leanna's turn to speak, and she stepped to the podium beside Doc Aus. The crowd clapped and whistled as camera bulbs flashed and strobe lights rolled across the assembly, demonstrating how many had come to see the promised miracle. Leanne spoke slowly and clearly, her voice slightly husky.

"Not since her tragic death on July 16, 1999, has this quiet corner of the city seen so much activity. Carolyn Bessette was a beloved member of New York society and the world. Her death left a void; we will never know her full potential." Leanna took a breath and quickly continued, "We will never see her grow old. We will never again appreciate her style and flair for fashion. We will never see the children her marriage to John Kennedy would produce. The dream of it all died with her that day." She paused. "Or so we thought."

Leanna turned and eyed the crowd sideways in a teasing manner, tossing back her ponytail curls flirtatiously. She returned the microphone to Doc Aus as 2 Unlimited's hit "Get Ready for This" blasted from the speakers—Guy's cue to enter with Ruby.

"I present to you … *Ruby!*" Doc Aus's booming voice took over as the musical accompaniment retreated from the loudspeakers. It was replaced by an audio track of a crowd cheering. A series of red firecrackers lit the sky, and confetti bombs exploded over the top of the stage. Guy led Ruby, who lagged unenthusiastically behind him, and he needed to tug the long glittering leash a little to coax her along.

"I present to you … *Ruby!*" Doc Aus repeated as Guy led her up a prop ramp onto an altar, where she sat elevated for all to see.

The crowd went wild, the press shoving one another to get a prized shot of Carolyn reincarnated.

"Guy, Ruby, over here!"

"Look here!"

"Ruby, Ruby!"

"Guy, Guy!"

"Over here! Over here!"

"Look here! Look here!"

It took more than five minutes for the fuss to calm enough for Doc Aus to begin speaking again. "Quiet, quiet!" He pleaded. "Please be quiet. We will now take your questions if you can just be quiet. Please address them in an orderly fashion. You first." He pointed at the ABC reporter.

"Yes, Doc Aus. Some rumors as to your credibility have come into question. What do you say to the threat of a multimillion-dollar lawsuit by the Christian Alliance? They claim that you are nothing more than a publicity-seeking farce," the reporter said seriously.

"I say, 'Call my lawyers in the morning.'" He laughed and pointed out another reporter.

"Doc Aus, what about this theory that Carolyn Bessette was pregnant at her death? Wouldn't those details have emerged in one of the recent biographies?" the BBC asked astutely.

"There are a thousand reasons why the information may not have been made public. My work is to examine the Esprit of this creature. I examine it through the transition from human to this animal state. Carolyn's Esprit is restless and eager for a conclusion. She has given us these clues, and we are listening. Next?" Doc Aus answered.

"What will happen to Carolyn's Esprit once the puppies are born?" MTV asked on behalf of animal lovers.

"Excellent question. The birth of the litter will mark the 'point of passing,' where the spirit fulfills its dying wish and, with no further business to attend to on earth, can fully cross over into the next world. Tonight, my friends, we bid our final farewell to Carolyn Bessette Kennedy," Doc Aus said almost apologetically to the surprised crowd.

"And what about the fact that you stole that dog from me, Guy Myles!" A familiar voice cut sharply through the night, sending the hairs on Guy's arms up into an alert state. He sucked in his breath. The dreaded moment had arrived—the twitch found them.

The media pack spun around to see who posed the question as the twitch emerged from the side of the street to the right of the stage. Members of the press who stood arm to arm stepped back and aside. This parting created an aisle for the woman to pass through. A group of Broomstick supporters trailed behind her as she sauntered toward the stage.

"That's right. You try to cower behind this ridiculous character." The twitch gestured toward. Doc Aus. "I want you to tell all these people who the rightful owner of precious Ruby is. You thief! You escaped into the night with our Ruby."

Guy gulped as Doc Aus came to his rescue. "Security!" the doctor called out as the twitch pushed past him up the stairs and toward the altar.

"Shut it, Osmond! The dog is mine." The twitch lurched toward Ruby with her arms outstretched.

Guy wasn't sure who initiated the defensive plan, but instantly, he found Leanna at his side. They stood shoulder to shoulder, creating a human shield to block the twitch from reaching Ruby.

"I want that dog! Give her to me!" The twitch tried to grab Ruby by ducking left and right around them to access the dog on the altar. Ruby, alarmed, jumped off the altar and darted down the opposite stairs. The twitch smiled an evil grin, gloating, "I've got you now," as she chased Ruby across the stage.

"No!" Harnessing all her strength, Leanna screamed and ran at the twitch with both arms outstretched. Guy lunged to grab Leanna's waist and swung her around him, propelling himself toward the twitch while sending Leanna toward the other stairs. After releasing Leanna, the exaggerated motion caused Guy's outstretched hands to push the twitch, who, in surprise, spun and staggered backward toward Leanna.

Leanna found herself face-to-face with the biker woman, Guy's horrible harassing neighbor and seized the opportunity for revenge. "Hey," she said, "time to have a little fun."

At that moment, a rogue confetti ball burst, causing a rainfall of debris to cascade downward, landing atop the twitch. Guy watched as the temporarily incapacitated twitch struggled to find Leanna through the shower of confetti. Her arms were outstretched, but she was blinded by the debris that continued to rain from the sky.

"I'll get you, Missie," the twitch promised.

Leanna pointed her index finger at the startled twitch and shook it in a tsk-tsk fashion. "No, I got *you*." And then, much to the surprise of Stacey and Tina, with a gentle gesture, Leanna hip-checked the dizzy, confetti-haired twitch, sending her cascading down the stairs.

"That's for all the nastiness you caused," Leanna whispered before turning to feign an expression of surprise that the twitch had fallen to the assembled crowd. Leanna smiled and shrugged her shoulders as the crowd gasped.

Once landing at the bottom of the stairs, the twitch stood unsteadily and stumbled across the base of the stage. Sensing her proximity, Ruby quickly darted out of the flap of the white tent and onto the street. Hot on her tail, the unsteady twitch parted the tent flap and stepped on the cobblestone road. Having never regained her balance from the confetti bomb and the hip check down the stairs, the twitch rolled her ankle on the uneven stones and ricocheted off her trailing posse of Broomstick supporters.

The twitch shuffled step-by-step before losing her balance entirely. In an almost slow-motion sequence, she tipped sideways into the void of sidewalk cellar doors opened to run electrical cords up to the massive light extravaganza. "I'm falling!" she screamed while descending into the dungeonous cavern before landing with a thud.

Press members dashed to the opening, snapping pictures of the fallen woman in the below street-level space. The more opportunistic journalists turned their attention back to Guy, who stood on stage with Leanna, shocked by the events of the twitch's demise. Without missing a beat, dozens of microphones poked inches from his face, and a frenzy of questions appeared out of nowhere.

"Guy, can you answer these accusations?"

"Is there truth to these rumors?"

"Guy, how can you explain?"

"Guy, Guy. Explain, Explain."

The reporters shouted in chaotic succession. He silenced them all by putting up his hand. "It is true that I am not the rightful owner of Ruby. But I did not steal her as accused. Ruby found me, and I brought her here, to New York, where the charm on her collar says to return her," he explained.

The quiet hush of the crowd after Guy's announcement was cut suddenly by Stacey's alarmed cries. "Something's happening to Ruby!" She pointed.

When Guy looked over, he saw the dog on the step of 20 North Moore. Ruby was arching her back profoundly, straining to push something out. In that instant, Guy knew that it was not a puppy. It was not coming from the place where puppies would. They watched as, one after the other, a series of small white balloons emerged from Ruby.

After producing a considerable pile, the task was complete. Ruby scratched her paws backward on the dirty sidewalk, shook, and went to sit by the silver hydrant to watch the assembled group's reaction.

A moment of stunned silence overcame the crowd, many of whom witnessed the event on various television screens set up for spectators without a front-row view. Even the seasoned journalists had trouble making a string of words to explain the event. If Guy could sum up the mood of the place, he would say that they were collectively dumbfounded.

One of the police officers assembled for riot control approached the dog and patted her on the head. Another walked past his partner to the mess. He stood and marked off the area with yellow tape, indicating that the site was now a crime scene. Then, he poked at Ruby's excrement with his baton and called for another officer to grab a bucket and some gloves.

Several officers returned. One took pictures, and two others collected the mini white balloons from the stoop. A few others stood around watching the recovery, speculating what could be inside. Guy and the girls heard the shocked gasps as one of the officers broke through a balloon to reveal the package contents.

"Did you know anything about this?" The officer shouted as he pointed at Guy.

"Not a thing," Guy answered.

"What is it?" Stacey asked.

"Well, this," the officer said, pointing to the balloon's contents, "I'd say is ice and a lot of it. Your Broomstick friend down there in the cellar used this dog as a mule."

The crowd booed as paramedics hoisted the bloody and disheveled twitch from the cellar. She was stunned by the fall and was barely able to walk. If life were in a cartoon, Guy thought, stars would surround her like a halo, and her eyes would be *X*s. The paramedics laid her on a stretcher and then rolled her into an awaiting ambulance. Two uniformed officers hopped in after the ambulance workers to escort the concussed twitch to the hospital.

Not wanting to miss a moment, the reporters filmed her departure. The ambulance switched on its sirens, navigated through the robust crowd, and drove off into the night. Once the wailing sounds were out of earshot, the CNN reporter's focus returned to the stage and Doc Aus, who had not moved or spoken since Ruby expelled her load on the sidewalk. He stood at the podium, speechless and ghastly white.

"Doc Aus, Doc Aus, what are your comments on what has transpired here tonight?" The CNN reporter did not waste a minute returning the attention of the evening to the Australian veterinarian.

"Fraud!" One person shouted among a stilled crowd, awaiting an answer, while another yelled, "Phony!"

"Where are the puppies, Doctor?" the CBS camera operator taunted.

"Doc Aus! Doc Aus!" they screamed for him, at him, demanding a response to the apparent farce.

Somehow, the word *faker* took hold of the group, and in no time, everyone shouted it in unison repeatedly. "Faker, faker, faker!" They chanted together.

Doc Aus's assistant raced up to the podium and offered only a brisk "No comment" as she shielded the humiliated doctor with her cape and escorted him back to the VIP tent.

Leanna took the initiative, grabbed the microphone, and announced to the crowd that the event was over. "Thank you, everyone. We thank you all for coming tonight. I assure you that Doc Aus will have a comment for you in the morning."

Tina and Stacey approached the podium and linked arms with Leanna, one on either side, leading her down the steps. Guy followed them from a distance behind while incessant flashbulbs documented their descent. Once they reached the street to join Ruby, a flash that must have come behind the threesome and Guy captured the most exciting shot of the night in pop culture permanence. It caught their four shadows against the exterior of 20 North Moore.

"And there they go. What a night! Well, folks, in a city like this, anything is possible. New York City is truly the place of dreams. I'm Justice Holliday, and we are out!" Guy heard the veejay say as the crowd dispersed into the city maze.

CHAPTER 17

BUBBY'S

Wednesday morning, Tribeca, New York

Doc Aus and his entourage disappeared into an idling limo before he and the girls could say goodbye. Guy overheard the cleanup crew speculating about a public mischief charge or something for Doc Aus and his assistants.

Ruby was frisky, and Guy noticed it immediately. When they returned to the tent, Ruby beelined for the craft table and barked. Guy knew what she wanted: food. He set her on the table and watched the dog devour all the meats, cheeses, and rolls. He laughed when she put her nose into the sushi and recoiled in disgust. It appeared that Ruby did not like wasabi or avocado, or perhaps she had an aversion to anything green.

"Wow," Leanna commented as Stacey continued to diarize the event.

"She sure is behaving like a dog now," Tina commented. "Poor thing. Imagine all that time she was full of drugs."

Guy was unconcerned about Ruby, who seemed thrilled to be rid of the stash's weight. She lay licking herself in full view. When done, she passed wind not once but twice. The second time, she looked back as if surprised by the sound. "Ruby! Such inappropriate behavior!" Guy scolded the dog while suppressing laughter.

"The doctor said she was pregnant but had drugs in her belly." Stacey paused. "Do you think it means that Carolyn was on drugs at the time of her death? Maybe that was why the plane crashed."

"Stacey," Tina gently clarified, "Doc Aus is a farce, sweetie. That means that nothing that he said held even a grain of truth. We drank the Kool-Aid and got swept up in the nonsense, that's all."

"But Carolyn was rumored to have done drugs," Stacey reminded them.

"Maybe, maybe not. Is it any of our business anyway?" Tina frowned.

Guy interrupted, "I guess it's just a rumor. And we all know how those can get blown out of proportion."

"Yes, we do," Stacey agreed, setting down her pen. "Ruby's a dog, nothing more."

As various caterers and production people disassembled the set, the tent, and the accessories, Guy and the girls remained to be questioned by the New York police department. Their interrogation lasted into the early hours of the morning. Eventually, the officers let them go, only after taking down their names and contact information. They cautioned the four to recall all details that could help "aid in the investigation." Either way, one assured Guy, the smuggling twitch would be going to prison for a very long time.

When they were eventually allowed to leave, a police officer gave Guy a slip of paper containing the nine digits of a phone number and a woman's name. The officer told Guy it would be a good idea to call the person, as they seemed to know about the dog. It was late, so Guy waited until the following day to make the call.

The line rang four times on the other end before someone answered.

"Hello?" The voice sounded like that of a child or perhaps a teen.

"Hi, I'm returning a message left about a lost dog," Guy said.

"Lost a dog? No, our dog is here." There was a pause, and Guy thought he heard a discussion. "Um, my mom wants to talk to you."

Guy waited as the phone shuffled from one hand to another. "Hello? This is Donna speaking."

"Hi, my name is Guy Myles. Officer Carl gave me your number about a lost dog. Did you lose yours?" Guy asked.

"Yes." Donna sighed in relief. "Well, my friend's sister did. We had just about given up on Ruby. How the heck did you find her in New York? Does she still have the Tiffany charm?"

"She sure does," Guy said, knowing he had found Ruby's owner.

Guy suggested the perfect meeting place and made arrangements for later that morning. When the time arrived, he and Ruby walked the twenty or so blocks from Anton's loft back to the belly of Tribeca. Ruby never looked up and zipped the entire time, nose down, generously sprinkling every planted tree she found. She was uncharacteristically lively as she zigzagged, sniffing everything she passed.

When they arrived in front of 20 North Moore, there was no trace of the tent, the confetti, or the crowd. Even the road appeared rinsed clean, disinfected of scandal. The police tape was gone, but Guy knew where it happened because Ruby made a beeline directly to the spot and refused to budge.

Guy suspected the second he saw them that they were the ones. They came directly over and exclaimed their delight in a craze. *Ruby!* The ladies finished each other's sentences and gushed their gratitude. Ruby seemed to recognize the pair, and her tail began to wag broadly from left to right.

"Oh my god!" Donna greeted Guy. "Thank you! We were all so worried."

Lydia pointed at the glass entrance marking 20 North Moore and said, "Really, it is still so sad about them."

"Yes, I still can't believe it." Donna shook her head.

"I remember where I was when I heard the news," Lydia confided. "I could not take my eyes off the television. It was surreal. I mean, after what happened to his father, who would have thought we could lose another?"

"Candles in the wind," Donna agreed.

"The coverage went on and on. I mean the search in the open water. Then when Carolyn, John, and Lauren were found dead, that was just horrible." Lydia shook her head. "So sad."

"You have that commemorative issue of *People*. Remember, Lydia?" Donna reminded her friend. "We read that one cover to cover."

"Sure I do. That one was priceless," Lydia said.

"God, if only. Such a shame," Donna said absently.

Looking at his watch, Guy saw that it was almost noon. He didn't want to be late for the girls. It was time to say goodbye. Guy gave Ruby's glittering leash to Lydia, who hugged him, exclaiming that her sister would adore the new glamourous accessory. The women both thanked him for returning Ruby. Not knowing what else to do, Guy bent down and scratched Ruby's head gently between her ears. She responded favorably and arched her back to meet the tickle of his fingers.

"Bye, Ruby," Guy said. "It's been quite the journey."

Ruby looked up, and Guy met her gaze for only an instant. He noticed something different about her. Their connection was gone, and she was like she was, as she should be, a dog.

"Bye, girl," Guy said.

Without fanfare, he said goodbye to Donna and Lydia, and as the women walked with Ruby to the east, Guy went in the opposite direction. In seconds, he arrived at Bubby's Pie Company, an all-American eatery that stood pleasantly on the corner of Hudson and North Moore. A broad blue-and-white-striped awning shaded the front and side windows like a sportsman's visor.

The outside patio, surrounded by a white picket fence, was inviting. Fortunately, a table set for four was newly vacant, save two empty coffee mugs and a torn pink packet of sweetener. Guy sat wobbling the table slightly with the knock of his knee. Instantly, he sensed the unevenness against the slope of the sidewalk. He folded the pink packet into four and inserted it underneath the table leg closest to his chair to steady the surface.

The air was heavy with the aroma of freshly baked pie wafting out from the café's open door. Guy noted the interior through the windows. The place bustled with activity against the creamy walls and arts-and-crafts décor. Dishes and cutlery clanked in a chorus while dark-aproned servers whizzed around the tables, balancing brimming beverages and hot food trays.

On the chair beside him, Guy found a discarded copy of the *New York Post* and read the front-page article headlined "Stooped!" Along with a play-by-play recounting the night's events, the journalist questioned whether Doc Aus was indeed a veterinarian, having so inappropriately diagnosed the dog Ruby as pregnant. They questioned everything: his education, wealth, nationality. It was the kind of stuff that sold papers.

Overnight, the sensation du jour seemed shredded into nothing more than table scraps for the hungry gossip hounds. And, Guy sensed, no one would be willing to let the story ease without a thorough postmortem. He suspected that that process would occupy Page Six for several more weeks.

Flipping over the cover story, Guy found a small box on page two, where the doctor announced his retirement in a statement that Guy took to be concessionary. The official quote read: "My gift of communication with the spirit world needs some revitalization." He planned to spend the next few years at an undisclosed location practicing "Eastern philosophy and meditation techniques."

"Hi, Guy," the girls chanted in unison as they approached the table, shopping bags in hand, wearing white I (Heart) New York baseball caps.

"Hello, ladies. Don't you look great in those hats," he commented.

"There's one for you, too, Guy!" Stacey exclaimed as she removed an identical hat and set it on the table. "Courtesy of Tina," she added.

"Wow, that's kind of you, Tina!" Guy smiled and folded the newspaper, returning it to the empty table behind him.

"That whole thing was weird," Tina said, noting the headline of the discarded paper.

"You're telling me!" Stacey agreed.

"Imagine all that time Ruby had a stomach full of drugs. I can't get over it. Poor thing. I hope she recovers," Tina said sincerely.

"Imagine Doc Aus convincing us she was pregnant and wanting to return to the homestead to have the puppies!" Stacey laughed. "Isn't it the stupidest thing you've ever heard?"

"Well, the guy was a phony," Leanna concluded as the waiter brought a handful of menus. "At least he got called out for it."

"And to think I started to believe it was something to do with her." Guy removed *Vanity Fair* from his case. In a tribute, Guy drew an extra chair up close to the table and leaned the magazine in an upright fashion so that the face of Carolyn Bessette Kennedy was staring back at them all, their dining partner. At that moment, the waiter returned to take their order.

"Wow," the waiter commented at the sight of the magazine. "After what happened around the corner last night, you're pretty brave for pulling that thing out. Plenty of people are upset at being tricked by that Doc Aus guy. She was a pretty good person, you know. She came in here a lot."

"Did you know her?" Stacey asked as she picked up her pen.

"Sure," the waiter remembered. "I saw her. She came with Kennedy and their dog. They were great, always playing footsie and touching each other. Really in love were those two. It's a shame about them."

"Yeah." Leanne nodded.

"What was their favorite menu item?" Guy inquired.

"I'll have to ask the chef if he remembers. You want to wait?" The waiter offered.

"No, I'll have one of whatever it is," Guy replied.

The girls ordered, and the waiter disappeared inside, coming out only moments later with four glasses of ice water. He placed them around the table, and Guy noticed they were so cold that beads of sweat were rolling down their sides onto the tabletop. He took a long gulp to the half-full mark.

"What will everyone do now?" he asked.

"I can tell you what I won't be doing," Stacey began. "I won't be setting up meetings with spiritual communicators anymore."

"Hindsight is often twenty-twenty, Stacey," Guy offered.

"Yeah," she said, appreciating his forgiveness. "I'm going to meet up with Herb and tour Columbia, I guess."

"That sounds promising. You must be excited," Guy said.

"I am. It's time I tried working toward something. Who knows? Maybe one day I'll wind up an editor like you, Guy." Stacey quickly wrote something in her journal while Guy moved along to Tina.

"Tina?" Guy asked.

"I'm staying here for my father," Tina announced. "He needs me after the breakup."

Guy was impressed by her display of compassion.

"What about you, Leanna? What's your plan?" Guy asked.

Her answer was interrupted by the meal's delivery. They ordered so much food that it took two servers to carry and set it on the table.

"Who's having the special?" the helper asked.

"I am." Guy indicated by raising a finger, noting a hefty fresh-baked blueberry muffin beside what he assumed to be a plain omelet.

"Isn't it funny that we've only ever had breakfast together," Stacey observed as she tucked her notebook back into her knapsack. "There are three meals daily, but road trips only seem to invite a stop for breakfast. Everything else is a snack."

"You are such an observant little wonder," Tina said, and Guy noticed that her comment sounded more like a compliment than an insult.

They ate their food in a peaceful, mild discussion about everything and nothing in particular. Then Guy remembered Leanna hadn't answered his question. "Remind me, Leanna, what will you do now?" Guy asked.

"Well," Leanna started and took a small sip of coffee, "I've decided to commit to big change. Honestly, I've spent the last few years angry about something that happened to me without realizing I can control the next things that life brings. Meeting you all, coming back here, and then the events of last night have made it clear that I am the limit to being me. It's time I lived again."

"Wow, can you repeat that?" Stacey asked as she dropped her cutlery to pick up her pen, "I didn't get it all."

"Leanna," Tina said, "You have a home here at my dad's place with me for as long as you need until you get on your feet."

"Aww, thanks." Leanna smiled.

"And Stacey, while we all look forward to reading your creation, you don't need to write every syllable spoken down in your book. Trust your smarts." Tina encouraged Stacey.

"Why, thanks, Tina. And if I had a sister, I'd sure like it to be you." Stacey said. "And you too, Leanna."

Simultaneously, Tina and Leanna reached across the table to touch the closest of Stacey's arms. "Thanks," they said together.

Guy knew the time was nearing. A glance at his watch told him it was one minute to the hour. It would soon be time for him to say goodbye and head to his interview at Ideal. He had not forgotten, but the job seemed less urgent to his happiness after the events of only a few days.

Leanna rose from the table, announcing that she needed to use the restaurant facilities downstairs. "Me too." Stacey quickly jumped up to join Leanna.

On their way, Leanna saw someone she recognized. "Christy?" She approached a woman at the establishment's entrance.

"Lea? Is that you?" Christy asked as the women embraced.

"Oh my goodness, It's been ages. What have you been doing?" Christy asked.

"I've been away for some time now, but I'm back," Leanna said.

"For good?" Christy asked.

"For good!" Leanna confirmed.

"Come and do yoga with me sometime." Christy passed Leanna a contact card with her info. "You look just the same."

"Thanks, you too." Leanna smiled.

The women embraced a final time before Christy went up to the bar to retrieve a pair of skinny cappuccinos the barista was frothing using the espresso machine's wand.

At the top of the bathroom stairs, Stacey grabbed the card from Leanna and read. It was confirmed, as she already knew. Christy lived at 20 North Moore in the loft vacated by John and Carolyn. She took her notebook and pen and tapped the gorgeous woman on the shoulders as she waited at the bar's side, announcing, "Hi, I'm Stacey, and I'm with Leanna. Do you mind if I ask you a few questions about your home?"

Guy and Tina were waiting together when Tina's cell phone suddenly began to ring. At first, she ignored it but then answered with a brisk hello.

"Mom?" Guy overheard her gasp. "Yes, I'm OK. Yes, that was me on TV. No, I won't be seeing Doc Aus again. Yes, I know he's bad news. Yeah, I'm staying with Dad. When are you arriving? OK, I'll see you then." She paused before adding, "I love you too."

"My mom's coming." She beamed as she gulped down the last sip of black coffee.

"That's great, Tina!" Guy congratulated her.

Stacey and Leanna returned from their trip to the washroom, Stacey giddy with excitement. "I just met Christy Turlington. She's even more beautiful in person. And she's so nice. I wanted to ask her all these questions about her loft, but she said, "I like to keep my private life private." I respect that. Also, there's a photo booth in the basement. Let's do a group photo. It makes four, so we can each take one."

"Great idea!" Tina exclaimed. "Come on, Guy!" They coaxed him out of his seat.

Leaving behind the beautiful sunny New York morning and a pile of empty dishes, the four proceeded through Bubby's large white entrance. They walked past the gleaming mahogany bar illuminated by a dangling row of white lanternlights. Behind this stood a wall of glass and liquor of various shades and potency. The bartender was chatting with Christy while steaming milk, and Guy overheard the conversation as he passed.

"Yeah, I always knew there was something funny about that guy. Anyone who wears that much makeup is sure to be a phony," said Christy.

"You are telling me! I totally saw that one coming!" The bartender chuckled.

Guy followed the girls down to the eatery's basement, where they found the photo booth. "Guy, you go in first since you're the tallest." Stacey parted the curtain.

Once he sat positioned on the seat, the girls joined him one after the other. They crammed so tightly that Guy felt his breath constrict in his chest. Leanna deposited their money.

"Whiskey!"

"Serious face!"

"Pouty face!"

"Angry face!"

The camera flashed four times as they made faces at the lens. When it was over, they pulled themselves off one another breathlessly, like school-aged children in the playground at recess. "That was super fun!" Stacey gasped. "Can we do it again?"

"It's not an amusement ride, Stacey," Tina reminded her. "And this beast can only do one thing at a time. We have to wait for the pictures."

"Right!" Stacey agreed.

The four stood together, waiting for the pictures to be processed. Guy thought it was Tina who made the first move. She linked her arms around his and Leanna's shoulders and then Leanna did the same to Stacey, causing a chain reaction until they hugged one another tightly in a circle.

"I'm staying here," Leanna confirmed. "In New York. I'm staying here in New York."

"That leaves you, Guy. I hope the manuscript edit all goes well," Stacey said.

"Well, it's in my bag. I will reread it all, but I have my plan." Guy felt more confident than ever.

Their pictures spat from the machine, and curiosity caused the group huddle to break apart. They spent a while passing the strip of photos, laughing at their images, and deciding who would take which shot. Eventually, they selected. Guy took the smiles, Stacey the serious, and Tina the pouts, leaving Leanna with mock angry faces that seemed rather comical. Guy tucked his picture into his wallet and checked his watch.

It was time for him to go, but ceremonious goodbyes were not his thing.

EPILOGUE

Stories from the *Tribeca Triangle* Podcast
Starring Jess Raven and Jenn Rosenthol

May 2016

JENN: Happy Cosmo Hour. I'm Jenn.

JESS: And I'm Jess.

JENN: Together, we are the wonder twins who bring you *Stories from the Tribeca Triangle*. We talk about the oddness of the zone and the weird stories of our neighborhood, Triangle Below Canal. So, how are you, Jess?

JESS: Great, Jenn. I've had a fun time preparing for this week's show.

JENN: Really?

JESS: Really! *laughs*

JENN: OK, big confession. Did you know that I was a Carolyn Bessette Kennedy superfan? I cut out pictures of her outfits from magazines, and, oh my god, I can't believe I'm admitting this … I scrapbooked them!

JESS: Please! *laughs* I cannot handle that so early into our cocktail hour! *laughs* But seriously, how am I your best friend and never knew this?

JENN: Guilty as charged! Do I have to sip this delicious cosmo for that revelation?

JESS: Yes, you must

JENN: Yes, I must. *slurp*

JESS: OK, so we are the same age, right?

JENN: Right. Seventy-eight.

JESS: For all our listeners out there, that means we were born in 1978. We are not actually seventy-eight.

JENN: Not that it would matter—we love our grammas. They are besties too!

JESS: Yes! Thanks, Jenn, we do! Shout out to Ricki!

JENN: And shout out to Pearl!

JESS: Wait! *laughs* Do you think they are having cocktails together right now?

JENN: We agree if you, the listener, can't hear our nodding heads!

JESS: OK, getting serious. Today's Tribeca Triangle focuses on Carolyn Bessette Kennedy, your girl crush.

JENN: *Groan* Oh come on. Don't make me regret telling you!

JESS: No guarantees, my friend. *laughs* But seriously, this story isn't only about Carolyn Bessette Kennedy. The weirdness came about a year and a half after she and her husband, John Kennedy Junior, died in that tragic plane crash.

JENN: So tragic.

JESS: Indeed. Do you remember Doc Aus?

JENN: The guy from Oprah?

JESS: No, that's Doctor Oz, Mehmet Oz. I'm talking about the dude called Greg Osmond, the Australian veterinarian.

JENN: Sounds vaguely familiar.

JESS: Well apparently he made a fortune selling debug software solutions to animal clinics across the US. This was in the late nineties, when people started freaking out about what would happen to computers with Y2K.

JENN: Oh I remember that!

JESS: It was a moment. Imagine if it was true and all the computers collapsed.

JENN: That would be, like, an entire other show.

ALLISON LANG COOK

JESS: Right! So this guy Osmond made all this money going around the country, preying on people's paranoia. And then the weirdness. (Music from *The Twilight Zone*)

JENN: Keep telling us about the weirdness!

JESS: OK! So once the doctor had the money, he reinvented himself as an animal communicator.

JENN: *throat clear* A what?

JESS: I'm not lying here. Doc Aus told people he could speak to dead pets.

JENN: Like the little dude in *The Sixth Sense*?

JESS: *laughing* Kind of. But no. He vibed it. People really believed it. I mean, he got a book deal and was on all the shows.

JENN: I think I saw him on Leno.

JESS: Yeah, me too! That was an epic episode!

JENN: OK, so please tell us more about the evil doctor who speaks to dead things.

JESS: After the Y2K computer debug success, he rented that cute brownstone in SoHo. You know the one?

JENN: The one with the iron gate outside?

JESS: That's it! *sound of a high five* He christened himself Doc Aus and set up an animal-communication headquarters. He hired a couple of Mossad-trained female bodyguards/assistants from Montreal to make it authentic.

JENN: No way!

JESS: *laughs* He costumed them all in green leather, velvet capes, and glitter makeup. He even adopted an Aussie accent.

JENN: Didn't anyone think to *google* him?

JESS: Well, you must remember that the Internet was in its infancy. Wikipedia didn't launch until January 2001. So when he was just getting started, he could say or do anything without people being able to fact-check.

JENN: *laughs* Without Jess and Jenn to fact-check!

JESS: We were around!

JENN: Yes, we were around! But we didn't even have smartphones.

JESS: We were babies.

JENN: College babies.

JESS: Those were fun years.

JENN: Yes, they were!

JESS: *clears throat* So, Doc Aus is all over the country selling his book on talk shows, making more money. But there is a wave of critics threatening to take him down.

(Doom music)

JENN: What! Did he summon the Hello Kitty ghost army to attack?

JESS: *laughs* Not quite but good thinking!

JENN: Hello Kitty. It was a real thing! *purrs*

JESS: OK, but seriously Jenn. This is when our Tribeca-triangle weirdness happens. So, a group of apparent road-tripper strangers arrives at Doc Aus's studio with a dog, Ruby. Doc Aus performs a séance and determines that Ruby possesses the spirit of Carolyn Bessette Kennedy!

JENN: Spooky.

JESS: On top of this, he claims she is pregnant and wants to deliver the dogs on the doorstep of Twenty North Moore.

JENN: That's' right around the corner!

JESS: It sure is! So, in mere hours, Dos Aus and his team have the streets barricaded off, tents erected, media, police, music, food, and fireworks. I mean, it was, like, a totally insane event.

JENN: Like a rock concert

(Van Halen guitar music)

JESS: You bet! For the listener, Jenn and I just rewatched the documentary that an NYU student made that night. The footage was raw, but you understood how the drama went down.

JENN: I love the part when the cop sticks his baton in the dog doo. Then the shot returns to Doc Aus, and you see the color drain from his cheeks.

JESS: Even with all that weird glitter makeup!

JENN: *laughs* And those bodyguards, the Mossad girls. They, like, freaked out and grabbed him and dragged him out of there. I've never seen such strength from relatively skinny girls. Can we watch that part again?

JESS: Let's do it!

(Audio muffled. Sounds of background noise.)

JENN: Yeah, that makes me want to do more CrossFit!

JESS: You and me both, sister. They are beasts! Look how they scoop him from under each arm and lift him off that stage! Like, poof! They are out of there!

(Audio sounds of bubbles bursting)

JENN: What happened to Guy? Those girls?

JESS: Great questions! So Guy is a big wig at *Vanity Fair*. I hear he goes by G now.

JENN: That makes sense. He was in the industry.

JESS: Yes, he worked for the now-defunct BlackJack. After people found out the stunt was all because of a Carolyn Memorial *Vanity Fair* issue, I think the magazine's sales increased by 75 percent. You know that Grayson Carter totally hunted Guy down and hired him.

JENN: Wow, that's a Cinderella story. And Stacey?

JESS: Stacey Crowe coauthored a book about the ordeal, *A Creature Unlike Any Other*. Ideal published it.

JENN: It was a pretty good read.

JESS: I liked it.

JENN: Oh and let's give an update on gorgeous Tina Mann.

JESS: Right? Tina starred in the reality dating show *Take Me to Montana*.

JENN: Did she find love?

JESS: Indeed she did! She gave her last horseshoe to that LA psychotherapist dude!

(Audio: "Bradley, I present you with my last horseshoe. Will you accept?")

JENN: Oh! Bradley was hot.

JESS: Yup! So hot! If you are listening, Bradley and Tina, we hope you live happily ever after!

JENN: We do! Whatever happened to Leanna?

JESS: Well, that's a good question. She was a somewhat controversial member of the pack. For a while, this video of a hissy fit she threw streetside kept airing. Until people grew bored of it, and it went away. You can still find it on YouTube if you google "Hot & Wild, meltdown" and "*Inside Edition*." To answer your question, I hear she is a wellness coach who specializes in people with anger-management issues.

JENN: That makes sense. OK, now what everyone really cares about. What happened to the dog?

(Audio: barking)

JESS: Aww, yes, sweet Ruby. She went back to her rightful owners.

JENN: Not those bikers?

JESS: No. She belonged to a lady from SanFran, some tech executive. She went back there.

JENN: *sigh* That's a relief!

JESS: She was an innocent victim. If you can hear us, Ruby, we hope you have an excellent life.

JENN: Do you think she ever actually had puppies?

JESS: Oh I wonder! They would be worth a pretty penny after all that went down!

JENN: Like, cha-ching!

(Audio: cash register sounds)

JESS: To wrap it all up I saved the best for last.

JENN: The biker chick?

JESS: You are a mind reader!

JENN: What happened to the biker chick? Remember in the movie when she falls into the street cellar?

(Audio: "I'm falling!")

JESS: I sure do! *laughs* It's my favorite part.

JENN: I mean, she just looked evil.

JESS: So ugly.

JENN: She needed a day at the Elizabeth Arden spa for sure. *laughs*

JESS: You know she chased Guy and his van across the country to get the dog back?

JENN: That's bananas insane.

(Audio song bite from Cypress Hill's "Insane in the Membrane")

JESS: *laughs* It's for sure dedication! Well, I guess the dope in the dog was some new kind of drug in a pure form that would have been worth millions on the street. That crazy event around the corner from here also brought down the some Broomstick baddies.

JENN: Using man's best friend as a drug mule seems so mean!

JESS: Horrifying. Those Broomsticks got what was coming. Like dozens of them got arrested.

JENN: And now they're all in Rikers?

JESS: Rotting.

JENN: Yeah! Let's drink to that! *sound of clinking glasses*

JESS: Well, that wraps up today's story about the weirdness that went down on North Moore, right here in Tribeca.

JENN: Friend, you did such a great job on this one.

JESS: Aww, thanks! Next week, we will talk about the spooky firehouse on Varick. Did you know it was in the movie *Ghostbusters*?

JENN: No, I did not

JESS: True story.

JENN: Well, thanks for joining us for this episode of *The Tribeca Triangle*.

JESS: Until next time. *clink of glass* Cheers!

JENN: Cheers! *slurp*

The End

BIBLIOGRAPHY

Allen, Mike, and Carey Goldberg, "Rescue Search in Kennedy Crash Ends; Coast Guard Tells Family There Is Little Hope." *New York Post*, July 18, 1999, A1.

Blow, Richard, *American Son*. (New York: Henry Holt & Company, 2002).

Bumiller, Elisabeth, "Enter Smiling, the Stylish Carolyn Bessette," *New York Times*, September 29, 1996, 31.

Carlson, Margaret, "Farewell, John," *Time*, August 2, 1999.

Charlton, Janet, "JFK Jr Baby Heartache," *Star*, February 11, 1997, 29.

Collins, James, "By George, He Got Married!" *Time*, October 7, 1996, 44–47.

Davies, Michelle, "Remembering Carolyn Bessette-Kennedy 20 Years after Her Tragic Death," July 11, 2019, *marieclaire.com.au*, https://www.marieclaire.com.au/latest-news/the-life-of-carolyn-bessette-kennedy/.

Davis, Boyd, *Narciso Rodriguez: Celebrating Beauty*, March 1, 2001, https://www.fashionwindows.net/2001/03/narciso-rodriguez/.

Duke, Lynne, "Bodies of Kennedy, Bessettes Brought to Shore," *Washington Post*, July 22, 1999, A1.

———, "Family Memorializes Another JFK," *Washington Post*, July 23, 1999, A1.

Family, Bessette and Freemen, "Statement of Grief by Wife's Family," *New York Times*, July 21, 1999, A20.

Fein, Ellen and Schneider, Sherrie, *The Rules*. (New York: Warner, 1995).

Fulsang, Deborah, "Carolyn Bessette Kennedy 1966–1999," *Flare*, October 28, 1999.

Ganem, Mark, "An American Princess Lost," *Ottawa Citizen*, July 21, 1999, A6.

Gerhart, Ann, "Bessette Tried to Avoid Kennedy Spotlight," *Washington Post*, July 18, 1999, A20.

———, "The Bridegroom Wore Blue," *Washington Post*, September 27, 1996.

Gilmour, David Jon, George Roger Waters, Richard William Wright. 1973. "Breathe (i the air)." *Dark Side of the Moon*. Composer Roger Waters.

Goldsmith, Olivia, "Kennedy's," *McCall's*, May, 1997, 45.

Grunwald, Michael, "JFK Jr. Feared Dead in Plane Crash," *Washington Post*, July 18, 1999, A1.

Hirschkorn, Phil, "JFK Jr.'s Magazine Salutes Its Fallen Leader," *Time*, August 26, 1999.

History & Culture, *Carolyn Bessette Kennedy*, October 12, 2022, https://www.biography.com/history-culture/carolyn-bessette-kennedy.

Jeffreys, Daniel, "Blonde Ambition." *Tattler*, 1996, 158–159.

Johnson, Tom and Fantle, David, "Carolyn Bessette Kennedy Echoes of Camelot." *Gold Collectors Series Magazine*, Fall, 50.

Kelly, Kate, "Friends Remember Lauren Bessette, Who Was Thriving at Morgan Stanley." *Observer*, July 26, 1999.

Kennedy, Edward M., *American Rhetoric Online Speech Bank*. July 23, 1999, https://www.americanrhetoric.com/speeches/edwardkennedyeulogyjfkjr.htm.

Kennedy, John F. Jr., interview by Larry King, *Larry King Live* (September 29, 1995).

Kennedy, John Fitzgerald, "NEWS CONFERENCE 12, JUNE 2, 1961." *JFKLibrary.org*, https://www.jfklibrary.org/archives/other-resources/john-f-kennedy-press-conferences/news-conference-12#:~:text=I%20am%20the%20man%20who,since%20our%20visit%20to%20Paris.

Kennedy, John, "Editor's Letter," *George*, October/November 1995, 9–10.

Kochan, Maureen, "John and Carolyn, Camelot's Golden Couple." *Gold Collectors Series Magazine*, Fall, 40–47.

Menkes, Suzy, "Fashion's Poet of Black: YAMAMOTO," *New York Times*, September 5, 2000.

Michaelis, David, "Great Expectations," *Vanity Fair*, September 1999, 130.

Muzio, David S, Demko, Steve, Elias, Dr. Bartholomew, Weston, Capt. P.D.,"Group Chairman Factual Report," *National Transportation Safety Board*, March 7, 2000, https://data.ntsb.gov/Docket/?NTSBNumber=NYC99MA178.

Nemy, Enid, "Anthony Stanislas Radziwill, 40, Award-Winning TV Producer," *New York Times*, August 12, 1999, C21.

Office of Sexual Health and Epidemiology, *Sexually Transmitted Infections New York State*, New York: New York State Department of Health.

Peretz, Evgenia, "The Private Princess," *Vanity Fair*, September 1999, 274–281.

Pyle, Richard, "Eulogy Speaks of Unfulfilled Potential," *Ledger*, July 24, 1999.

Roshen, Maer, "Prince of the City," *New York Magazine*, August 2, 1999.

Seligmann, Jean, "Sunday in the Park with George," *Newsweek*, March 10, 1996.

Service, Gannett News, "Anthony Radziwill, JFK Jr's cousin," *Courrier News*, August 12, 1999, 99.

Services, Bee News, "Brits and Bessette-Kennedy Make Best-Dressed List," *Sacramento Bee*, April 23, 1997, F2.

Services, News, "JFK JR. UNDERGOES SURGERY ON HAND," *Chicago Tribune*, October 10, 1997.

Smolowe, Jill, Elizabeth McNeil, KC Baker, Matt Birbeck, Jennifer Longley, Eric Francis, Ellen Illgian, Linda Kramer, "To Have and to Hold," *People*, July 24, 2000, 100–109.

Solomon, Cindy and John South, "Wife Catches JFK with Ex-Love Daryl," *National Enquirer*, March 25, 1997, 4–5.

Staff, "25 Things You Didn't Know About Carolyn Bessette." *Globe*, October 15, 1996, 36.

———, "A Man in Full," *People*, August 2, 1999, 66–71.

———, "Crazy for Carolyn," *Newsweek*, October 20. 1996.

———, "JFK's Bride Is a Tragic Anorexic," *Globe*, February 11, 1997, 3.

———, "JFK's Lawyers Called In to Gag His Wife's Ex-Hairdresser," *London Times*, October 27, 1997.

———, "JFK JR. Captured in All His Glory." *Gold Collector's Series Magazine*, Fall, 58–65.

———, "JFK JR. Heartbreak: Bride Hated Being a Kennedy," *National Enquirer*, February 4, 1997, 8.

———, "JFK Jr.'s Secret: Bride Is 9 Weeks Pregnant," *Star*, October 8, 1996, 3.

———, "Kennedy Was 'Man Accompanying Carolyn Bessette,'" *Orlando Sentinel*, July 20, 1999.

———, "Messy Split, Bye George," *New York Daily News*, May 16, 1997.

———, "NOAA Ship *Rude* Has Wreck-Finding Expertise," *CNN. com*, July 20, 1999, accessed Feb 23, 2023, http://www.cnn.com/US/9907/20/rude.profile/.

———, "Say Goodbye to The Pretender," *Newsweek*, October 11, 1992.

———, "The Look of Yohji Yamamoto." *In Style*, July 1999, 260.

Staff, *Washington Post, The Life of JFK Jr: Crash and Search*, July 16–22, 1999, accessed February 23, 2023, https://www.washingtonpost.com/wp-srv/national/longterm/jfkjr/recovery.htm.

Printed in the United States
by Baker & Taylor Publisher Services